THE CRIMSON CORD

THE CRIMSON CORD

Louis Green

iUniverse, Inc.
New York Lincoln Shanghai

THE CRIMSON CORD

Copyright © 2005 by Louis E. Green

All rights reserved. No part of this book may be used or reproduced by any means, graphic, electronic, or mechanical, including photocopying, recording, taping or by any information storage retrieval system without the written permission of the publisher except in the case of brief quotations embodied in critical articles and reviews.

iUniverse books may be ordered through booksellers or by contacting:

iUniverse
2021 Pine Lake Road, Suite 100
Lincoln, NE 68512
www.iuniverse.com
1-800-Authors (1-800-288-4677)

ISBN: 0-595-33372-9 (pbk)
ISBN: 0-595-66875-5 (cloth)

Printed in the United States of America

Contents

Characters		ix
Prologue		1
Chapter 1	The Certain Man	3
Chapter 2	Childbirth	6
Chapter 3	Calamity	8
Chapter 4	The Crimson Cord	10
Chapter 5	Confusion	14
Chapter 6	A Call for Caregivers	17
Chapter 7	The Committal	23
Chapter 8	Conflict	29
Chapter 9	Compatibility	32
Chapter 10	The Concubine	36
Chapter 11	Commerce	39
Chapter 12	Circumcision	44
Chapter 13	Concern: Interlude of Explanation	49
Chapter 14	The Complex: Chamor Rosh	51
Chapter 15	The Confident One	54
Chapter 16	Conversation with His Confidant	57
Chapter 17	Conversation with a Corpse	62
Chapter 18	The Coming Crisis	66
Chapter 19	Carnage of Childhood	68
Chapter 20	Comrade of the Chaberim	75

Chapter 21	Coconspirators: The Criminal from Crook Street and His Former Concubine	83
Chapter 22	Confrontation & Chaos	87
Chapter 23	Convicted by the Council	96
Chapter 24	No Consolation	111
Chapter 25	The Caravan	113
Chapter 26	The Far Country	120
Chapter 27	Casting off the Coast	130
Chapter 28	Carnival in Canaan	135
Chapter 29	The Convert	140
Chapter 30	Collapse of the Canaanite Civilization (and Zerah's Conscience)	150
Chapter 31	Joined to the Certain Citizen	156
Chapter 32	Coming to	163
Chapter 33	Coming Home	167
Chapter 34	Celebration and Contempt	175
Chapter 35	The Conclusion	180

Acknowledgement

The story line for this book originated from a conversation by and between me and a few close friends as we sat around a campfire on the Green Mountain Ranch somewhere around the turn of the twenty first century. It was impossible to think of anything but heaven while staring at a starry setting such as the one we witnessed on that crisp clear night. There aren't many sights that compare to a "Texas Hill County" night sky whose only competition is a flickering camp fire unfettered by bright city lights. Just as "The Crimson Cord" is about two brothers, uncannily it was two brothers, "The Ewing's," from Louisiana that provided the entertainment for our guests that evening. Both of these brothers are special to me and I gladly say that they never behaved like the sons of "The Crimson Cord" story.

One could hear a hint of sadness in Hammer Ewing's voice as he sang a few country tunes that soon crossed over to our favorite gospel songs that evening. We both feared that his brother Gary was gravely ill and probably would not be with us much longer. So when Gary asked me, "What will we do for entertainment in eternity;" he reminded me of a traveler preparing to go to an unfamiliar place and he wanted to know what to do when he got there. I had been Gary's pastor some years ago, even better, we became very close friends. You might even call us "buddies." My answer to him was that I would enjoy going back in time to see "replays" of biblical events. Saint John 21:25 records, "if all the things that Jesus did were written, the world could not contain the books." So we may conclude that many of the stories of the scriptures are condensed versions, that provides us with vital information, but does not have enough room for every detail.

Hence, I know that I can never exhaust the material, but I have begun with the parable of the Prodigal Son. It is possibly the second best known story all of the scriptures. My quest has been to expand a brief twenty two verses into a comprehensive story. "Gary, if there any parts of this story that I have omitted, you and I will watch them again when I join you in heaven."

Other than the brothers, I am grateful for my Parents, Bill and Roxie, who never dissuaded me from exercising my imagination, even when in 1957, I was sent home from school for convincing my classmates that we were under attack from the Russians. My pretentious panic prompted my "chums" to duck under their desks and cover their heads! Likewise, I took some "imaginative liberty" in the writing of "The Crimson Cord," all the while attempting to underscore the story with scriptural accuracy and historical facts. It took little imagination for me to describe parts of this novel that I have lived out. I too departed the teachings of my youth, but like the rebellious runaway of the following pages, I returned home because of the unrelenting power of the love of parents.

However, I can't give much credit to my daughter Becky for teaching me how to love a rebellious child, simply because she never was one. Well, at least not often enough for me to catch on. I do trust that this book will inspire those who struggle with disobedient children, to remember that unconditional love is the one thing that will bring our prodigals home at the appointed time and that God's hand of protection will rest upon them until that day comes.

One of God's greatest gifts to someone is for them to know that there is another they can always count on, regardless of circumstances. Which brings me to thank the one person who has the bigger part of any success that comes to my life, that being my best friend, Judy. She is living proof that "a friend loves at all times." She says she is my biggest fan and if she were the only one, I would be fine.

I acknowledge Michael and Annette Kelly, my awesome pastors, who shepherd Church of the Hills, and likewise, my fellow parishioners who each in their own unique way inspire me. Special thanks go to all of my educated friends and family, who helped undangle my participles and review the edits. But mostly, my sincere thanks goes to those of you who read "The Crimson Cord," as we pray together for a Godlike ending to all of our life stories.

Characters

Chavvah. Eve, mother of all
Qayin. Cain
Nachash. The serpent
Abiel. G-d who is Father
Ebed. Manservant
Ammah. Mother of twins
Ormah. Mother-in-law
Shiphrah. Hebrew midwife
Pharez. The one who tears
Zerah. Son of the morning
Egla. The calf
Naarah. The girl
Eleazar. Help of G-d
Hiphil. The one who circumcises
Machir. The salesman
Anan. Sorceress
Eli. High priest

Prologue

THE CRIMSON-COLORED CLOTHS OF CANAAN

The *coccus ilicis* was commonly known among the ancient Canaanite people as the crimson (scarlet) worm. Although the worm is the size of a small berry, it identified an entire race of people. The "Kinakhnu," as they named themselves, means "the red people." They acquired this name as a result of their use of the scarlet worm in the making of dyes. As the female worm species prepared to give birth to her young, she attached her body to the trunk of a tree, affixing herself so firmly and permanently that she never left again. She deposited her eggs beneath her body and protected them until the larvae hatched and entered its own life cycle, then she died, leaving a crimson fluid that stained her body as well as the wood of the tree. The rare and beautiful dye came from the remains of the dead worm. Once the dyes were applied to fabrics; the "red people" shipped the famed cloths from their ports to the entire known world.

A simile of the life cycle of the scarlet worm opens our story. A young Hebrew mother loses her struggle with death as she gives life to twin sons. Her attending midwife tied a crimson cord around the ankle of the first of the twins that pressed his way from her womb. The cord served to designate his order of birth for the purpose of determining birthrights, but fate intervenes as the would-be firstborn is pushed aside to a different destiny. He forsakes his family and its values to stain his life with strong drink, satanically inspired worship and sexual deviancy, all common to and propagated by the Canaanite culture. The "red people" colored more than fabrics with their dye. Their lascivious lifestyle tainted the lives of many a wayward prodigal. The "Kinakhnu" religion was both captivating and dangerous. Although history condemns and denounces it for the thousands of innocents who perished as human sacrifices on the altars of its lust, it repeats itself in every generation. It may cloak itself in new white robes to conceal its bloody crimson purpose, but it is everybit as deadly now as then.

The father of the twins in this story is simply identified in the Biblical parable as "a certain man." We will put a name, a face, and a life story to this "certain man." The word "certain" in the Greek language is "*tis*" which can also mean "every." Whether you are a man, woman, boy, or girl—"every" one of us can find ourselves in the pages of this book. Regardless of where you are in life, may this story help guide you home.

The question is: Can love, even if not perfect in every way, and perhaps misplaced or misunderstood prevail over unholy providence? Sometimes, a heart has to be broken before it can release the love it holds!

CHAPTER 1

The Certain Man

It had been over a millennium since the first mother of the new earth conceived a child with her husband, "the red dirt man." On the heels of their terrifying serpent encounter, Chavvah experienced something entirely different and frightening as she gave birth to Qayin. His name means "to wail." Chavvah yelled out in such pain, that the sound of his name became a funeral chant. Chavvah gave birth painlessly, before death slithered into paradise lost, but entertaining the serpent brought a curse of excruciating pain upon her. She revengefully repeated prophecies that G-d spoke to her. "My offspring will crush your head. Hear me O'Nachash; we will crush your head." From that day forward, of the tens of thousands of Ibriy births, every mother and father bore the hope that their child of birth would be "the serpent head crusher."

The third Sabbath of the month of Abib dawned upon the serene and prosperous city called Jerusalem. The Sabbath was the most important day in the life of those dwelling in Jerusalem. Religious practices dominated their culture. However, today was to be more than sanctimonious exercise for one of Jerusalem's most promising, fledgling citizens. Although Abiel was only twenty-nine years of age, the people of the city respected him as much as they did their elders. He was not so good-looking as to intimidate other men; nonetheless, his manliness attracted men of strength. Yet he possessed an aura of gentleness that assured the timid and assuaged the weak. He could have taken a wife some years ago. Girls and women alike were enamored by him and eager to be in his company. Unfortunately for them, he was more interested in the affairs of his father and family concerns than romance. That is until he met and married

Ammah. Unlike other doting women, she was the first girl who ignored him into relentless pursuit of her. She was the "forbidden fruit" of Chavvah's garden, which he could not resist. His young bride, Ammah, was a soul match for her husband. She spent the first sixteen years of her young life desiring only the company of her mother, her father's concubines, and her aunts. Under their tutelage, she learned to bake bread, cook stews, make cheese, ferment wine, and spin clothing. These skills made her most desirable as a wife who would be capable of managing a large household. It was fair to expect that she too would become the mother of many, judging from the fact that she had nine brothers, all born without complication or loss. Ammah was not delicate or frail. She was robust and had the appearance of one beyond her years. Many prospective husbands sent their fathers to Ammah's house with a bride price. They all left disappointed and spurned. That is until the day when Abiel's father visited. A blissful nine months passed as swiftly as a weaver's shuttle for Abiel and Ammah. For years, they had no thought of being with one another; now they could never remember being apart.

It was unusual to find Abiel sleeping as the first rays of morning light pushed the last vestiges of night over the western horizon of Jerusalem. At the same moment, Ammah desperately battled the pangs of childbirth, as her fetus pushed its way out of the darkness of her womb toward the dawn of its first sunrise. Abiel's manservant, Ebed, had faithfully kept a vigil throughout the night and morning watches. Just as a cock noisily began crowing just outside the window of Ammah's bedchamber, Ebed respectfully but firmly shook the covered leg of Abiel. Even though Ebed was twice Abiel's age and had been a servant for his family long before Abiel was born, he did not usurp his seniority. Ebed's voice rose from a whisper as he competed for attention with the noisy bird outside. He exhorted, "Abiel, wake up…master…master…wake up, master. It is time; Ammah's midwives have called out to me and it is time!"

Exhaustion sent Abiel spiraling into a deep sleep. His fatigue was intensified by the lingering hurt of his father's death. Shortly after gaining the hand of a bride for his son, Abiel's father lost his life to the pitiless hand of death. As the eldest son, Abiel assumed responsibility for overseeing the bountiful inheritance bequeathed to him and his brothers. The past few nights, images of Abiel's departed father filled his dreams. In these night visions, his father offered guidance concerning how Abiel should administer the family birthright. These cogitations were vivid, and Abiel would awaken strengthened. At other times, he became anxious over his duties. His father's mantle fell heavily upon his shoulders, even though he had spent most of his life preparing to wear it. A second cloak of responsibility loomed as G-d had blessed him to have a child of his own. He hoped the baby would be a male that he could train up to help with the family affairs. In addition, having a son would assure him that at the appointed time of his death, the family inheritance would pass on to yet another generation! Abiel hoped that someday he would have as many children as his father, if not more. He was the eldest of five brothers and twin sisters.

Meanwhile, Ebed continued shaking the slumbering father-to-be. One final robust jolt from Ebed roused Abiel, causing his senses to rush at him like a hungry lion chasing a frightened gazelle. It took a few moments and a shake of his head for him to grasp that it was not his father's spirit prodding him to get up and be about his business. Abiel jumped up from his bed as he roused to the realization that it was Ebed waking him with the news that his baby was being born. He hastily washed his face in the cool water that Ebed had drawn and poured into a basin. He halfheartedly commenced praying his customary morning prayers. He trusted that G-d would forgive him, if just this once he hurried past the rituals that he practiced since the time that he could speak well enough to utter a few sentences. Nonetheless, Abiel made a feeble attempt to lay aside his pardonable distraction and pray, "Hear, O Israel, Hear, O, Hear…The Lord our God is…I hear Ammah, I hear my wife calling for me."

Abiel waited many weeks for this moment, and his anticipation served to strengthen his heart through some dreadfully difficult times. Some of the land that Abiel inherited was as rough as the back of a crocodile and as unforgiving as a coiled viper. It did not resemble the earth that his ancestors and other ancients described. They told stories of a bountiful garden, wherein every variety of plant and animal flourished. Supposedly, it was a paradise watered by mystical dew from heaven every morning. Pristine rivers containing an abundance of varied species of fish and other aquatic life divided the land. Albeit most days and nights with Ammah made life seem as good for Abiel as paradise. He dared to think, "Who can tell; it may be that a child born of my lineage will be the seed of Mother Eve that fulfills the promise of God to crush the head of the cursed serpent and to put an end to the injustice and suffering that is common to all men."

CHAPTER 2

Childbirth

As remembrances of Mother Eve appeared from antiquity, they apprehended Abiel's attention. A shrieking cry from Ammah abruptly reminded him that her curse of agonizing childbirth was present, like an unwelcome guest, at this gory sacrament to the perpetuation of life. A deafening silence interrupted the commotion that came from Ammah's room. Abiel hurriedly made his way down the long hall leading to Ammah's bedchamber. He halted in half stride, paralyzed by an eerie pall of quiet that hung like a heavy curtain separating him from the room where his beloved wife walked amid the dark shadows of the valley of death. Ammah did not have the luxury of stopping as she struggled for her life, and the new life entangled in a web of death with her. She fought valiantly to wrest spoil from the hold of death, humankind's mortal combatant.

Just then, the resonance of mingled cries pierced the silence. For a moment, Abiel's heart seemed it might never have beaten again, but then it began to pound wildly. It beat as if it passionately danced the *hora* with Abiel's as its partner. A pity, this was anything but a wedding feast. His subsequent impulse was to push open the closed chamber door so he could see the curious events transpiring just out of his sight.

Tempted to act rashly, he refrained, as his ever-stately mother-in-law, Ormah, stepped into the hall from inside Ammah's bedchamber. Out of character, she appeared bedraggled, but Abiel did not notice. His eyes strained to see what his ears had alerted him to. In the brief moment the door was open, he discerned the cries of two infants. His heart ceased dancing. A menacing notion swooped down on him like the attack of a hunting falcon. He counted aloud, "one, two…one, two…two, yes two voices." His behavior bewildered Ormah. "Who is he talking to?" she wondered as she listened to him counting.

She had no hint of what he was thinking. His mind raced toward an unwanted conclusion. "Twins," he said aloud, "twin girls, just like my twin sisters." If the tone of his voice did not betray his disappointment, the look on his face bespoke the emotion welling up in his heart.

Ormah, perceiving Abiel's sentiment, yearned to console her son-in-law. Just as she rendered relief to her daughter by holding her throughout the agonizing watches of the past night, she embraced him with her words.

She agreed, "Yes Abiel, you are the father of twins." These words tore at the dam holding back his river of tears. Abiel was nearly angered to see Ormah break into a wide smile. Drops of disappointment joined by angry ones threatened to betray his manhood, but before his first tear fell, Ormah mercifully and gleefully sang out, "Twins, twin boys! You have twin sons, Abiel."

CHAPTER 3

Calamity

The floodgates of Abiel's eyes broke open. The tears of disappointment that threatened him gave way to a river of salty joy streaming its way down his face. He laughed and shouted out praises to the G-d Most High and to Ammah. He wanted nothing else but to go to Ammah's side. He would kiss her hand and share the joy of this moment with her. Then to hold his sons! Wiping his tears away, he realized something was amiss. The euphoria of his own emotion blinded him from seeing that Ormah was weeping. The tenor of her lamenting was not one of gladness. Grief-laden sobs were something that he recently became painfully familiar with. Ormah's cry sounded much like the grief that overcame his mother the day she received the news of her husband's death.

He reluctantly probed, "Did we have three sons and one has died?"

Ormah paused to collect herself for a prudent answer to his question—one moment too long for Abiel. He bolted toward the door leading into Ammah's room, but Ormah reached out and firmly, grabbed hold of his arm. Her strong grip spun him around, aligning his face directly in front of hers. He was in no way prepared for what he saw in her misty eyes, much less what she was about to tell him. She could not decide what was worse, the throbbing pain in her own breast or being the messenger of death to her son-in-law. She loved Abiel long before her daughter did, having been acquainted with Abiel's father and mother years before Abiel was born. They were good, decent people. Ormah remembered Abiel from the day he was born and even as a child, he remained respectful, never doing anything to mar or tarnish the reputation of his respected family. Ormah played a big role in arranging her daughter's marriage to Abiel. She assured Abiel's father that his bride price was acceptable, unlike others before his. He was everything that a mother-in-law could ever want for her daughter. Now Ormah had to plunge a dagger deep into the heart of this wonderful man.

Her words resisted forming on her lips with the tenacity of a small animal hiding in its nest, fighting death from a predator. Her hesitancy to speak told Abiel more than he wanted know. In full panic, he jerked his arm from Ormah's ever-tightening grip. Four frantic steps and he found himself engulfed in a shroud of darkness. Mere moments ago, the anticipation of new life was as bright as the morning sun peeking through the eastern window. His hopes broke apart like a small boat dashed on the jagged rocks of sorrow that unfortunately are ever concealed just below the calm shallows near the shores of life.

This impetuous act by Abiel was possibly the most imprudent thing that he would do in his entire life. None of his life experiences prepared him for the ghastly scene that unfolded before his eyes. His wife's uncovered body that he so cherished as a husband, lay still, but warm from the heat of convulsing. She slumped down on the birthing stool upon which she sat and ruled as the queen of life for the past few hours. All that held her upright was a rope firmly suspended from a roof beam. Her right hand still hung in the loop that she used to pull against it as she strained to deliver. The rope showed of bite marks. Ammah had chewed on the rope incessantly during her ordeal, endeavoring to muffle her screams. The blood-covered midwives did not hurry to move Ammah. They never suspected that Abiel would dare to enter the room. One bathed the twins with water, as another rubbed them down with salt and oil.

"Bring me some long strips of swaddling," Shiphrah ordered in a snappy voice, not attempting to hide the fact that she was upset. Her helpers moved through the room like a swarm of ants. They may have looked disorganized, but everything came together with purpose. The wrapping process now complete made the boys look more like Egyptian mummies than Hebrew children.

No one in the room dared to speak to Abiel. There was no counselor to advise him, yet his paternal yearnings compelled him to attend to his sons first. It was not that he felt no concern for Ammah's fate or was unmindful of her. Nature's survival instincts told him that there was nothing he could do for Ammah; yet all would not be lost if their sons survived. He felt his heart split in two between grieving for Ammah or providing for his newborn children. The rush of opposing emotions left him standing still, looking nowhere, and wondering everything.

CHAPTER 4

The Crimson Cord

As Abiel counted the fingers and toes of the twins, he noticed that one of his sons had a conspicuous red mark on his forehead. However, something drew his attention away from the inspection of the twins. Whisperings among the chambermaids and midwives distracted him.

"Quick, help me." One said.

"Over here." Said another.

"Let's get her down." They agreed.

"What a terrible sight for Master Abiel to see."

"Someone get a blanket."

Reluctantly, he turned his head just enough to see one of the maids cover Ammah's body. Several other women strained to lift her enough to get her arm free of the birthing rope so that they might move her up onto her bed. Abiel's admiration for the women who labored as midwives rose as he surveyed the bloody scene. His churning stomach dispelled any notion of helping them lift Ammah onto the bed. He felt queasy and faint even though he was accustomed to blood. Abiel had cut hundreds of rams and cattle.

"I must not let the women see me like this. I must hold on," he reassured himself, besides, his participation would lend credence to the reality of what he just witnessed. His best friend for now was denial. Returning his attention to his sons eased his sickness.

As his head cleared, he vaguely remembered something unusual about both of his sons. Looking at them again, confirmed that indeed one son had a reddish birthmark. The mark was big and ugly. It caused Abiel to gasp! The other son had a red-colored cord tied around his ankle. Abiel knew that midwives customarily tied a colored cord somewhere on the body of the firstborn of twins so as to tell them apart. The cord identified the firstborn. It assured him of his preeminence in the family.

Abiel finally collected himself to the point that he could look around the room without it spinning. He saw one of the midwives of reputation that he knew by name. The women of Jerusalem agreed Shiphrah was the best midwife around. She possessed the skills of an accomplished surgeon when she took up a knife to assist in delivery. No other midwife possessed her knowledge of herbs and potions used to control pain and induce labor. Some even accused her of being a witch. That is unless they required her services. Labor pains and its terrors had a way of transforming her into an angel. Shiphrah possessed all the physical qualities necessary for her profession. Her hands were small, so little that they looked out of place next to her large forearms. Conversely, her tiny hands were perfect for comfortable entry into the birth canal. Once there, her fingers detected things known only to her and G-d. In spite of small hands, if the baby needed turning in the womb, she seemed to possess supernatural strength.

Without looking toward her, Abiel called Shiphrah. "Shiphrah, come. I need to speak with you."

Shiphrah, hearing Abiel call her name, dreaded what would ensue. Knowing that he would ask for an account of the things that just transpired frightened an otherwise brave woman. She whispered to one of her helpers, "Can you tell? Is he angry?"

A shrug of the shoulders from someone not wanting to be involved was not much help. Shiphrah was not a stranger to blame coming from an upset husband for a birth-related death. Her face grew hot as she crossed the room.

Her pace quickened as he insisted, "Shiphrah."

She questioned herself, "How can I explain things that my own eyes don't believe? In all my years of experience in midwifery, never have I seen anything to rival this."

The closer that she got to him, she sensed hurt, not anger. Shiphrah thought, "A hug would help more than trying to answer the questions that will surely deepen his hurt more so than comfort him." She did not know Abiel well enough to embrace him.

Without lifting his head to address Shiphrah, Abiel queried, "This son, the one with the cord around his ankle, you did mark him with a cord as my firstborn, did you not?" His body and his voice shook with emotion.

Her reply shook him even harder, like an aftershock of the earthquake that hit him when he entered this damnable room.

She began her defense, "Abiel, you know my reputation as a midwife or else you would not have allowed me to have been called to your wife's side. I am a truthful person. I would not make mention of my truthfulness and reputation, if it were not for the fact that what I am about to tell you is so incredible."

He interrupted, "Yes, yes Shiphrah. I acknowledge that you are renowned for your character. Please, just answer me."

This eased her just a bit and she started in, "Your son, the one with the cord tied around his ankle; I tied it to his ankle when his foot first appeared from Ammah's womb. It terrified me when I saw a foot come out first. I saw that the child needed to be turned. This kind of birth usually causes awful pain and death."

She resisted the urge to rush, in spite of the impatience on Abiel's face. She continued with deliberation, "What occurred next is so astonishing that I, along with the other women present, including Ormah, your mother-in-law, have a hard time believing what we saw. Just as I got the cord tied around the ankle of the baby, his foot withdrew into the womb."

She paused to swallow, hoping to get some moisture into her throat, which suddenly was as dry as the great Egyptian desert. "Master Abiel, forgive me for talking so plainly."

"Go on. I insist. Go on," he chided.

Gulping again, she continued, "Scarcely had that happened when, the head of another baby started coming out. Your sons fought to see which one would arrive first. Their contention created a deadly situation for Ammah. I'm not telling you these things to upset you; I just want you to hear the truth."

Shiphrah paused, needing assurance that Abiel really wanted to hear the rest.

"Go on," Abiel urged, with somewhat more of a begging tone. "Please, I must know everything."

But before she could continue, he exclaimed, "You are telling me…You are telling me that the son who wears the cord was being born first, but was pushed aside by my other son? Consequently, the first was born last and the last became the first?"

Something in his voice made her feel like a liar. She responded in a voice that convincingly had a tone of strength and confidence. "Yes, and what is even more amazing, Ammah survived the entire ordeal and remained responsive enough to name your sons as they were born."

Abiel's total immersion in what he was hearing kept him from noticing Ormah walk up beside him. Her voice startled him as she enjoined the conversation asserting, "Abiel, I witnessed the things that Shiphrah just told you. Every word of it is true."

Hearing confirmation from Ormah, one that he trusted implicitly, assured him that he should believe, no matter how incredulous the story seemed. Even so, he could not resist asking, "Ormah, you heard Ammah name my sons?"

"Yes," she replied without hesitation. "As impossible as it seems, Ammah called out your son's names as she was dying."

Abiel could hardly breathe, but managed to continue, "Tell me, Ormah, tell me their names."

"Ammah named your firstborn Pharez and your second son, the one with the cord around his ankle, she called Zerah."

He wondered aloud, "Surely you are mistaken in saying that the second son was the one with the cord around his ankle."

He was ashamed of himself for voicing his innermost thoughts without consideration of the rudeness and disrespect he showed. "I shouldn't question mother. Not here and now."

Ormah took no offense, making allowance that Abiel was stupefied by the events of the morning. She asked Abiel to come and sit down next to her on the bench in the hall just outside the bedchamber.

She whispered, "Son, this may take some time and it will be painful for both of us, but it is imperative that you of all people grasp what happened."

CHAPTER 5

Confusion

Raising the tone of her voice ever so slightly, Ormah began, "I know that I confused you by attesting that Zerah, the son with the cord around his ankle, was born last. Still, listen carefully. As Zerah was coming out of the womb, the midwives saw that something was terribly wrong. Zerah's foot came out first. Shiphrah knew that he was breach. Anyway, Shiphrah hurriedly put a cord around his ankle. She was going to attempt to turn him."

Abiel groaned, and she paused long enough to move down the bench to him, taking his hand in hers. "This happened just as the first shafts of the morning light came. Ammah saw the baby's foot and called out the name Zerah."

Abiel enjoined, "I see the meaning of that in our tongue; Zerah, "rising of light" or "son of the morning."

Ormah nodded her agreement and continued, "Even though the child was not yet completely out of her womb, the name unquestionably was appropriate. Then, the strangest thing happened. Just as Shiphrah told you, Zerah's leg went back into the womb. As it did, Pharez's head pushed its way out. The pressure of the unborn pushing on each other produced an insufferable strain on Ammah's womb."

The palms of Abiel's hands were sweating so profusely that it prompted Ormah to ask if he wanted her to continue. Neither of them noticed Ebed standing down the hall. He scurried faster than he believed his aging legs could take him, and soon reappeared. He excused himself for entering their private moment, as he brought them cool water from the courtyard well. Abiel furiously splashed the water onto his hands and face, as would an otter frolicking in a marshy wadi. Ignoring her own pain, Ormah took the towel and wiped Abiel's face. As quickly as she wiped away the water, his perspiration replaced it as if she had not dried him at all. He blinked at Ormah as the salt of his sweat burned his eyes. "Mother, I am all right. Please, continue."

The next deep sigh came from her. "As the second son appeared, Ammah shrieked out the name Pharez, meaning, 'I am tearing', and that is exactly what happened. She was incurably injured. We were unable to stop her bleeding. Shiphrah did everything possible. It is because of her that Ammah lived long enough to deliver both Pharez and Zerah."

Abiel's family pride surfaced though his hurt long enough for him to exclaim, "Shiphrah will be handsomely rewarded."

Ormah acknowledged his remark with a deliberate gesture of her head, but wasted no time getting back to her story. She hastened to be done with this, not knowing how much longer she could hold back before giving way to her own grief.

"As Pharez pushed past Zerah's foot, Zerah's heel pressed against his brother's forehead as if to stop his birth. Zerah's heel caused a huge bruise on Pharez's forehead."

"Mother, I know. I have seen it and it is awful, isn't it?"

"Yes son, it is, and I don't know if it will go away with time. Shiphrah does not think it will. Anyway, our 'son of the morning' retreated into the darkness of the womb, taking the red cord with him. Ammah could not see what was happening. I am not as sure as the others are that she knew that there were twins. She possibly said the name Pharez thinking that Zerah was still coming out wrong. She knew he was breach. Shiphrah attempted to turn Zerah but was unable. Zerah, not Pharez, was the one born breach."

This dumbfounded Abiel. He sat in quiet contemplation of this story as deep as an unsolvable mystery riddle recited by a king's jester for the entertainment of his royal court.

The names Ammah gave to their sons added to the mystery of this most incredible story. Abiel double-checked himself several times by spelling and respelling the names of the twins forwards and backwards. "Pharez," "zerahP," "Zerah," "P-hareZ." Surely, Ammah could not have thought up such a riddle, especially as she passed through the door of death. "Breach" and "son of the morning" have no similar meaning, yet the name Pharez is Zerah, when spelled backwards.

"What was happening to him and Ammah? Was there a spiritual significance to the struggle in Ammah's womb? Zerah's name means 'son of the morning', like that of the fallen angel Lucifer. Ammah is dead, leaving our firstborn disfigured. G-d marked Cain, the firstborn of Eve, because of the murderous anger with which he coveted his brother's blessing. My ancestors, Jacob and Esau, wrestled over their birthright until Jacob grabbed Esau's heel while still in Rebekah's womb. The head of the serpent should be bruised, not the head of my firstborn. Furthermore, I never will believe that one of my seed could behave like Lucifer." Abiel rebuked himself for entertaining thoughts that bullied their way into his mind, like an uninvited guest to a party. Then an even more frightening thought seized upon him.

The battle for Eden was for ownership of the birthright of the sons of G-d. It began never-ending struggle to determine who should have dominion over the earth. "What if Pharez and Zerah…?" he wondered.

Surely, any moment now, Ebed will rouse me up out of my bed, and this hideous nightmare will end! The sun will rise on a celebrated Sabbath day, and the shadows of frightening night visions will retreat in its light!

CHAPTER 6

A Call for Caregivers

Abiel's hopes for awakening from a bad dream disappeared as Shiphrah's voice called him from his stupor, "Sir, I have something for you...Sir."

With a start, he turned to see her holding the boys. She nodded approval for him to hold out his arms, which he did, but with reluctance. Not because he did not want to, but because he had never held anything so precious, so fragile. She handled the boys as if they were unbreakable. Shiphrah placed the swaddling-wrapped twins safely in his strong arms, saying ceremoniously, "Master, behold your sons." At that moment, stark reality fell on him with the force of Elijah's mantle. Pharez and Zerah nuzzled against his chest, hungrily searching for their mother's milk. Not finding what nature normally provided for babies, the twins demandingly made their needs known. Their famished cries forced Abiel to abandon his fears and attend to their needs. He soon learned that he lacked more than milk when it came to mothering.

Mother-in-law was thinking far ahead of him. Before Abiel thought of milk, she dispatched Ebed into the streets of the city to inquire of prospective caregivers for the babies.

She barked at Ebed, "Get going, man. Do you want these babies to starve?"

Ebed got a move on, not accustomed to this kind of demeanor from the usually meek Ormah. He rightly suspected that he would have no difficulty finding wet-nurses, after witnessing numerous infant funerals every day. It was commonplace for babies to die during birth or early in their infancy. Many of the young girls who lost their children were extremely poor. Most of them would welcome a chance to live under the roof of a wealthy family for a season.

What complicated Ebed's task was that Ormah instructed him to fetch two caregivers, one for each child.

He didn't normally curse, but the thought of two more women coming into the house perturbed him, causing him to mouth the words, "Bleeders controlled by the sun, the moon, the stars, and only G-d knows what else. I must be sure that the two that I pick will not cause any problems in the master's house."

Before making any final decisions, he determined to go to the main gate of the city and converse with the elders to inquire of the reputations of the women that he might select. Shrewdly, this would take the burden off him if anything went wrong. It was time to move with urgency. Two voracious babies waited to feed from the breast of a woman. This is all that will quiet them. Ebed gave pause, "I must think of more than food for the twins. Nature is a wonder, the way it works for survival. Strangers bond as mothers to children who are not of their flesh. I have seen goat's nurse orphaned sheep."

He determined to take extreme caution in creating any union that likely would remain years beyond the time of weaning or childhood.

Soon the city was astir with the news of Ammah's death. Word was out that Ebed sought wet-nurses for Abiel's twin sons. Ebed's assumption was right and by mid morning, a number of women seeking employ gathered at the house of Abiel. The faithful old servant was glad that he would not have to search the city. The city came to him.

There was such a clamor in the courtyard; Ebed could not talk to the women one at a time. He went out to them, if for no other reason than to quiet them.

As he entered the yard, he kept his distance from the women, fearing that they might mob him. It took several strapping servants to keep the desperate ones off him. There was one that did not join the throng of girls. She stood back maintaining a certain air of dignity that almost cloaked her need. Ebed recognized her, and called her name as he motioned for her to come to him.

"Egla, come over here. You other women make way. Let her through."

He heard that her little boy died a few days ago. It was in a tragic accident that also left her husband severely crippled. As he watched her make her way to him, he marveled at how courageous this woman must be. To lose her only child just days ago and bravely come forward for such a difficult assignment as this had to be difficult. He would surely approve of her as one of the women that he would hire. He even allowed himself a fleeting fantasy that he was a man of youth and wealth and that he could take her as his own.

The usually fluent Ebed stumbled at his words. "Egla, it is good to see you. I mean, I am surprised to see you out so soon. I am sorry, I did not mean; what I mean is…I really am sorry about the death of your son. Are you sure that you are up for something like this?" It was uncharacteristic for Ebed to be so awkward. Being awake all night and enduring the fatal goings-on of the morning took a heavy toll on him. He was fond of Ammah. He could not have hurt worse if he had fought and been beaten by one of the giants of Gath.

Egla demonstrated her excellent character. She, noticing his discomfort, mercifully interrupted, "I thank you for your kind words concerning the loss of my son, but please understand that he is the reason that I have the courage to come here. You may not know this, but I have no other children. I poured all of my love into my child. Now I am as though my womb is barren. I am lost without someone to hold and nurse."

Ebed wiped his running nose on the sleeve of his outer garment.

"If you should hire me," Egla continued, "I will provide much more than the milk from my body and the comfort of my breast to the child that you ask me to nurse. I know that if I give love again, it will heal my broken heart. The accident that claimed the life of our son injured my husband. We desperately need this chance."

Egla's words so moved Ebed that he struggled to keep his composure. He worried that with all of his pent-up emotion, he would embarrass himself if he bared his feelings.

Fortunately for him, she continued by requesting, "And if you would be so kind, sir, please consider my friend Naarah. Her baby girl died just one day after its birth. She is so very young and is the concubine of a wealthy but cruel man who is displeased with her for not bearing a male child. Rumors are that he had something to do with the child's death. I will see to it that she causes no problems, and that no request of Abiel or his family goes unmet. For this, I give my most solemn word. I beseech you, kind sir; listen to the words of my heart and look favorably upon my request. Send the other women away, and allow Naarah and me to remain with you and the household of Abiel."

Ebed longed to tell her immediately that he granted her request. Nevertheless, his servant mentality demanded that he seek guidance from the elders of the city. He excused his indecision because he knew nothing of Naarah. Unwittingly, Egla put herself in a precarious position. She faced rejection if the elders deemed Naarah unsuitable. Ebed twitched his finger at Naarah as he and Egla departed from the courtyard to make their way to the city's main gate.

With an air of authority, he said to her, "You, come; go with Egla and me. You other women wait here until I return or send word to you."

It was a typically quiet morning as the three of them made their way down the narrow streets of Jerusalem toward the Damascus Gate. They took care that their shoes did not make too much sound on the rocky pavement, so as not to violate the Sabbath. As it was, before the day was over, they would exceed the distance limits allowed for walking on this holy day.

Ebed grumbled, "I hope motherless and hungry babies qualify as 'an ox in the ditch' exception to Sabbath law. I do not have time to go offer sacrifice for some unnecessary offense."

Ebed was not sure if there would be a quorum of elders gathered at the gate. With all of the vendors and markets closed, it was possible no one except the watchmen would be at the gate. Secretly, Ebed hoped that this would be the case. Attempting to seek counsel from the elders was the equivalent of dutifully honoring them. He then would be justified in making his own decision concerning the women.

"Walk softly," he admonished as they drew near the Damascus Gate.

Ebed's wish failed. Upon arriving at the gate, he saw elder Eleazar in attendance. If just one of the elders had to be present, Ebed could not have asked for anyone wiser or more reasonable. Eleazar, watching Ebed and the two women approach the gate, anticipated the nature of their business. The news of Ammah's death and the call for wet-nurses preceded their arrival. Nothing notable ever happened in the city that news of it did not fly first to the main gate. Eleazar was relieved when he saw Naarah and Egla with Ebed. He knew much of these two women.

Naarah was reputed to be an unfortunate girl, taken as a concubine by a wealthy man whose reputation was less than golden. She always looked dark-eyed and frail, a telltale sign of her abuse. Now that she failed to produce a son for her master, he would be glad for someone else to care for her. Eleazar had no proof, but he believed that the baby girl born to Naarah had a deformity, and her husband destroyed the infant and fed to his dogs. Naarah's husband wanted to sell her and would have if it were not for the protection of the law. People said of her that she was a loyal person. She must be staunch not to have run away long ago.

Contrastingly, Egla made a striking appearance, as beautiful in her spirit as in the flesh. As the trio drew near, Eleazar couldn't help but notice fresh lines of pain in Egla's pretty face. However, her sorrow failed to distract from the natural grace with which she carried herself. Eleazar did not understand why her parents named her Egla, meaning "the calf," unless they intended it as a spiritual thing, such as "a most expensive offering to G-d." It certainly had nothing to do with her physical appearance, which was stunning.

Ebed spoke first, "Greetings in the name of Abiel, my master whom I have come to this gate to represent."

Eleazar responded, "Greetings to you and my respect to the house of Abiel. What is your cause?"

Ebed made it known, "I have come to inquire if there is any reason why the two women standing with me should be forbidden to enter into the service of the household of Abiel as nurses for his sons, seeing that as of this day, their mother has died."

As presiding elder, Eleazar raised his hand to his face and stroked his long but thinning beard several times, feigning to be deep in thought. Then with a voice that sounded much stronger than expected, he announced loudly, as he would have done if speaking to a vast assembly, "I know only good of these women that stand in the gates of the city this day. Go in peace and render service unto the household of Abiel as you would render faithful service unto G-d."

Alas, after so much had gone wrong for much of the day, Ebed finally reckoned that G-d smiled on him. Here was some good news to bring to Abiel.

He quickly thanked Eleazar for his blessing and turning to the women, he said, "Hurry, go to your houses and collect your belongings. There are two hungry children awaiting you. I will go, dismiss the other women, and give the good news to Abiel. I will send servants to your houses to help you with your belongings."

Naarah remarked that she had little and required no help. The ever-helpful Egla said that she would bring Naarah to her house, and the servants could find both of them there.

As Ebed neared the courtyard of Abiel's house, he noticed that the women who gathered earlier were leaving. The sun's position indicated that it neared midday. The sweltering heat made it easier to give up hope. Besides, staying away from their homes any longer would put them in peril of disregarding the Sabbath. There was but one woman remaining inside the courtyard. She took refuge in the shade of the lone tree in the center of the yard. It surprised Ebed to see her standing there. Her dark dress nearly hid her in the shadows and strangely, she did not call out to him.

"This poor soul must really be desperate to remain standing out in the heat of the day without any assurance that I would even return."

Even so, he had no need for a third person. He thanked her for coming and abruptly told her she could leave. Without intending so, he bordered on being rude to the woman. It did not matter. She left quietly as if she did not hear what he bothered to say.

He was anxious to get inside the house and give Abiel the news of the nurses. Entering the house, Ebed asked one of the servants if they would inform Abiel that he wished to speak with him. Ebed was disappointed to hear that he could not see Abiel right away. He was busy preparing to offer sacrifice to G-d, and instructed several of his servants to fetch a choice calf. Religious law did not require him to offer anything to G-d for the death of his wife, nor for the birth of his sons. This would be a free will offering. Had Ammah lived until the fortieth day after birth, she would have been required to offer sacrifice for her cleansing. Her midwives were defiled, and Ammah's death did not release them from their obligation. Abiel arranged to pay their offering price for them. Likewise, he reminded his treasurer to send five shekels of silver on the thirtieth day after birth to pay the price of redemption for Pharez. There was much to do. Only a man strong in body and in spirit could hold up under the load on his shoulders. Thankfully, he possessed faith like iron. However, even iron will bend if excessive heat is applied to it.

CHAPTER 7

The Committal

Having just buried his father, Abiel was well acquainted with the details involved in planning a funeral. Burial was an arduous task, and it threatened to overwhelm him. He turned to a steady source of help. Ormah! "Mother, I know that I have asked much of you…"

She stopped him before he finished, "You and the twins are all that I have left of Ammah. What do you require? Whatever it is, I will consider it an honor to do."

It was humbling for him to confess, "I cannot manage the affairs of the family and make proper preparation for our precious Ammah's funeral. I need…'"

Again she cut him short, "I know exactly what to do. Leave it under my care. I will attend to everything."

She left the room before Abiel could reply, going straightway to the bed where Ammah's body lay. She gently placed potsherds over her daughter's eyes and prepared to have a final conversation with her daughter. The private nature of their talk prompted Ormah to find an excuse to clear the room. She sent servants to fetch oils and spices to prepare Ammah's body for burial. Under Ormah's direction, Ebed dispatched others to purchase a coffin, to hire "mourners" to walk in the procession to the family gravesite and laborers to open and close the tomb. Shiphrah's birthing chest contained more than enough swaddling cloth for the babies, but no one anticipated using it to wrap and tie up Ammah's corpse.

Once alone, Ormah rehearsed, "Ammah, I know that you hear me. The day that I brought you into the world was a bright and sunny day much like today.

You always brought light into my world. Not one dark cloud have I seen since the first time I held you. No storm will end our time together. I will sit with you and be your 'watcher'. I will comb your hair, bathe you, and make up your face until time for me to take you to your new home. There were long pauses between each statement. Ormah waited for responses that only she could hear. Please allow me to break our custom and bring food into the room. You must be hungry after your struggle. I will have the servants bring fresh bread, just like the bread that we so often baked together. It will remain uneaten, but we will smell it together. I will take some wine that you made and pour it out to you in your honor. In the morning, we will dress you for your journey. Your attire will not be as pretty as your wedding dress was, but I promise you that you will be beautiful."

She was not finished, but a gentle knock on the door interrupted. She pulled a cloth over Ammah's face and bid the caller to enter.

It was one of the temple priests and Abiel.

Politely, Abiel whispered, "We aren't coming in. The priest just came by to check on us and remind us of the laws of burial."

Even though they did not linger, Ormah overheard the priest as he and Abiel went down the hallway, "Ammah's body must be buried quickly. In fact, at dawn tomorrow."

Ormah spoke as if expecting a response, "We don't have much time left, my child. I thank you for your pain and your struggle to leave part of yourself with us. I will love your sons as if they were you.

The entrance of two strange women escorted by servants carrying baggage cut short Ormah's and Ammah's goodbye. Shiphrah was not far behind with Pharez and Zerah in her sturdy arms.

Sabbath law prohibited burial on the rest day. The law created an awkward situation, in that Ammah's body remained in the house overnight. All the while, women who just yesterday were strangers to the family held and nursed Ammah's babies. The nurses and the babies took up residence in the same room with her lifeless body. She rigidly remained a silent sentinel, keeping watch over the morbid events. Every time one of the babies cried, the women in the room looked in unison toward Ammah's corpse. It may sound foolish, but they shared a fleeting thought that Ammah should get up and do something.

All through the night, Ormah repetitively sang the same lullaby.

> *"If you live on a hill, In a city in the sun, And you play in the shade of an olive tree,*
> *And at night you get tired, Though you've had a lot of fun,*
> *Say goodnight first of all to the olive tree.*
> *Leaves of silver shine in the moonlight, Olive branches wave in the moonlight.*
> *Dream of an olive tree, Its roots so deep, Dream of an olive tree while you are asleep. You are young, You are old. You are warm or you are cold.*
> *You can rest in the shade of an olive tree.*
> *At the end of the day, though you nothing more to say,*
> *Say goodnight last of all to the olive tree.*
> *Though the fruit of the tree, can be bitter as can be,*
> *There is food for the world in the olive tree.*
> *And a place for the birds, What a melody is heard.*
> *Go to sleep to the tune of the olive tree."*

Some members of the household thought the song to be beautiful, others thought it mournful. The unfortunate ones slept through it.

Daybreak postponed its appearance under the unrelenting stubbornness of a lingering dark night. There was barely enough light to make out the images of twelve women dressed in black garments gathering outside Abiel's house. Luckily for them, no one reported their crass talk or their occasional laughter. It was out of place for such a time, appreciating that in moments they would wail like the end of the world was upon them. Their arrival signaled that it was time to begin the procession to the gravesite. The "mourners" began warming up. Several of them beat on their breasts, while each in their own way made woeful noises. Jerusalem was in for a rude early awakening.

Ebed looked on with care as several of the strongest of the menservants lifted Ammah's stiffened body, placing her in a roughly hewn box that was her coffin. The clamor of activity awakened the twins. As only infants can, they managed to sleep much of the night, while Egla had not slept at all. Ormah's lullaby mesmerized her. She used to sing the same song to her child at his bedtime. Watching from a corner in the room, she nursed Pharez and revisited her own grief. She fought back tears in fear that her sorrow would get into her milk and poison the baby at her breast. Naarah joined Egla in the corner, clutching at Zerah so tightly that he yelped in discomfort. She hid behind him more so than she held him.

Egla scolded her, "Naarah, what are you doing? Surely, you hear him crying. Girl, feed the baby. Feed him."

Egla looked away from Naarah to see Ormah staring at them, placing her finger over her mouth, signaling for them to quiet down. She complained to the other servants, "What is the matter with these girls? They know that the dead can still hear. Ammah will not rest if she hears her babies crying."

Naarah stared back at Egla, her face, a mixture of embarrassment and a hint of resentment in one look.

The servants strained, letting out a half-awake grunt as they hoisted the heavy wooden box up on their shoulders and made their way out into the courtyard. By this time, the courtyard was bustling with activity as family and friends joined the "mourners." Ebed barely recognized Abiel or Ammah's father Hiphil. He had never seen either of them with their heads shaven. Abiel, Hiphil, and Ormah joined the servants, placing their shoulders under the coffin as the procession made its way out into the street that led to the Dung Gate on the east side of the city. From the gate forward, a path wound its way down into the Kidron Valley.

Once in the street, the hired mourners began beating on tambourines and small drums, letting out bloodcurdling cries, tearing at their garments, and heaping ashes into the air. Soon the procession passed through the Dung Gate and down the incline that led through the deep ravine of the Hinnom Valley. Hardly could anyone imagine a scene any more dreadful. The smoke of the perpetual fires in the valley refused to allow the full brilliance of the early morning sunrise to illuminate the landscape. Instead, it caused a reddish hue to descend across the path that the procession followed. The charred debris of the altars of Moloch and Baal, amidst the strewn weapons of defeated armies, resembled foggy evil spirits desiring to possess any passerby. This view, mingled with the awful smell of burning rubbish, smoldering flesh of cremated criminals, and the shrieking cries of the mourners, made for a scene that reeked of "hell." This was Tophet at its worse and best.

One of the aged relatives of Ammah determined not miss the chance to tell her grandson who walked at her side the story of "Toph."

"This is the vale of 'the drum', she said. Worshipers of the false god Baal beat on drums to drown out the cries of the children being offered as sacrifice to their bloodthirsty gods." The little boy grabbed his grandmother's leg and that just in time.

Ammah's mourners stopped beating their tambourines and drums as they descended into the valley. No one said a word. The babies that perished in the fiery sacrificial arms of idols deserved solemn remembrance. The shuffle and tottering of feet sliced through the peculiar quiet. Without warning, the temporary lull shattered as hordes of overfed, black vultures lifted up from a heap of waste just off the pathway. The flap of hundreds of powerful wings beating in rhythmic unison caused a rush of air that produced a noise sounding like that of drummers. With everyone's emotions already on edge, the vultures sent a sudden panic through the followers. Some dropped to their knees while others ran in terror. Abiel and Hiphil were the only two that kept the presence of mind to cling to the coffin. Their resolve kept the heavy box from dropping into a narrow ravine. It would have been nigh impossible to retrieve the coffin from such a deep and inaccessible place.

Abiel called out to Hiphil, "Sir, are you all right?"

"Yes, I think that I am, but quick, call the servants. I can't get up with the weight of this casket sitting on my arm."

Abiel let his end of the casket down to the ground and hurried to lift the heavy box off Hiphil's skinned, but otherwise unbroken, arm. He did not have to summon the servants. Having run away, their pride hurt worse than Hiphil's arm, and they returned almost as quickly as they fled. Fortunate they were to have a master who did not beat his slaves.

Soon the mourners regrouped and were once again under way. Some aloud and others under their breath swore at Tophet. "Cursed place. May my feet never pass this way again?"

Abiel could hardly wait to get out of Hinnom and up to the other side of the Kidron. As the procession neared the cave of burial, the mourners attempted to avoid defilement by stepping around or over the shallow graves of the poor. Small rain-hewn ditches running down the hillside served as inexpensive burial sites for the unfortunate. Kidron was a highly sought-after burial ground. According to tradition, Messiah would first appear there to resurrect the dead ones. It relieved Abiel to see that gardeners took care of moving the stone from the mouth of the sepulcher. There would not be any delay in the proceedings. One part of him hated to see the funeral end. It represented the finality of many things. Another part of him could not wait to be away from this place. His dread gave way to formality as a rabbi spoke a few verses from the Psalms, ending his remarks with, "Yahweh has loaned, and he has come for what is his. May the name of Yahweh be praised!"

Abiel did not recite the holy writings. He secretly prayed, "G-d, I beseech you that the next time that I come to this place, that it is I who is borne upon the shoulders of my servants that I may sleep in death with my fathers and my wife."

All of the life had gone out of him. As Hiphil and Ormah escorted Abiel out of Kidron, his last recollection was turning to look back toward the cave, making sure that the workers put the tombstone back in its place. Everything else was a blur until he arrived home. A house with four new occupants never seemed emptier. It was now time to start *shiv'ah*.

CHAPTER 8

Conflict

Preferential treatment for Pharez began from day one. As the friends and family gathered for *shiv'ah*, Abiel was careful to introduce Pharez as his firstborn, seeing that he represented "the redeemed" first fruits of Ammah's womb.

Proudly holding him high over his head and turning around so that everyone could see became a ritual when guests arrived. Abiel would exclaim, "Look at this man-child. How strong he is. My firstborn. Surely he is blessed." Abiel chose not to see the veiled reaction of forced smiles and pretentious compliments. Those who saw only the bloody birthmark on the baby's forehead did not share the sightlessness that Abiel suffered from. The birthmark overshadowed any other features that Pharez possessed.

"Yes, Abiel. What a fine son. Ammah would be so proud," seemed to be the polite and possibly only response. However, hardly out of the door and into the street, those leaving the house of Abiel could not stop talking about Pharez's blood red birth mark.

"Did you…?"

"How could I not?"

"Do you think that Abiel could help but see it?"

"I would think that it is impossible that he doesn't."

"I wonder if he realized what we were thinking. I tried to smile as best I could."

"I did too, but I felt like such a hypocrite."

"But what could anyone say?"

"I am not that wise. My thoughts are it would have been better for the poor child to die along with its mother."

"Amen."

Without exception, as guests left the house, Abiel could be heard saying, "Pharez, my firstborn,…my firstborn,…my firstborn." He said it with the conviction of someone attempting to convince himself. Regardless, he was undaunted in his determination to have Pharez be his firstborn. He put Pharez on the bosom of Egla, who was very buxom. Apart from her apparent physical attributes, she exuded the spirit of motherhood. Physically and emotionally, she was ready to receive a child into her arms and her heart. Nurturing came natural for her.

Contrastingly, Naarah was noticeably tense and unsure of herself. She lacked physical appearance, being of slight build. She looked malnourished when compared to Egla. Her demeanor was of one in turmoil, and it rightfully worried Ormah. She questioned if the situation warranted her apprehension. "Is my judgment tainted because another woman stands in my Ammah's place? Should I bother Abiel with this? It cannot be jealousy, for I don't feel the same of Egla."

Although the twins were just a few days old, Pharez grew and gained weight, as one might expect of a baby boy. It was noticeable that everything about Egla agreed with him. Conversely, Naarah's anxieties affected the flow and the quality of her milk. Unquestionably, performing the most mundane of tasks made her uncomfortable. Zerah cried constantly, and his discontentment demanded that someone do something. As Ormah dutifully watched over the twin, she decided that she had to bring this matter to Abiel. Little Zerah was not doing well and likely would die if his situation did not soon change. Ormah reluctantly approached, "Abiel, I know that you have been occupied with the many duties of the family business and this household. Perchance you have not notice what is happening with Naarah and Zerah."

Her conversation caught him off guard. Any mention of Zerah or Pharez got his attention.

"What is it? What situation?"

She hoped that she had not offended Abiel by suggesting that he was not dutiful.

"I cannot altogether blame the girl, but it is clear that she has not bonded with Zerah," Ormah explained. "He is not doing well. I would hate to dismiss Naarah and send her back from whence she came, but our first concern is for the well-being of your sons. I know you agree."

He cautiously nodded in agreement, not knowing exactly where Ormah was going with her talk.

"Abiel, you are wise beyond your years, much like your father; what are your thoughts on this matter?" Ormah asked.

Any compliment comparing him to his father made him wary.

"Mother, I too have noticed that Zerah is not doing as well as Pharez, but I do not reckon that it had anything to do with Naarah. I trust your judgment in these matters. I am sure that you are right in your opinion. If you feel that we should keep Naarah, I can only suggest that we try letting Naarah and Egla take turns nursing the twins. Put Zerah with Egla, and Pharez with Naarah. See if Pharez can adjust to Naarah. If not, we will have to consider replacing her. First, speak with the women, see if they are agreeable to such an idea."

Egla's maternal drive goaded her to accept responsibility for Naarah, even though Naarah was barely younger. She intended to make good on her promise to compensate for any shortcomings that her friend might have. Egla too noticed how poorly Naarah did with Zerah. She contemplated secretly nursing Zerah, knowing that the consequences could be dire. If she were caught attempting such a thing without permission, it would be the same as stealing a portion of the inheritance of the firstborn. Even the best milk belonged to Pharez!

Ormah found the two of them together. Even though she made it sound like a request, Egla and Narrah knew an order when they heard one.

"Abiel and I have spoken about the plight of Zerah. We would like for both of you to consider a change as it relates to nursing the babies."

Egla smiled her approval, but Naarah feigned not to understand the "suggestion."

"What do you mean, change the way we nurse? I did not know that there was two ways," Naarah sarcastically challenged.

Egla pinched Naarah so hard that she flinched. Not that Naarah really cared which baby she nursed, for truthfully she cared nothing for nursing either of them. She was fearful of change, knowing that one son rejected her. What would happen if Pharez rejected her too?

Motherly Egla wasted no time protecting her promise. "Naarah was making a jest. Weren't you?"

Feeling Egla's fingers tighten on her buttocks, Naarah replied, "Yes, of course I was."

Ormah was not that naive. She got what she wanted, but would continue watching Naarah with the eye of an eagle.

CHAPTER 9

Compatibility

Fate once more made its presence known as Egla took little Zerah up into her arms. Egla's love was a salve for her own wounds. Understandably, she might mistake her own needs as love for Pharez. Although, something real, perhaps even mystical, happened to her the moment she first held Zerah. Egla imagined holding her own son again. He was back from the grave. Whatever occurred affected Zerah as well. He quieted down and contentedly nursed as Egla sang softly and swayed rhythmically to sound of his suckling. As part of the lyrics of her lullabies, she unwittingly called Zerah by her dead son's name. His name was Benoni or "son of my sorrow."

On the other side of the room, Pharez got his first taste of the bitterness that worked its way through Naarah's spirit into her physical body. Neither her milk nor her gaunt body agreed with him. Her bones were not as comfortable to lie against as Egla's soft flesh. Nothing she did quieted him. Egla and Zerah shut the rest of the world out, making themselves oblivious to Naarah and Pharez's dilemma.

Not Ormah! She watched as her compromise unraveled like poorly spun wool. It did not take long for her to get enough of watching Naarah's frustration.

Naarah sat, stood, sat, walked, rocked, sat, and swayed. Nothing assuaged Pharez's discontentment.

Rather than say anything unkind or something that Abiel would not agree with, Ormah decided to pray. Slipping quietly out of the room, she made her way to her guest chamber where she had stayed since the day of Ammah's death. Once behind the closed door of her room, she knelt to pray. First, she asked G-d to give her wisdom that she might deal with Naarah's inadequacy. Ormah was no stranger to fervent prayer. She was a godly woman. The loss of her daughter forever softened her heart.

She cried out, "Oh, G-d, you have taken my daughter into your bosom where I know that she is safe, cared for, and fed. I pray that I have found favor in your sight. Show me your way, that I may provide the same care for these precious sons that you have blessed us with?"

A strange sensation coming from her breast interrupted her prayer. She looked down at the front of her clothing and saw that it was wet. "Could it be?" She ran her hand inside her garment, touched her breast, and quickly brought her hand to her mouth. "It is milk. This is G-d's answer," she shrieked in elation. I will help Naarah nurse my daughter's children.

Ormah had mixed emotions about telling Abiel. A short while ago she thought only of criticizing Naarah to Abiel, and now she could hardly wait to tell him about her prayer and its answer. Many questions flooded her mind: "What will Abiel's reaction be to my experience? What would happen if he let Naarah go and something happened to my milk? How would Egla react? She is so outspoken about her feelings for Naarah. We could not afford to lose Egla. How will my husband feel about my nursing our grandchildren? My nursing should not seem that strange. I am not past the age of bearing children."

Ormah's excitement overruled her fears and questionings. The oozing evidence of her answer to prayer still showed on her dress as she scurried out of her room to find Abiel. She muttered as she went, "Poor man, how many more changes can he withstand?" Her joy had to wait awhile. Abiel gave instructions to his servants that he was not to be disturbed. He went to rest from the rigors of mourning. The long visits with his many friends were both comforting and disconcerting. Upon awakening, the first thing he wanted to do was to see his sons. He could not have anticipated the sight that greeted him as he entered the room where the twins were. On one side of the room, Zerah lay sleeping with Egla's arms embracing him. Naarah and Ormah sat side by side across from the bed. At first glance, the scene appeared normal. Ormah stayed close to Naarah the past few days. But, as Abiel's eyes adjusted to the dimness of the room, he saw Ormah holding and nursing Pharez at her breast. He could hardly resist the urge to rub his eyes and look a second time to see if his sight deceived him. He quickly shifted his eyes back to Naarah's face, so as not to stare at Ormah. They blankly looked at each other until the soft, comforting voice of Ormah ended the uncomfortable silence. "Abiel, if you would, please wait for me in the main room. Pharez will be asleep soon and I will come out to you and speak of these matters."

Abiel labored not to be annoyed. It was his turn to mutter as he backed out of the room, "Women, they are so unpredictable. Who can ever figure them out?"

He was not the only male in the family that was confused and impatient. Nursing from his third "would-be mother" in less than one week proved too much for Pharez. Egla perfectly suited him, but not so of the immature girl who was unsure of herself. Now he lay in the bosom of his grandmother who was struggling to come to grips with her newfound role. If the adults involved in this confusion could not figure out what to do, what chance would an infant have? Pharez finally fell asleep, more so from exhaustion than satisfaction.

Ormah laid Pharez down in his bed as Naarah slipped in alongside him, expecting that her presence would calm him and that both of them could get some much-needed rest. Ormah experienced an uncertainty in her heart as she stepped out of the room to speak with Abiel. She prayed that she had not become overly protective of the twins and allowed her emotions to entice her to do something unseemly. "Abiel," she whispered, "please, step away from the door. Pharez is having a difficult time sleeping as it is, and we certainly do not want to disturb him. I know that what you just saw must have you terribly confused, but I trust that I can explain. You know I have been concerned that Naarah is inept at nursing. Furthermore, she is very awkward at doing anything that pertains to motherhood. I am not suggesting that she is not trying. I just know that for the good of our children, we had to make some changes. Rumor had it that her master would not care if she never came back to him if it was not for the money that he would lose if that happened. I dread to say anything bad about Naarah in fear that I will bring more trouble to her life. It is already pitiful."

Ormah tried not to pause or give occasion for Abiel to get a word in. If she finished the entire story, the better her chances would be to convince Abiel to see things her way. She continued, "I was so disturbed over the situation that I went to my room to pray. That is when milk began to flow from my breast. It is G-d's way of showing me that I should nurse my grandsons, just as Ammah would have done if she had lived."

Abiel breathed in as though he would speak, but before he could say a word, Ormah pled, "I humbly ask that before you answer me or make any decisions that you pray for G-d's guidance in this matter."

There was little that Abiel could or would say after such a presentation. To deny Ormah's request would be tantamount to calling her a liar. She boldly said that G-d had spoken to her. She was not the kind of person to make something like this up.

"Yes," Abiel said. "I will pray and meditate until I am confident and at peace."

CHAPTER 10

The Concubine

The next morning, as he arose for prayer, Abiel was ashamed to acknowledge his suppressed passion. He willed to always put his sons first, but caught himself staring at the gaunt but exotic-looking Naarah. She was not as pretty as a mature woman would be, but there was comeliness about her youthfulness. Even the fire of her dissatisfaction with life's circumstances burning in her dark eyes was captivating. The very thought of sending Narrah back to the house of another man seemed wrong to Abiel, but then he reluctantly rebuked himself, knowing full well that he had no claim to her. Lustful thoughts had no place in him, especially as he mourned for his departed wife.

With yearning, he sought G-d, "Help me O' G-d to purify my thoughts concerning this girl Naarah. You know my heart. I love my wife, but I am just a man more so than a just man." As he prayed, he heard the voice of his soul tell him to redeem Narrah from her master and take her unto himself as a concubine. It would be a mistake to trust that everything would work out with Ormah, Elga, and Naarah. Pharez and Zerah would be the ones to suffer for the problems of the women. Ormah had not yet informed Hiphil, her husband, of the developments, and he may not understand or allow Ormah to pursue what she believed G-d would have her to do.

The days ahead did not look easy. If Naarah had similar feelings toward Abiel, she could comfort him. The strength of her youth would be helpful in the house and the fields. Abiel's mind swirled like a dust storm howling in from the desert. He considered what others might think of him.

"There is only one person that I can tell my feelings to. If she understands, then nothing else matters. Ormah is my best friend. I trust that she always tells me the truth. After all, she is the one who told me to pray about this."

He took a deep breath and prayed again, "G-d of mercy and compassion, I ask that you help me rightly decide in this matter. Most of all, I pray that I never do anything to bring a reproach upon you or my family. May I never speak one offensive or hurtful word to Ormah. Guide me in your paths. Grant me a portion of the wisdom that my fathers possessed. Amen."

Ormah rose earlier than usual this morning. Between times of nursing Pharez, she dozed off, only to fret over her reoccurring dream, awakening to a compulsion to pray for Abiel. The dream's meaning was not clear. It was much like peering into fog. She saw Abiel in the market, buying sheep. He did not choose the best of the flocks, but bought ewes that were sickly. His chief shepherd questioned him about the wisdom of his choices. He berated the shepherd, telling him that he did not know business. Abiel wanted to buy the sheep at a good price, make them well with the green grass of his pastureland, and sell their lambs for a great price. Ormah interpreted the meaning of her dream to be that it would take time to know the wisdom of Abiel's decision. Ormah decided to agree with Abiel's decision, in spite of her ominous feelings. She awakened sure that Abiel would keep Naarah. "What could be wrong with that?" she questioned. Unwittingly, she answered her own question, "He will redeem Naarah from her master and take her as a concubine, and it might happen because of my pressuring him."

She was just about to say, "G-d forbid," as Abiel entered the room. It was an awkward moment. They gawked at each other; neither of them prepared to initiate the conversation that was about to take place. A lengthy pause of silence finally ended as Abiel mustered his courage and began, "Ormah, I heeded your advice and prayed about my decision concerning Naarah and what we should do about her inability to nurse Zerah or Pharez. It appears that G-d intervened for us by allowing you to make milk and giving you the desire to nurse your grandchildren. Have you spoken with Hiphil about any of this?"

"Yes, Abiel, I did speak with my husband, and he agreed that we all should do our best for Pharez and Zerah, even if it means making sacrifices." He could no longer avoid asking Ormah the question: What if he decided to take Naarah as a concubine? She relieved Abiel of his painful duty by unexpectedly telling him about her dream. She left nothing out, including her premonition that he would redeem Naarah from her master. As she related the dream, she saw that it did not have the intended effect. Abiel took her dream as a confirmation of the correctness of his intentions.

"You see!" he shouted. "It is the will of G-d for Naarah to be with me."

Ormah could not resist. She was always honest. "Take it as a warning, Abiel. The shepherd knows more of the sheep than the merchant."

His countenance fell.

It had been days since she had seen even a semblance of happiness in Abiel's face. So she softened her words, saying, "But what would I know? I am but a keeper of the house."

She forced a smile to form on her lips.

Looking rather sheepish himself, Abiel managed a compromise. "Good, after the last day of *shiv'ah*, I will go and meet with Machir. He is Naarah's master. I will see if we can arrange to redeem Naarah. Please inform Naarah of our decision. Make sure that she helps you in any way that you require. Try to instruct her in the ways of womanhood."

She forgot or underestimated Abiel's cleverness. Within minutes, his decision became their decision. Ormah noticed that Abiel intentionally used the word 'we' instead of 'I', when he spoke of gaining Naarah's redemption. He included Ormah in his plan whether she wanted in or not, and he was not finished. "I want you to put Pharez back with Egla and you nurse Zerah. I will be true to my responsibility of honoring my firstborn son."

As he turned to walk out of the room, she remembered that Hiphil needed to talk with Abiel about the circumcision, tomorrow being the eighth day. Keeping with tradition, Hiphil would perform the ritual. He wanted to hear straight from Abiel which of the sons would have the distinction of being the firstborn. Hiphil had heard conflicting accounts of the birth of the twins. He wanted to be sure.

The morrow would be a momentous day—redemption for his concubine and circumcision for his sons.

CHAPTER 11

Commerce

Abiel knew nothing about Machir so he instructed Ebed to go to the Damascus Gate and inquire of the elders. His father trained him to learn as much as he could about a man before attempting to negotiate with him. Once again, Ebed was fortunate enough to find Eleazar sitting near the city gate on this Sabbath day.

"Ebed, you come again so soon. To what do I owe the honor of this visitation?" Eleazar said.

Ebed worried. He could not tell if Eleazar was sincere or using sarcasm.

"If I came to this gate seeking your council every day, I could never exhaust your wisdom, kind sir." Flattery always worked.

"You are welcome to come here anytime, Ebed."

"A thousand thanks. My master seeks to redeem the wet-nurse Naarah from her master, one known as Machir, but knows nothing of the man."

"I know him far better than I wish to." Eleazar retorted.

"Master Abiel believed that you would. Master seeks to gain some advantage by learning what he can about Machir."

The wise sage of the gate was his usual helpful self.

Eleazar started in, "Machir is a man appropriately named. His name implies 'the salesman'. He owns several bazaars in the city. He is reputed to be as crooked as a viper's body. Abiel best watch him carefully. He will buy, sell, or steal anything. He likes stealing the best. The authorities believe he collaborates with a band of marauding thieves that bring him their plunder. He obtained his concubine Naarah from these thieves after they stole her from her family during one of their raids."

Ebed did not anticipate anything as bad as this. He respectfully thanked Eleazar for his help and headed home. It unsettled him, being unsure how this news would affect Abiel. As he walked, he caught himself wishing that Abiel's father were still alive. He would know exactly what to say and do!

As Ebed neared the house, he uttered a quick prayer, "May the wisdom and strength of his fathers be with him." He wanted to pray more, but there was not time enough. He was afraid for his Abiel. Eleazar said Machir was a snake. "What chance would a dove like Abiel have against a snake?"

He regrettably thought, "It is hard to envision the child that I bounced on my knee as a warrior. That is what this will be. War! And what will be the prize?"

A short time later, Ebed related Eleazar's message to Abiel. Abiel's facial expression changed from one of interest to a look of raw determination. His jaw twitched several times as it stiffened in rebellion. Abiel was not one to give up when things got rough.

Ebed remembered, "I should have known—the boy ever determined to win at any game he played. He cried in anger if he lost and heartily celebrated when he won. His unrestrained delight sometimes offended those he bested. He may have the nature of a dove, but he possesses the will of an ox."

Ebed could read Abiel's mind. He often quoted word for word the things that Abiel said. His lips moved as Abiel started his tirade, "Who does this 'salesman' Machir think he is? Does he think that he can steal and sell the souls of people?"

He stopped just long enough to scold Ebed. "Would you please stop mocking me? I am serious."

"As G-d liveth, I will find a way to deal with this jackal. I know his kind. His arrogance will become his snare and pitfall."

There was a growing tone of anger in Abiel's voice. He had no use for this dog or his kind.

Abruptly, Abiel fell silent. He stopped ranting long enough to consider the message.

"Did you say that Eleazar told you that Naarah was taken from her family by force?" he asked.

"Yes master, that is what Eleazar said."

"I can not redeem her, Ebed. I can not redeem the poor girl."

"Redeem. Did you say redeem, sir?"

"Yes, redeem. You didn't know what I planned?"

"No. I did not know. It is not my business, sir."

Abiel could not redeem Naarah with money. She was stolen property and he could not possess her!

Abiel tucked his head and walked away, but Ebed knew that Abiel would not quit, not that easy!

Early the next morning, Abiel sent word for Naarah to join him. Without a word, he took her hand and started out of the house. Naarah sensed that something unusual was happening.

She was afraid to ask what it might be and even more frightened of the answer.

"Abiel, do you mind telling me just where it is that we are going?"

Curtly, he answered, "To the heart of the city where the bazaars were set up."

The smell of the fresh bread rising from the ovens over on Baker's Street drifted up her nostrils. Memories that were long since buried resurrected, causing terrifying recollections to rush at her. "Thieves tied me like an animal and brought me to this place against my will," Naarah remembered. She wanted to bolt and run away but Abiel's iron grip on her hand reminded her that it would be futile. The part of the city they were heading into was no place for women or children. At this moment, Naarah felt like both. There were poor children everywhere begging for alms and bread. They argued with the prostitutes standing about, attempting to gain choice position on the valued street corners. The corner that Abiel and Naarah just rounded to walk down was the exception. It was as frightening and as empty as a gateway to hell.

It was a muddy, narrow, winding street, appropriately named "the street of the crook." Naarah forsook her thoughts of running away. She squeezed Abiel's hand tightly, tighter than he had been holding hers. Abiel regretted that he had not brought his servants along for protection. However, he did not want to appear fearful or intimidated by Machir.

Just a few more quick steps and they stood in front of Guwr's Bazaar. Abiel paused long enough to say, "Naarah, you are not to say one word to anyone. I brought you here to listen so that you will fully understand what transpires in the next few moments. You will have a lasting decision to make once I conclude our business with Machir. The other reason I brought you with me is that I have never met or seen this man. I need you to point him out to me. Do you understand?"

She really did not but said, "Yes" anyway.

Abiel responded, "Good, let us go inside and find him."

Machir was easy to recognize even without Naarah's help. A grotesque physical appearance combined with a boisterous laugh betrayed his identity. Abiel pushed angry words through his gritting teeth, "Just as I envisioned him!" Machir's laughter choked in his throat as he spotted Abiel and Naarah approaching. Abiel moved with the fortitude of a soldier running into battle. Naarah was not as brave. She marched behind her captain, half bent over in fear. She wrapped around him to hang on and used her freehand to point an accusing finger at Machir. Her trembling finger struck with the power of a sword. Abiel made for an imposing shield. The spectacle sent a shiver up and down Machir's spine. Abiel left no room for doubt. He meant business. Without introduction or formality, he went straight to the heart of the matter.

"Machir, you know that Naarah has been under my hire while staying at my house for one week. You have wrongfully neglected to send any provision for her care."

"Yes, so?" was all Machir could muster.

"Under our laws, once you stop providing food and other necessities for a concubine, you must grant her freedom."

"Yes, so?"

"The only way that you could continue to claim her would be if she had bore you a male child. I have knowledge that the only child that Naarah bore for you was a daughter, and that child died."

"Yes, so?"

Machir attempted a tough front. Abiel knew the real meaning of "Yes, so?" and it spelled weakness.

He threw Machir's words back at him. "Yes, so? I intended to offer you money to redeem Naarah, until I received a report that you engage in theft and slave trade. I am sure you obtained Naarah illegally. If necessary, I will summon the authorities to come and examine this matter. Perhaps they will question some of the prostitutes on this dirty and crooked little street. Let us see if any of the women and men have stories to tell of how they got here and to whom they bring their money."

Machir lost his nerve. His face turned as ashen as a corpse. By contrast, Abiel's face flushed red with indignation.

"I shouldn't, but I am willing to leave you to your nasty business as soon as you write a release for Naarah, granting her freedom from you forever."

Machir grabbed for his parchment and ink like a hungry street beggar fighting for a dropped piece of bread. His street instincts told him that he got a good deal. He had to get Abiel out of his shop as quickly as possible.

Machir knew better than to say one more word.

Abiel and Naarah were back out in the street and on their way home. Only now, their roles reversed. Abiel trembled like a terrified little boy. His shaking was not out of fear, rather a release of emotion. The frightened little girl Naarah no longer existed. She had stared down the demon that tormented her and broken his power. Self-assurance replaced the fear that possessed her earlier. She held a parchment, with the word "freedom" on it. She no longer needed anyone to hold either of her hands.

"I am not servant, not a concubine, nobody's slave. I am free to go anywhere I want."

Then she remembered what Abiel told her earlier. "He said that I would have to make a big decision. I guess this is it. Somewhere, I might have a family, someone who misses me or wonders if I am alive. I can hardly wait to get home and tell Egla everything that is happening. She will help me think this through."

Abiel also was in a big hurry. He was already late for his sons' circumcision.

CHAPTER 12

Circumcision

Hiphil was apprehensive as the appointed time for the circumcision ceremony came and passed. It would be most unusual for Abiel to be late for any event, much less one of this significance. As Abiel rushed to get home, he hoped to find Hiphil waiting for his arrival before beginning the ceremony. However, Hiphil religiously made a practice of punctuality. Importance or insignificance made no difference to him. The military trained him well.

The women worried that they could only keep the twins calm for a short time.

Ormah questioned Egla, "Where do you think he is?"

"I don't know. He and Naarah left early this morning, going somewhere."

Hearing the women speculate only made Hiphil all the more anxious. He liked to be in control and errantly mistook womanly concern as an affront to his leadership.

"Why don't you two take care of the babies and let me worry about Abiel and his whereabouts?"

Ormah and Egla gave each other that smug look, the one that says, "We will see about that."

He would soon regret wrongfully assuming that Abiel went to the fields and would not return until dark. Tradition demanded that the circumcision be done on the eighth day after birth. Hiphil was sure that Abiel's wishes would be for him to proceed in accordance with customary law. Accordingly, he picked up his knife and went to the room where Ormah, Egla, Pharez, and Zerah retreated after upsetting him.

The last Hiphil had heard, Egla nursed Zerah. Ormah and Naarah took care of Pharez. Upon entering the room, he asked Ormah to hand over the child that she held. He was not aware that Abiel made the nurses exchange babies a second time. He did know that Pharez had a red birthmark on his forehead. Hence, before cutting any foreskin, he looked closely to make sure he held Pharez in his arms. As Ormah picked Zerah up out of his bed, she failed to notice that he slept with his forehead against the post of the bed. This caused a temporary redness.

This being Hiphil's first circumcision, Ormah did not know what procedure Hiphil would use. So, it did not alarm her when Hiphil took Zerah first. She assumed that he would also take Pharez and lay the boys side by side before beginning the ceremony.

It was unusual for Pharez to whimper, much less cry, especially if Egla held him. However, from the moment that Hiphil took up Zerah, Pharez started crying, as if to register his complaint over being second in line. His sniveling temporarily distracted Ormah, and she turned to help Egla determine what caused Pharez such distress. Her attention shifted back to Hiphil when she heard the Zerah cry out in obvious pain. Hiphil stood tall, proudly holding Zerah's bloody foreskin.

In panic, she blurted out, "What have you done?"

"What have I done? Can you not see for yourself? I cut the child according to our custom. That is what I have done."

"No, no. I understand that, but you cut the wrong child first."

"I cut the child of the bloody mark. He is Abiel's firstborn."

"The bloody mark?" she questioned. "Zerah has no bloody mark, and he is the child that I held at my breast."

At the same moment, Abiel made his way down the hall toward the room where the ceremony was under way. He paused just outside the door to listen. He heard two babies crying. The sound of it carried him back to the day the twins were born. Understandably, the recollection made him reluctant to enter the room. Eight days ago, the cry of his sons had been the harbinger of death. It was not going to be easy to get over any of this.

Hiphil decided to go ahead and circumcise the second child. It could not make things any worse and maybe, just maybe, Abiel would never know the difference. As he took the second baby from Egla, he could not help but look. Sure enough, the glaring crimson birthmark told of his error. He picked up his knife, but just as he moved to make the cut, he heard the door open.

With renewed courage, Abiel stepped inside the room.

"I see that you are about to start without me."

Abiel's voice startled Hiphil so; he dropped his knife to the floor. He confessed, "I am afraid that I have done something wrong, Abiel." The twins lay beside one another, and Hiphil awkwardly pointed at them. "See, they both have red marks on their forehead." To his dismay, what he presumed to be pointing at did not exist. "The mark—it is gone! I swear by…" He stopped, knowing better than to swear.

Abiel looked on in confusion. "I don't understand. What is happening here?"

Hiphil had no ready answer. Ormah broke the silence, directing her words to her husband as if Abiel were not anywhere around. "I believe you circumcised Zerah first."

Not giving in, he lamely defended himself. "But, the red mark; it was a red mark I was told to look for. How else could I know the identity of our firstborn son? If I circumcised Zerah, why did he have the red mark?"

Ormah answered, "I didn't notice a red mark as I handed the child to you. However, Zerah slept with his head very near the post of the bed. Perhaps this explains…"

He broke in, "But why didn't you tell me? You knew what I was to do. Are you sure it is Zerah that I cut first?"

Ormah suggested, "The eighth day is accomplished. We can unwrap the swaddling. Remember, Shiphrah placed a cord around Zerah's ankle. No one removed it. I helped wrap the twins. The cord will still be in place, and we will know for sure which son is circumcised."

Egla picked up the baby she believed to be Pharez. He bawled as though he was the one circumcised. Ormah nervously begged, "Would you please forget his crying and help me unwrap this circumcised baby?" As she loosened the binding on his upper body, he quieted. A hushed peace came over him. Egla took the wrapping off the baby's right leg.

Naarah entered the room just in time to see everyone standing in a circle around the babies. As she and Abiel neared home, she had collected herself enough to be respectful and follow behind, leaving her to be the last to arrive. Everyone except Pharez was holding their breath in anticipation. Naarah should have held hers, but her new found freedom made her bold.

There it was, the cord, dangling from Zerah's ankle, exactly where Shiphrah tied it.

This small piece of rope drastically affected everyone in the room.

Hiphil shook his head in utter disgust, chastising himself, "I failed my sons. I have cursed them with confusion for the rest of their lives."

Ormah felt every bit as responsible as her husband did. She did not lift the knife, but she humbly accepted the blame that Hiphil spoke over her.

Egla, caring for Zerah as she did, gloated in satisfaction. It was her opinion that the first few days of life for the twins unfairly favored Pharez. This made it all the sweeter to see the one that she believed wronged, to have his moment of recognition.

Abiel refused to allow this setback to rob him of the satisfaction he got from putting Machir in his place. After dealing with a hardened criminal like Machir, other challenges did not seem so insurmountable.

"Enough of this uncertainty," he protested. "Hiphil, hand me the knife."

Hiphil looked disappointed. "Abiel no longer trusts me. I have lost the honor of circumcising Pharez."

Abiel consoled his father- and mother-in-law, "Our faithfulness to G-d's ordinance is the important thing, not the ceremony. There are other ceremonies yet to come. I will pay the price of redemption for Pharez as my firstborn and this controversy will be over and settled."

What he did next surprised everyone in the room. Instead of cutting Pharez, he put the knife to the cord on Zerah's ankle. Then he handed the knife back to Hiphil. "You did nothing wrong." Abiel held Pharez as Hiphil finished the work of circumcision on the angry firstborn. No one had to guess how Pharez felt about the proceedings. He continued to bellow out his displeasure.

Zerah lay quietly, making contented facial expressions.

Naarah resented seeing Zerah gratified. Unwisely taking advantage of her liberty, she went on the attack, "There is not any reason why Zerah should turn away from me. I was nearly sent back into Machir's slavery."

Abiel admonished her, "Naarah, stop."

There was no turning back for her. "Look at him," she pointed at Zerah. "You can see it. He will steal his brother's birthright and bring confusion to this family."

Hiphil resented her mention of "confusion." He took it personal, as if he caused the problem. Joining in, he complained, "This family, you say. Since what day did you become part of this family? You have no right to speak this way."

Undaunted, she had more to say. Egla saw Naarah inhale to speak. She made a quick move to put her hand over Naarah's mouth before this went any further. She managed to muffle what sounded like a remark about Ammah's death. Naarah pulled Egla's hand away just as Ormah and Egla managed to escort her out of the room.

Hiphil looked down at his bloodied knife. "Too bad I cannot circumcise her lips."

CHAPTER 13

Concern: Interlude of Explanation

Seven Years Later

Seven years ago, Abiel imagined a life of harmony and peace with his wife who would train up his children from infancy. When of age, his sons came to work with him to learn religion and business. He began teaching his sons the path to righteousness, just as his father had taught him. Abiel was sure that his guidance and the teachings of the rabbis would develop the boys into the manner of men that any father would be proud. Sadly, life was not working out the way that Abiel had hoped. He worked diligently to undo the unfortunate circumstances that accompanied their birth. The harder that he tried to better the situation, the worse it became. It was astonishing that two sons looked so identical, but were completely opposite in nature. From the time that Pharez took his first steps, he was his father's little shadow. Zerah cared only for the company of other children and women, especially Egla. Pharez did not seem to miss the nurturing of a mother. Although, he did pay attention to the things that Naarah said to him. It was disconcerting that Naarah was not always the best influence on Pharez. Much of the conflict between Pharez and Zerah would not exist, absent an adult agitating the problem. Naarah's resentment of a child rejecting her as a wet-nurse was indicative of her plaguing emotional problems. Her emotionally scarred past drew her to the birth-scarred Pharez, prompting her to seize upon every chance to criticize Zerah. In her eyes, he could not do anything right.

Abiel struggled to sort out his attraction to Naarah. To be so shrewd in business, he could not discern his true feelings for the woman. For one, he still grieved for Ammah. His faithfulness to her memory left little room for a relationship with another woman. He did not deny his feelings for Naarah. It may have been pity, but viewed through eyes that occasionally gave in to lust, it resembled love. Even during moments of lust, he restrained himself out of his fear of conceiving a child with her. Abiel never got past thinking of the deformed baby girl that Naarah birthed. Worse yet, she failed in her attempts to nurse and mother either of his children, both the one that she loved and the one she hated. Abiel could not commit to a woman who may not be able to conceive, give birth, or properly raise a child. Some days, he thought of asking her to be his wife, other times he wished that she would leave for good.

CHAPTER 14

The Complex: Chamor Rosh

Abiel knew that there was a good reason why Pharez preferred being with him instead of playing with the other children.

Still he encouraged him, "My son, you know that I love having you with me, but you are missing so much."

"No, father. I miss nothing by being with you. My greatest desire is to learn of the land and the animals. I love to sit with you and the shepherds under the stars and hear stories of the exploits of men of old, to be near you in the presence of the holy men, and learn to love our G-d. What more could there be for me?"

"That is my point. You are but a boy. The time will come for you to be a man. I will celebrate your mitzvah with you when the day arrives. But until then, you need to play and make friends."

"You are the only friend that I need, father. Ever since I can remember, you called me your man-child. Please, do not make me act like other boys. I have no need to play with children who are not like me."

Abiel was at a loss for words. Admittedly, Pharez made a good argument. It disturbed Abiel to hear a trace of pain in Pharez's voice. He chided himself, "I feel so bad for the boy. I as his father should know what to do for him. Perhaps I should get some help. I try to be a good person, but that alone may not be enough to make me a good father."

Abiel made time to speak with a priest of the Holy Temple. Merely thinking of the meeting caused him a sense of dread. He wanted to learn but was afraid of what the truth might be. Needless to say, he was relieved when the course of the conversation turned to the nature of children.

The priest lectured, "Abiel, for all the good that there is in children, they can be extremely cruel. They learn to speak long before they mature or develop judgment. Babies they are, with little or no wisdom when it comes to speaking out or remaining silent. Frankness in speech has its place. As it is said, 'Out of the mouth of babes comes the truth.' However, words spoken out of turn are sharp arrows that pierce the heart. Name-calling is one thing, but making fun of someone's physical deformity is cruel."

"This is exactly what happens every time Pharez ventures out to play with other children," Abiel explained.

"You should continue encouraging him to play with the children. I have found that children resolve their difficulties and get over their hurts much quicker than we adults do."

"I have and I do continue to encourage him, and you are so right about children. However, I recently found out that the father of a boy that Pharez quarreled with has gotten involved. The children laugh at Pharez and call him names. Sometimes the names are just names that children have always called one another. Pharez was able to handle that. The man, who chose to act as a child himself, called Pharez 'chamor rosh.' Several other boys heard the insult and thought it was funny. 'Chamor rosh' has become the nickname for Pharez. I even had to punish Zerah for using it."

The priest admitted, "This is terrible. Perhaps I should speak to the man."

"It may come to that, but the man is not a worshiper. A worshiper of G-d would never act like that. Anyway, at first, Pharez did not realize what 'chamor rosh' meant. He asked me. I had no idea that anyone had called him that, or I would not have told him. I wrongly suspected that he heard the words in the market. When I told him it meant 'an ass with a red head,' he grabbed his forehead and ran away from me. I could not decide what to do. Should I run after him or give him time to be alone? I chose the latter because I did not know what to say if I caught him."

Pharez ran fast and hard into an experience that changed him forever. He never forgot the first time that he saw his birthmark for himself. Hiding from Abiel, he sought refuge in Naarah's room. He waited for a long time, hoping that she would come in and comfort him. After some time passed and no one came in to see about him, he looked around the room. His eyes went to a highly polished brass mirror, lying on a small table next to the window. He knew better than to meddle with any items that belonged to the women. Yet, the chance to see his face for the first time was irresistible. Naarah was in another part of the house when she heard a loud noise come from the direction of her room. She hurriedly left what she was doing and went to investigate the source of the clamor. She found Pharez crying hysterically, his face covered with both his hands. The mirror lay on the floor across the room where Pharez threw it.

The innocence of his childhood disappeared as swiftly as the image of his marred face appeared in the reflection of the brass mirror. If not bad enough to have a disfigured face, the distress of seeing it affected his speech. From that day forward, he spoke normally when around Abiel or Naarah; however, when a situation became the least bit awkward or uncomfortable, he stuttered horribly. Of course, Naarah blamed Zerah for the stuttering, and her work of provoking jealousy between the brothers became easier than ever. She even convinced Pharez that Zerah was responsible for "chamor rosh."

As the years passed, Pharez heard a lot of talk about his G-d-given birthright. Truthfully, there were days when he would have traded away his birthright to rid himself of the birthmark and the stammering of his lips.

CHAPTER 15

The Confident One

Pharez lived life beset by reality and serious complexes. He experienced the pain of rejection and the hurt of a brother who was ashamed of him. Whereas Zerah journeyed through life amused and lighthearted, making the world his playground. No one called him bad names, but they always called him to play. If a game required choosing sides, he never worried. He was a leader, and as such, he did the choosing. It pained and angered Pharez that when Zerah led in choosing, he always avoided selecting him. Embarrassed and degraded, Pharez, always the last one left unchosen, was out of the game.

He decided to confront Zerah only to find that it is not wise to attempt intimidating an intimidator.

"Lii…ittle bbrottther," he began, "I neeed…dd tooo talk to tooo youuu."

He knew that Zerah did not like the name little brother. It did not set a good tone for the conversation.

Zerah impatiently rejoined, "Go on, but make it quick. That's right, you can't. I have other things to do."

"Why dooo do yooou treat me worse thaaan a stranger? Ddddon't yooou you know that weee willll always beee be tooo…together? I…I knooow that yooou don't wa wa want to admit it, bbbut it wa wa wass G-d that favored mee me over yooou. St…st stop blaaaming meee and ggggive mee me the honor that I…I…I have been gggranted."

Zerah's next words were poisonous, and his venom went straight to his brother's heart.

"If it is G-d that gives the honor that you possess, you can have it all. You have had a look at yourself and you still want me to honor you? The day will come when you will realize who it is that deserves honor and who it is that is cursed. Anything else, big brother?"

Relations between the brothers deteriorated until it seemed they could not worsen. It happened one afternoon as Zerah played in the street with a few of his friends. As part of the game, he ran to hide from them. Choosing to hide in an empty box under a neighbor's window, he got on his knees and crawled in it. For the longest time, he stayed quiet, hoping that his friends would not be able to find him. As he knelt in the darkness of the box, he heard voices coming from the open window above his hiding place. Whoever it was speaking, oddly enough, was talking about him. For the first time in his life, he heard the story of his mother's death. He listened so intently that he forgot about the game. He did not even hear his friends shouting out as they attempted to find him.

Zerah heard, "Whatever possessed Abiel to choose the deformed one as his firstborn?"

Another spoke, "Yes, he ignored the cord that the skilled midwife placed on Zerah's foot."

Back and forth it went, "Just look at the boys. Zerah is such a handsome boy and quite a leader. Pharez cannot even pray without stuttering." Someone laughed. "He must know that G-d is mad at him."

"It probably has something to do with their mother's death; you know how some have blamed it on Zerah."

"It had to be Pharez's fault, pushing past his brother in his mother's womb, to wrongfully take the birthright. After all, Ammah called out the name, "I am tearing," as she gave birth to Pharez. She knew who it was that caused her to bleed."

By this time, Zerah could not take any more. He learned secrets never breathed in his house. Out from under the box he came, running as fast as he could until he was home. His friends spotted him and chased after him, thinking his running was part of the game.

Zerah wasted no time going to the upper room of the house, hoping to be alone. He needed time to figure out what to do next. Instead of answers, his questions loomed ever larger as the evening shadows fell across the room. What he needed was the truth from someone who did not care about an inheritance or anything else but him. He needed a friend. He needed Egla.

There was one and only one reason why she was still under Abiel's roof. Her husband died during the first year that she was under hire as a wet-nurse. Out of loneliness, she chose to stay on as a servant. This was her seventh year of service to Abiel. The law of Deuteronomy allowed her to be free from her servitude. As before, she requested to remain. Accordingly, Abiel pierced her ear with an awl, signifying that she would forever be in service to his family. Death and loneliness were her excuses for staying. Zerah was the reason. He was as close to Egla as he ever let anyone get. "Why didn't she tell me about these things? Why didn't anybody tell me?" Zerah wondered. He wondered if Pharez knew. The neighbor's words rolled over and over in his mind.

CHAPTER 16

Conversation with His Confidant

Egla could tell that this was not going to be ordinary conversation, not child talk. She could not remember ever seeing such a look on a child's face. The one who always smiled looked serious. His look reminded Egla of a scholar rapt in study of sacred mysteries.

"Gracious, Zerah, whatever is wrong with you?"

His voice cracked with emotion. "Yesterday, as I was playing, I hid under the window of a house down the street. The people in the house had no idea that I was there. I heard them mention my name, Pharez's, and that of our mother. They said that some have blamed me for my mother's death. What did they mean by that?"

Egla gasped. "Since the day that Naarah went on her tirade, Abiel forbade us to speak of these things. This poor child had to hear of them from the mouth of strangers."

She wished for Abiel, but he was away. No one would distract Zerah from demanding answers to his questions. Egla tried to distract him with a warm embrace, in hope that love would suffice. For the first time ever, Zerah pushed her away.

Refusing her affection, he repeated in an angry tone, "What did they mean? Did I cause my mother's death?"

Before she could answer, other questions came gushing out like a waterspout. "How did my mother die? Is Pharez the firstborn? Is this why my father prefers Pharez to me? What did the people mean about a cord around my ankle? Why does Naarah hate me?"

Egla never imagined that such emotions lurked unseen and unspoken in the heart of this young boy. "How could I have been so close, yet so unaware of his feelings?" He hid them well, concealed behind the mask of his fun-loving nature. She understood the questioning of his mother's death. It is common for a child coming of age to wonder such a thing. Nevertheless, the thought of Abiel favoring Pharez was hard to comprehend. Naarah hating someone was altogether possible.

Egla did her best to remain calm in the midst of the storm. She reached for Zerah's hand. "Son, come and sit next to me." There was hurt, and Egla longed to heal it with soft words and loving touches.

She lovingly spoke to him, "Zerah, you are mistaken to believe that your father loves Pharez more than he loves you."

Impatiently, Zerah interrupted, "Then why is Pharez always with him?"

"You will have to be patient and let me try and answer your questions. Tell me all that you are feeling, but please allow me to answer each question. Pharez is often with your father because that is where he wants to be. You know that your brother does not like to play as much as you do. Abiel would love to have you with him, every bit as much as Pharez. Your father knows what you enjoy. It is out of love that your father allows you to do what makes you most happy."

"But Egla, there are times that I want to be with you, but father makes me stay with Naarah. She has never liked me. When I try to tell father the things that she says and does to me; he refuses to hear of it. She too told me that Pharez is father's favorite, and there is nothing that I can do about it."

Egla answered, "I am not trying to take up for Naarah. Perhaps, when you get older you will understand some of the problems that she has that affect her feelings. She had a difficult time with you when you were a baby. She resents that you rejected her. As a child, evil men took her as a slave and brutally abused her. Zerah, I know that it is asking a lot from you, seeing as you are still a child, but try and put yourself in her place. She really doesn't know how to show love."

"If that is true, why doesn't she have problems with Pharez like she does me? She always tells Pharez how much better he is than I am. But she is careful not to do it in front of any of you."

Egla had no idea that a situation this critical existed. She resolved to have a stern talk with Naarah. Evidently, Naarah had been very sly in her deception. Egla had suspicions that ill feelings existed, but never imagined that Naarah would stoop to childlike behavior.

"Son, just because Naarah seems to love Pharez more than you does not mean that she doesn't love you. Just think, I love Pharez and would do anything for him, but you have always been special to me. Perhaps this is the way Naarah feels toward Pharez."

"But Egla, you never say anything bad about Pharez to me. Why does Naarah try to cause trouble if she loves me?"

"I can't explain everything she does, but I promise I will talk to her. She may not be aware of what she is doing, or how it makes you feel."

"Oh please, don't tell her that I said anything. I am afraid of her and what she will do next if she thinks that I am telling on her."

In a strange way, it relieved Egla to hear there was something or someone Zerah feared. His bravado worried her.

"Are you really that afraid of her?"

"Yes, she tells Pharez to call me names and tries to make him hit me. She even tells him that it is my fault that he has that red mark on his face and that he should make one on mine. I have bad dreams that she is going to do something to me."

This kind of talk made it difficult for Egla to maintain her composure. She felt guilty that these things happened right under her nose and that she did not see it. She pulled Zerah ever so close and kissed his cheek in hopes of dispelling his worrisome thoughts. The kiss worked for a moment, but he had more questions. "Why would anyone blame me for my mother's death? Did I do something to cause it?"

"You are much too young to understand, but many mothers die as they are giving birth to their children. It is something that no one can control. It is in G-d's hands. You must not blame yourself or Pharez."

This would have been the right answer for most children, but Zerah was different. The concept of a G-d that wanted his creation to fear him caused a problem for him.

"Are G-d and Naarah a lot alike? If they decide that they don't like you, they make life hard," Zerah argued.

"I, like you, have asked difficult questions about G-d and what he does and does not do. Let me put it to you this way. I did not know your mother, but I hear that she was a wonderful person. I accept that I will never be her. However, my child and my husband died while you were a baby. G-d knows best what we need. When we experience loss, G-d gives us something else to take its place. I consider you to be the son that I lost. I hope that in some way, I can provide the love that your mother would have given you. I do love you, Zerah."

The sincerity of her love dispelled his anger.

"I am sorry that I raised my voice to you. I feel better, but why did mother give us the names that we have? The people that I overheard talking said I was the firstborn. The name that mother gave to my brother makes me think that he hurt her as she gave birth to him. Why did she name me 'son of the morning'?"

"I wasn't there when you were being born, but I am told that you came just at sunrise."

"Then you are saying that I was born first. Why does not father acknowledge me as the firstborn?"

"I told you, I was not there."

"You said that 'son of the morning' is my name because of the sunrise. Why does Naarah say that my name is the name of the Devil?"

Egla forced some sternness into her voice, in hopes of avoiding answering the question, more so than to show displeasure for the questioning.

"It is not my place to get involved in family matters."

"But I thought that you were part of the family."

"In love only, Zerah, in love only. Not in legal matters."

This was somewhat over Zerah's head. He failed to see a difference. Hence, he pressed even harder.

"Do you think that mother tried to tell us something through our names? I learned the spelling of them and our names contain the same letters, yet they are backwards. We are twins, but I am nothing like my brother. He treats me as if I am much younger than he is. He is bigger and stronger than I am, but I can run faster. I know that I am smarter than he is. If he is the firstborn, other children should favor him, but they do not. They laugh at him. I am ashamed to call him my brother."

"Zerah, you shouldn't talk like that. He is your brother regardless of which of you should happen to be the firstborn."

Zerah risked one more insult.

"Even the girls make fun and will have nothing to do with him."

Egla seized the opportunity to get away from serious conversation. She teased, "Why Zerah, what do you know about girls and who likes who? Maybe I shouldn't be kissing you if you are starting to like girls."

He refused to quit. "Thank you for the hugs and kisses, Egla, but there is one other thing that I overheard. The neighbors spoke of 'a cord' tied around the leg of the firstborn. Just tell me, was it on my leg?"

"As I told you, I was not there. Enough for now, there are children waiting outside for you. Go and play."

Egla's hesitancy about the cord aroused Zerah's curiosity more than ever. He was onto the secret that held the answer to everything that troubled him. He decided to get a piece of colored cord, tie it around his ankle, and see what happened.

"I know," he said. "I will get a piece of red-colored cord and tie it around my ankle. If I am right, it will not take long for me to find out what the cord represents."

CHAPTER 17

Conversation with a Corpse

Egla did her very best to answer Zerah's questions, but her wavering fell far short of satisfying Zerah. As he contemplated Egla's reluctance to provide answers, a second devious plan came to mind. He deliberated, "Putting that cord around my ankle created chaos in this house. However, if father knew what I am thinking to do now, it would be worse. I have to get to my mother. Even father's religion teaches that the dead ones speak to the living."

It was easy for a smart boy like Zerah to find his mother's burial place. He did not dare ask anyone the whereabouts of her tomb, fearing to raise suspicion over what he planned to do. He waited patiently. Then one bleak, rainy morning, he heard the mournful noise of a funeral dirge. Zerah wasted no time changing into some old clothing. He knew he was going to get wet, and did not want to upset Egla. Once out into the street, he managed to join in the procession unnoticed. Funerals attract large crowds of onlookers, and the throng provided the cover he needed. His good fortune continued. The deceased woman happened to be a person of wealth. Her tomb was a preferred site near Ammah's grotto among the ancient olive trees. Zerah listened intently to the conversation of the mourners.

One of the family members remarked, "We will bury our cousin in a wonderful place. Close to the family of Abiel. I know because I walked in the procession to bury my friend Ammah, Abiel's wife. The garden around her tomb is well kept."

"You mean Abiel, the righteous man from the east side of the city?"

"Yes, that family. Our family owns the sepulcher next to theirs."

Zerah made sure that he stayed close to these people. They unknowingly directed him to his destiny.

As the family neared their plot, the one who earlier spoke of Ammah, said in a respectful whisper, "Over there. That is the tomb of Abiel's family."

Zerah resisted the urge to run to the tomb. He argued down his emotions, "Now isn't the right time. There are too many people watching. If someone recognizes me and tells father, I will be in big trouble. It will be safer to return another day."

His remaining indecision washed away in the dreary drizzle, as it turned into a cloudburst. The crowd scattered for the trees or any other cover they could find. The storm raced across the valley and over the Judean hills as if it did not care to tarry any longer than necessary. However, it lingered long enough to dump its fury in torrents. The power of the rushing water unearthed many shallow graves as it ravaged the small ravines. The sight of decaying bodies in rotted boxes descending the drenched hills toward the valley floor almost defied description. The only way to describe it is that they looked like small boats absent a helmsman, caught in a riptide, sweeping them out to sea. Getting the bodies back into their makeshift crypts would be no small task for the gardeners of Kidron. Several distant flashes of lightning, trailed by peals of thunder, signaled that the storm had passed and it was time to get out of the valley.

No one needed a second chance to leave. The family and their friends hastened to get out of the valley. Their movement reminded Zerah of sheep, herded by an overly aggressive dog. Every man, woman, and child gaped in wide-eyed fear. That is, all but one. The one child who felt at home here would have stayed if given the chance. Zerah remembered the rabbinical teaching, "Heathens believe in storm gods."

He rationalized, "I can believe in a god that has the power over the storms. He just spoke to me. I do not know his name, but he spoke to me. He washed opened the graves, as a sign to me. He will open mother's grave when I return. She will speak to me as a mother speaks to her son. I wonder if she and I are heathens."

Zerah sauntered about in a maze of sopping wet robes, hoping to catch a glimpse of Tophet. No one stopped moving long enough for him to get a good look. What he did manage to see flashed as quickly as the lightning of the passing storm. His brief glance only added to his confusion. "Why is everybody so afraid of this place? Yes, there are strange things scattered about in the rubble.

Yes, the smell is awful, but I see nothing to be afraid of." He could hardly wait to return.

The day finally came when Abiel went away on business. Zerah got up early that morning and made an excuse of going out to play with his friends. The house servants likely would not miss Zerah. They tended to relax and become a lot less watchful when Abiel was away. This made a perfect opportunity for Zerah to return to Kidron to search for the secret that up to now evaded him. Fortunately for Zerah, the watchman at the Dung Gate stepped away to relieve himself. Zerah scurried through the gate undetected and hurried down into Hinnom.

It took all of the resolve that he possessed to keep from stopping to look closely at the things that fascinated him during his first trip through Tophet. His mother's tomb beckoned him to a mitzvah. Even at his early age, he disdained his family's religious traditions. Ceremonies held no attraction for Zerah, but this walk through Hinnom touched a spiritual place in him that he did not realize he possessed. With every step, he unexpectedly recited ritualistic words that parents customarily speak over their sons during bar mitzvah. He chanted, "Blessed is he that has released me from the punishment of this one. Blessed is he that has released me from the punishment of this one." The symbolism of the words is that the boy is now a man and his parents are no longer responsible for him. Zerah added, "I don't need a priest to make me a man. Coming here on my own proves that I am as brave as any man can be." The experience empowered him. To him, his visit here was not rebellion; it was freedom! His biggest surprise came when the questions that he planned to ask his mother no longer seemed important. He single-mindedly wanted to be someone's "firstborn," made to feel needed above all else. Whether real or imagined, a soothing warmth enveloped him as he arrived at Ammah's tomb. In that instant, he rested sure that he felt his Ammah's arms around him. He stretched his arms to return her embrace.

If repeating parts of a bar mitzvah was strange, what happened next startled him. His voice reverberated off the rocky crags of Kidron's caves and echoed down through the valley as he shouted out, "Son of the morning, I am the son of the morning." The returning sounds of his voice were so sharp and clear, they caused Zerah to duck down and hide. He thought that someone shouted back at him. Realizing that the sounds were nothing more than his echo, he stood up and screamed again, "I am the son of the morning." He shouted out several more times. The repeating voice did not sound at all like his. This fascinated him. Daring to try again, he determinedly announced, "My father and my brother do not acknowledge my birthright. My mother, you make the rocks cry out for me. They know who I am! I am the son of the morning."

Zerah stood trembling in the evening shadows of the cedar trees. A sharp breeze whipped at the tree's limbs and across his skin. He mistook the sensation of the chill for exhilaration, until he realized that the valley was rapidly cooling down. The sun began to set in the scarlet-colored western skies over Jerusalem. He had just enough time to look around in Tophet, if he were to make it home before dark.

Zerah had to be extremely careful where he stepped. Smoldering ashes from burning garbage were everywhere. Ignoring the danger, he left the main path to explore the mystery of this place. He had to look down in order to choose each step carefully. His eyes caught sight of a small metal figure. He picked it up with the nimbleness of a thief, even though he did not consider himself one. In the twilight, the image appeared to be half man, half bull. The statue had writing on it, but Zerah was barely able to make out the words in the approaching nightfall. Straining his youthful eyes to read, he sounded out the words on the image, "GUWR-BAAL." Something about the name was familiar, but Zerah did not have time or light enough to stand around and think about it. He quickly made his way back to the path and ran up the hill toward the Dung Gate as hard as he could. Zerah ignored the emphatic demand of the gate guard that he stop. He narrowly avoided the grasp of the extraordinarily plump watchman who attempted to lay hold on him. Just a few more steps down very familiar streets and Zerah would be home, and none the worse for any of his deceit. He thought as he ran the last few steps, "Even if I get caught, any punishment would be worth what I found."

Zerah's daylight visit to Kidron left him with the impression that he was born the "son of the light," but the years ahead proved that his late evening rebirth cast a dark shadow over his life that transformed him into a "son of darkness."

CHAPTER 18

The Coming Crisis

Seven Years Later

Zerah and Pharez neared their sixteenth birthdays, having accomplished their ritualistic passage into manhood three years ago. Their respective behavior proved that ceremony and age does not make a man out of a boy who refuses to mature. However, a child who is eager to submit to the rule of elders will become a man. Pharez, no longer his father's shadow, stood strong as his father's right hand. Zerah developed physically, but remained a child in a man's body. Unfortunately, the underdeveloped child in an overdeveloped body found empowerment from the wealth of his guilt-ridden father. Zerah masterfully misused his father's misguided feelings. He was the one chink in Abiel's armor. Aside from Zerah, Abiel was shrewd and an astute manager of wealth. He just could not succeed at getting Zerah under control. Abiel's weakness was unmerited guilt in disguise. He was not as confident of his decision to make Pharez his firstborn as he pretended to be. His uncertainty cast a spell over his judgment. Abiel knew what Zerah was up to, but lacked resolve to refuse him anything he requested. Regrettably, Zerah not only squandered the family's financial resources; he spent the fortune of his family's "reputation" as if it had no end. Abiel's heart was laden with grief and his sorrow showed as silver streaks of gray in his otherwise ebony hair.

Pharez, always mindful of respecting his father, refrained from telling Abiel everything he knew about Zerah and his behavior. That was about to change. The contention between these two brothers became dangerously critical.

Pharez's feelings spilled over as he complained to Naarah, "It just is not fair. I work night and day at father's side to protect our wealth. My brother labors just as hard to destroy it. He lives only to please himself even if it means defying everyone else."

She egged him on, "I know; your father will not even let me correct your brother. Any time that I try, I am the one that is scolded. The way Zerah speaks to me is shameful. Even worse, Abiel allows Zerah to wear that cord on his ankle."

"I will not speak against my father, but I hear there was a time when he cut that cord off of Zerah's leg. The day will come when I will do the same. If he resists, perhaps I will cut off his leg and he can suffer shame as I have. He wears the cord next to the same foot that caused the mark on my face."

Abiel's house became "a house divided," but Naarah devised a plan that could change all of that.

CHAPTER 19

Carnage of Childhood

It disturbed Egla to see the drastic changes in Zerah. The past few years were torturous for her. She loved Zerah as much as a woman could love her own child, but he pulled away from her. He even went so far as to tell her that his life was none of her business and she wasn't his mother. His attitude problems began when he visited his mother's tomb some years ago. The little boy that left his house that morning never came back. The individual that returned from "the visit" believed himself as grown up beyond his years. The once respectful boy reveled in rebellion. It changed his calm and courteous nature into calloused cynicism that was uncommon for someone his age. His thirst for pleasure was insatiable. Life is supposed to be a sip of water to go with our daily bread, but Zerah tried hard to drink the well dry every day.

There also was a frightening side to all of this. First, Zerah insisted on wearing the crimson cord around his ankle. The cord insulted Pharez and challenged Abiel's authority. Zerah just as well call his father a liar and his brother a thief.

Worse yet, Zerah engaged in the worship of an idol. The small relic he found on the day of "the visit" obsessed him. He set the thing up in his room and resorted to soliciting its help in certain matters. The twins relentlessly argued over the cord and the idol. Abiel tired of separating them. Of necessity, he gave Pharez a room of his own. His worst fear was that someone, perhaps even Pharez, would put the word out that Zerah worshiped idols. The priests would have no choice but to inflict severe punishment for such a practice. Under their law, Zerah would be stoned and his body burned along with his half-man, half-bull god. Abiel sternly warned his servants, including Naarah, not to mention a word to anyone concerning this matter. He could not be convinced that Zerah was actually worshiping the idol. He was aware that Zerah had the relic, but assumed that it had meaning to his son because of when and where he found it. Still, Abiel did not approve of Zerah having it, but up until now, he failed to persuade Zerah to get rid of it. Zerah emphatically told Abiel that he would leave home before parting with the relic.

Nightlife in Jerusalem contrasted to the daylight activities of the great city, giving the impression of two different cities. Jerusalem's activity by day centered in and around the great temple. Habitual calls to worship and prayer from priests in brightly colored robes, surrounded by gold, gild, and glitter defined the opulence of G-d's house. Mix in the distressed sounds of hundreds of sheep, goats, cattle, and oxen that preferred green pastures to the dusty holding pens of the profiteers from the big business of religion. Singing birds and cooing doves, unaware of their fate as offerings of preference for the poor, sweetly softened the troubled lowing of the other animals.

However, the daytime Jerusalem rolled up its religion along with its vendor tents and streets at dark, surrendering the night to those who disrespected G-d's commandments and violated his law. Sanctimonious sounds gave way to crude solicitations of prostitutes mingled with mirth and cursing of drunkards as night set in. The blood of sacrificed animals that ran like a natural spring by day gushed as a river of wine and strong drink by night, not that the night did not have blood of its own. Mornings always brought to light the bloodied bodies of those that dared to wade too deep into night's dark waters.

Zerah knew that his father did not want him going out at night, especially venturing into certain parts of the city where trouble was inevitable. For a time, disobedience pacified Zerah, but as the nights wore on, he needed more. He wandered further away from his neighborhood, away from his childhood friends, who of late bored him silly. Wine did little for him. He looked for more than what he ate and drank at his father's table. The fare bored him even more than his friends did. Why should G-d concern himself with what someone ate or didn't eat?

A young man with rebellion in his heart, excitement on his mind, and money in his pocket smelled like the carcass of a dead animal to the vultures of the night. They had no problem finding each other.

Drugs dulled his youthful strength, but fired his passion for defiance. The identical twins, rebellion and drugs, joined him as constant companions. As if these two were not wicked enough, he made the acquaintance of a third person who proved to be the most deadly member of an "unholy trio." Providence strutted onto the stage of Zerah's life drama as a villainous player that ever dons a different mask.

It happened one fateful night as the 'would-be firstborn' stumbled into the abyss of the vilest quarter of Jerusalem. The practices of those who frequented this quarter of the city were punishable by death, that is, if street murder did not get them first. The weak and innocent survived here only if under the protection of a "guardian angel."

Zerah's lips were numb as he put his cup to his lips one more time. Sipping deeply, he succumbed to the sway of the intoxicant. The potency of his drink persuaded him that everyone around him wanted to hear his story. It healed him to tell others of the wrong done to him by his father and brother. He wanted to make them pay one way or another, if by no other means than smearing them to other people who always reciprocated by retelling some worn out story sadder than his.

Little did he know he was under the watchful eye of one regarded as the most contemptible man in the entire city. That person was about to signal for his thugs to rob and kill the brash visitor who refused to stop talking. As Machir lifted his hand to order his men to move, he heard the young stranger say the name Abiel. That name slapped Machir flush on his face with a menacing memory that he recalled as readily as if it happened yesterday. His henchmen were perplexed when Machir waved them off from proceeding with their deadly duties. It was not like him to pass up such an easy quarry, as this drunken boy assuredly would be. Machir did not need time to plot. Evil came natural to him. "No one ever humiliated me as Abiel did the day that he and that worthless concubine came trampling on my territory. Tonight, Baal delivered a gift into my hands and I will have something better than blood or money. Ahaaah, the sweet nectar of revenge!"

"Young man, my name is Machir and who are you?"

"My name is Zerah, but why do you ask?"

"I heard the things that you were saying about your father and your brother, and it caused me to remember some painful things that happened to me when I was a young boy. Here, first share a drink with me. If you don't care to talk about this, I will walk away."

"No, please, give me the drink and go on with your story."

Zerah was so taken with the powerful presence of this stranger, he didn't notice the tattooed and muscled-up man who placed the wine bowl up on his table. He was anxious to hear more from the man to whom he was instantly attracted. He dipped his cup into the bowl as Machir continued, "My father loved my brother more than he cared for me, and it hurt me deeply. Until one day, I realized that I could be a man on my own and that I did not need either of them. It was not that easy at first, but I learned not only to survive but also to prosper. You do not know who I am, and it is not that important right now, but for the sake of what I am telling you; if you stay around, you will find out that I have done extremely well here. I don't have to depend on anyone."

Machir said all the things that Zerah wanted to hear, plying his craft as a salesman as artfully and skillfully as a weaver creating patterns on a loom.

He continued, "I haven't met your family, but from what you have said, I think I know them. They must be very much like my people were. If I had stayed with my family, I would have been a son in name, but little more than a servant. My father never let me be myself. He always wanted me to be my brother. He never loved me; he just needed me in the family to carry out their wishes. How old are you anyway?"

"Almost sixteen, Zerah replied."

"The exact same age that I was when I realized that it was time for me to get away and seek my own path. I never looked back. I believe that you and I are a lot alike, and I can help you get free if that is what you want to do."

Machir laughed under his breath as he connived, "Abiel stole my concubine. I will steal his son."

Zerah did not want to appear weak. Albeit, he had to fight back tears as he thought, "If only my father understood me as well as this stranger."

Remembering the question, he affirmed, "Yes, absolutely yes. I do want help. What will you do?"

"Good, the first thing that we can do is to let you experience the life that is here for you. I know there are many things that your father and his religion forbid you to do. It is just so they can control you. Come on, go with me and I will show you what I mean. Enough talk."

Then in a challenging tone, Machir said, "That is if you think that you are ready."

Something about the demeanor of Machir gave Zerah a momentary pause, but the drugs he consumed overpowered his reluctance.

Zerah responded, "I've been ready," and with those words, he and Machir walked out of the dim light flickering from the oil lamps, stepping out into the darkened streets, a darkness only outdone by the blackness of Machir's heart.

Machir wasted no time putting his impious plan to work. He headed straight for his bazaar down on the street of the crook, where he knew he had plenty of elixir to mix with wine. He planned to serve his unsuspecting guest a concoction he called the "spirit" drink. The combination of fermented wine and potent drugs was a secret told to Machir by his necromancer. Along the way Machir queried, "Tell me Zerah, have you ever been with a woman?"

"Me, why yes, yes I think, I don't, I mean I'm not sure."

"Zerah, Zerah, slow down. It is all right. I had not either until I got away from my father. Would you like to?"

"Sure, you know that I would. But I don't have any woman to go with."

"Don't worry, Zerah; let's have another drink and then we will see what we can do. I have a drink for you that is better than anything that you have ever tasted."

At that moment, they arrived in front of Machir's shop. Several lamps provided just enough light for Zerah to make out the words, "Guwr's Bazaar."

"I know this name. I have seen this name somewhere before."

"What name is that, Zerah?"

"The name Guwr."

"And why should it be so strange to you that you have heard the name of my bazaar? You know it to be a common word."

"Machir, you don't understand why I am so taken by the name of your place. I have heard the word before, but some years ago, I found a strange relic. It has special meaning to me. The relic bears the inscription GUWR-BAAL. I tried to make sense of the meaning, but no one wanted to help me. You barely know who I am, and you seem interested in what happens to me. Then I see the name Guwr on your shop, and it makes me believe that I am in the right place with the right person."

Machir breathed a sigh of relief. For a moment, he thought that his prey might escape from the trap. To his delight, the trap was intact and its victim secured.

"Don't worry, Zerah; I have many things to tell you. We have plenty of time. Let's have that drink first."

Once inside, Machir hurriedly enticed Zerah to drink his mixture. Just one sip and doors opened to a new world that Zerah never knew existed. He stepped through the portals into a realm of demons, fortunetellers, mind-altering drugs, and perverted sex. Machir's plan worked flawlessly. Without leaving Jerusalem, he sent this boy on his way to a strange land, and he intended to leave him there to die. If, perchance, Zerah ever wanted to go home, he would return to his father's house as someone his family would not recognize.

Zerah slurred, "You said that you would tell me the meaning of Guwr. What does…?"

Machir interrupted, "In time, but not tonight. The rest of this night is for playing." It sounded so innocent, but this was anything but play. If a game, it was a lethal one.

"I asked you earlier about women. You said that you wanted to…"

"Yes, but I told you that I don't know any."

"Enough about what you don't know and what you don't have. You are with me, and I will take care of you."

"But why? You and I just met. I don't understand why you are so kind to me."

Machir did not miss one word. After all, words were the tools of his trade. When Zerah used the word "kind," it told him that he had this boy right where he wanted him. "This fool thinks that I am being kind to him," Machir thought.

"I told you that our lives are very similar. Sometimes, old men think they can relive their lives through the young. I want to spare you some of what I endured. That's all."

The son of the morning struggled to get out of the bed somewhere around midday the next morning. The bright light of a sun that rose up long before him caused his head to pound harder than he ever remembered. It was a strange sensation, not knowing exactly where he was or how he got there. An unruly laugh just outside his door jogged his memory.

"Machir. Now I remember. My friend Machir."

Zerah was about to open the door when it dawned on him that he was naked. He looked around for his clothes, only to discover that they were scattered all over the room. Strangely he thought, "Egla would never permit such clutter."

Machir heard the bumping noises coming from inside the room and made his way to the door. Zerah almost jumped out of his skin when Machir banged on the door and laughingly inquired, "Are you alive in there? Do I need to send one of my girls in to see about you?" The challenge prompted Zerah to dress faster than he ever had. In his haste, he put his outer garment on backwards. He was a site to behold as he stepped out of the room. His eyes were the color of the blazing sun outside, his hair disheveled, and something else he had not yet discovered. Machir gaped at him. He could not have been more pleased. "And this is only the first night. Just wait until I am through. If Abiel could only see his son now."

Then he howled in laughter and lustily whistled as he pointed at Zerah's neck. He did not stop whistling until he feared he might make too much of a spectacle of the boy.

"You must have been a real man with those women last night. Are you sure that you had never…?"

"What are you talking about?" Zerah asked as he reached up to feel his neck. His head was hurting so bad that he had not even noticed the painful bite marks all over his neck and chest.

"What you need is some wine. Trust me, it will make your head feel better. Not to worry; it is not the strong drink. We will save that for later. Tonight we will celebrate you becoming a man."

CHAPTER 20

Comrade of the Chaberim

Chaberim are included in the Ugaritic inscription of Ras Ibn Hani, a list of evildoers, where it may mean those who magically bind people to do them harm. The root is also the source of the word meaning "comrade," in the sense that the comrades are linked together by sworn oaths.

On several occasions, Zerah stayed out all night, but he had never been gone from home for any number of days. It entered his mind that if he stayed with Machir for a few days, perhaps his family would realize just how badly they needed him. Besides, he had many questions for his new mentor.

For the past several years, he dreamed of being with a woman and regretfully, he could barely remember the past night. He knew for sure his neck was sore as could be and wondered if that was all that there was to sex.

His lustful thoughts left him as he heard Machir call him. He just finished gulping down a cup of wine and went back to his room to lie down for awhile. He could tell by the tone of Machir's voice that there was not to be any sleeping today. That would be all right, too. He was anxious to talk.

"Yes sir, I'm awake. I will be right out."

"Good, there is something important I want to show you."

"What is it?"

"I can't just tell you; I need to show you. So hurry; the day is passing us by."

As Zerah stepped out into the shop, Machir continued, "Last night, you seemed intrigued by the name of my bazaar. You said that you found a relic with the inscription GUWR-BAAL, and you asked me to explain the meaning to you. Was that just the drink talking or do you really want to know?"

"No sir, I mean yes sir; what I mean is no sir, it was not the drink and yes I do want to know."

"You must never tell anyone that you saw what I am about to show you. Do I have your word? If I do, I want you to swear an oath."

"How do I do that? I am willing, but I never have and I don't know how."

Machir couldn't help but think that this boy was a lot like the sheep that the money-grabbing priests easily lead to their slaughter.

"It's easy. Just think of the most important thing in your life and then say that you swear by it."

Without hesitation, Zerah said, "I swear an oath upon the crimson cord of my birthright that I will never tell anyone what you are about to show me."

Machir cast a fleeting glance at Zerah's ankle. He had previously noticed the red cord and now he knew that it must hold some great value to the boy.

"That was a strange oath, Zerah. You and I will talk about your ankle cord later, but for now follow me." Once Machir lit a lamp, he lifted a rug that covered a hidden door that led down into a cellar. As Zerah made his way down the steps, something reminded him of the late evening that he explored Tophet. The soft glow of the lamplight was about the same as had been the hue of the setting sun on that eventful evening. It too scarcely illuminated the landscape, but provided enough light that one could see objects up close. His eyes blurred from the drink, but he could see well enough to distinguish the shape of a large golden bullhead. Machir moved the lamp ever closer to the base of the object, revealing the words GUWR-BAAL.

"Machir, where did you get this?"

"Now, now, that is not a question for you to be asking. Be contented to see what you are looking at and for the answer to one of your questions." Stolen property from a temple of an idol god would have been the truthful answer, but truth is the one thing Machir was not capable of giving.

"But seeing this doesn't answer anything. If anything, it raises new questions."

"Come on, let's get out of this cellar before someone discovers us. I will explain everything to you. Is what you just saw the same as the image that you said you found?"

"Yes, exactly, only yours is much larger. What are these things?"

"GUWR-BAAL is the god of the Canaanite people who live to the north of us. At one time, we worshiped Baal here in Jerusalem, but crazed reformers came and destroyed everything. The name on our idols means 'god of the stranger'. I feel like a stranger in this city, when it comes to its citizens and especially its religion. Your family's invisible god will never understand people like you and me. His followers seek to destroy our god and they will stone us if they ever found out that we had his image in our possession."

"You believe it is possible that my fathers worshiped Baal?"

"There is no doubt they did, the hypocrites. They accuse Baal of being a god of violence even as they daily fill the streets of Jerusalem with the blood of animals and of those who oppose their religion. I have been to the city of Gubla in Canaan, and I practiced the worship of Baal in his majestic temple. Zerah, you must see this for yourself. Baal is a god of love and prosperity. Look at how he has rewarded me wealth. The Canaanites have massive trade ships that carry their goods all over the world and return with every kind of merchandise imaginable, unlike the impoverished shepherds and fishers of this cursed city. If it were not for the slaughter of sacrificial animals, this economy would collapse. You probably do not understand what I say, because you are young and by Jerusalem standards, your family is wealthy."

Zerah resented Machir identifying him with his family. "You are wrong about me and my family. I told my father that he must let me keep Baal or I would leave home. I would leave now if I had a place to go."

"I can't make that decision for you, but I can tell you from my experience that you will never be happy until you are free of people who deny you the privilege of serving a god as great as Baal. If anything, they will destroy you or have you killed if you insist on following what you know in your heart is right."

In spite of the strong feelings between the brothers, Zerah never imagined that one of his own family members might kill him. Machir's words brought the possibility to life and the proposition stunned Zerah. He needed something to hold him up. "Do you have some more of your 'spirit drink'? You said that we could celebrate my manhood. If you say the same, we can drink to our belief in Baal.

Machir tried to sound confident, yet he worried about creating a zealot. Too much open talk could draw unwanted attention. Unbridled devotion would be dangerous.

"Sure man, I have all the drink that we need, and we will drink to our god. Baal is not like your father's god who denies you all earthly pleasure."

"You said it is dangerous, but I am willing to take a chance if you come with me. I want to make an oath to Baal just as I made one to you. Can we go to the cellar again? It won't take long."

"Only for you, Zerah."

Machir relit the lamp and they hurried down the steps. Zerah ignored the last four steps, leaving his counterpart halfway down and in glee at the sight of his convert, the son of his enemy, kneeling before a powerless god. In Machir's religion, god was convenience. God was gratification. God was money. God was anything but real or interested in the lives of people. In this ruse, Baal served Machir's purposes perfectly.

Zerah earnestly entreated, "O Baal, I am 'guwr' in this land and to my family, but in you and through your servant Machir I found the truth. I swear an oath to you, on my mother's tomb. I will serve you all the days of my life."

Zerah never suspected that Machir's only interest in him centered around a diabolical ploy to get even or better yet, ahead of Abiel.

The second night of revelry fulfilled every expectation that Zerah had of life. There was acceptance, wine, drugs, friendship, sex—condoned and encouraged by his god. In the days and nights that followed, the people who came and went fascinated Zerah. Women brought the money that they earned with their bodies, but as Machir said, "They are well kept and fed, unlike the women that beg for food, and besides, my women enjoy themselves."

The participants in the nightly rites taking place at "Guwr's Bazaar" intrigued Zerah the most. The "conjurers" could tell fortunes by reading the stars or the clouds, lucky and unlucky days, good and bad omens, the flight of birds, or the entrails of beasts. One particular "conjurer" kept Zerah spellbound. He never tired of watching or listening to Anan's incantations and divinations. Likewise, she took a special interest in Zerah. Machir accepted "conjurers" not for the authenticity of their prophecies, but for their entertainment value. Anan's job was to supply the ingredients for the "spirit drink." Other than that, she was simply amusing. Machir's frivolous attitude toward witchcraft angered her. She, of all people, knew that her gift was imperfect; nonetheless, so much better than religion. Reading Zerah provided an opportunity to impress Machir and improve her reputation as a "diviner." No one had to know what happened sixteen years ago.

She stood in the courtyard of Abiel's house and spent most of her day waiting for a man named Ebed to come and hire her as a wet-nurse. Of all the women who gathered in hope of finding work, she was most patient. As the day wore on, the rest gave up and left. Anan remained alone, driven by dire need. When Ebed returned, he hardly noticed her. With nothing more than a feeble thank-you for her trouble, she returned to the street. Tired, hungry, and alone, she never expected to encounter any of this family again.

It took her some time to make a connection between her past and the handsome young man who sat across the table from her the past few weeks. Actually, it came back to her in a dream. Today, the time she spent some years ago, hopelessly waiting in the hot sun for word from Ebed would finally pay off. The hours that she lingered in Abiel's courtyard helped her glean a wealth of information about his family. There she talked with the servants, learning that Ammah died while giving birth to twins and that there was much confusion over which of the twins was the firstborn. She also learned the names of the twins.

Anan did not need much information to fashion a believable story. Until now, her sustenance had been paltry in spite of the fact that she was good at what she did. Her hopes were high to change all that. Reputation is everything in her business. The news of an accurate and profound reading would spread her fame like fire. A good test would be to see if the skeptical Machir would be impressed.

Anan walked into Guwr's Bazaar with her face set like stone. Machir greeted her with his usual harsh laugh. She completely ignored him as she made her way to a table in the corner. He noticed that she had something wrapped in a piece of sackcloth in one hand and a small knife in her other hand.

"My but aren't you friendly tonight," bellowed Machir.

Uncharacteristically, she did not answer him. In a tone of voice unfamiliar to him, she chanted, "I must see the prince."

Machir attempted to make light. "The prince? You must be in the wrong palace, my queen. There are no princes here."

She repeated, "I must see the prince."

About that time, Zerah came in from off the street, suspecting that Anan had arrived. He hoped she would mix the strong drink he came to crave, but unexpectedly walked in on something more intoxicating than her drugs.

She pointed her finger in the direction of Zerah and said, "Prince, come and sit with me at the table."

He and Machir looked at each other as they both shrugged their shoulders.

A crazed look contorted her face as she repeated, "You must come and sit with me at the table of your destiny."

Intrigued by the turn of events, Machir motioned to Zerah to do as she said. He sniggered, "This might be entertaining."

Zerah did not have time to think anything. He obediently took his place on a stool across the table from Anan. His willingness changed to apprehension, when she unfolded her sackcloth bundle, revealing a bloody liver from a freshly killed calf. She fretted to herself, "This had better work. I am out a handsome sum of money, and Machir will not give it back to me. Not even for a good laugh."

She bought the liver in the "black market" run by the priests of the temple. They had oversight of the sacrificial animals and used animal parts for their own gain.

She went to work, mustering all of her skills of sorcery, uttering words that no one else in the room understood. Simultaneously, she waved her small knife in rhythmic patterns in the air. She ceased gesturing with the knife long enough to say, "May the spirit of this calf that shed its blood for us tell us the things that have been, so we might know the things that shall be hereafter."

She carefully brought the small knife down across the center of the liver, exposing several arteries that ran in the same direction. She made a small but decisive cut on one of them and blood spurted out. Without pause, she cut the other artery, but no blood appeared. Looking up, she fastened her eyes steadfastly on Zerah. He was sure he felt heat coming from her stare. In a strange sounding voice, she told him, "Your mother died as she was giving birth to a child, but your father is still alive."

The knife went back to work with aplomb, this time exposing one artery going into the liver and a second one leading out. Two smaller arteries connected the two vessels. Without changing expression, she assertively said, "Twins."

There was excessive blood from the cutting. It helped Anan disguise her "magic." It worked in her favor if she could be the only one looking, not that Zerah had the stomach to look anymore anyway.

She continued, "One of the vessels is wrapped around the mother artery and has caused it to die. That is why it has no blood. Wait, the same vessel is wrapped around its twin vessel." She snapped her head up again, staring straight into the eyes of Zerah. Her voice sounded like the hissing of a snake as she spewed out, "Your twinnn killlled your mother with hiss greed and now heee desireeess to kill you!"

She slowly lowered her head until it touched the liver.

When she looked up, there was a huge bloody mark on her forehead. Zerah thought he saw his brother's face and it paralyzed him with fear, leaving him unable move or speak. It got worse when she raised her knife high over her head. For a moment, Anan appeared possessed by the spirit of Pharez. Zerah felt sure she or he would plunge the knife into his chest. He flinched as she jammed the knife, blade first into the table.

"Whhoooo!" He blew all of the air out of his lungs and followed with a sigh of relief.

Her performance was not over! She tore into the bloody meat with her fingers, all the while stammering unintelligible words. She paused while her lips twisted into a big sneer. "Good," she said. "Good, it is good."

She violently ripped off a piece of the liver and began a mantra, "Pharez, the one who tears, you will be torn. Son of the tearing, you will be torn asunder."

She held the piece of meat above her open mouth and tightly squeezed it, making it drip blood. Once her mouth was full, she swallowed it down and declared, "I drink your blood and rob you of your power to destroy."

Then she dropped the meat into her mouth and eagerly chewed at it until it became pulp. She swallowed hard and it was gone. "I eat your flesh, just as you consumed the flesh of your mother and would do likewise unto your brother."

Zerah was astounded. He just heard this woman tell the story of his birth and call the name of his brother. Machir, the unbeliever, was not too steady on his feet. He stumbled for a place to sit down.

Anan's intuition told her that her performance was perfect so far. "Now for the finish." She reached her hand down into her pocket and pulled out a long piece of cord. Anan held it over her head and waved it around. After speaking a few more strange words, she rolled the cord around in the excess blood from the liver. The cord soaked up the deep crimson color. Zerah's shock intensified when she informed him, "You wear a crimson-colored cord around your right ankle, don't you?"

With a quivering voice, he answered her, "Yes, but how did you…?"

She did not let him finish, "I am enlightened by the power of Baal. Give me your right leg. Lift it up to me."

Without hesitation, he lifted his leg toward her while precariously leaning back on his stool. She jerked the small knife out of the table and used it to cut the bloody cord in two pieces, holding one-half of the cord over the flame of the lamp. Zerah wanted to say something. His anklet had been symbolic and special to him for a long time. "Why did she burn it?"

Before he worked up courage to ask her aloud, she explained, "For many years you wore this cord as a reminder of your rightful place in your family. You wore it wrongly. You concealed it under your garment where it was hardly visible. Having it close to your foot signified that you were under the heel of your father and your brother. As of this night, you will wear a new cord around your neck. With it in full view, everyone who sees you will know your power and that you are to be the head of your family. It is decreed by our Lord Baal."

She placed the bloody cord around Zerah's neck and as she tied it, she said, "As I place this blood-soaked cord around the neck of your servant O Baal, I invoke you to promote him to his rightful place that he might serve you. May he honor me, your mouthpiece, with the fruits of his sustenance? Cause him to prosper in this place. Give him treasures hidden in the night. Let him no longer be known as "son of the morning," but henceforth be called "prince of darkness." Make him obey the wishes of his father Machir, the one who can teach him the true ways that are your ways. I will be 'Lamassu' and allow Machir to be 'Shedu.'"

Zerah had no idea what the strange names meant, but they resonated with his mood. Later, he discovered "Shedu" to be his reincarnated male ancestral protective spirit and "Lamassu" his feminine guardian angel sent to help him realize who he was destined to be.

CHAPTER 21

Coconspirators: The Criminal from Crook Street and His Former Concubine

If Anan hoped to impress Machir, she succeeded in a big way. She soon found out thieves resent someone stealing from them, especially if you steal their glory. There was room for only one "prince of the night" on Crook Street, and Machir claimed the title. He fumed, "Who does the "hora" think that she is, coming into my bazaar handing out titles like they were treats for her guests? Besides, she has no idea what I intend to do, and it certainly involves more than getting a few coins out of Zerah. I will kill him and lay his body at his father's door or sell him into slavery. If I castrate him, I can get a high price for him as a 'temple eunuch.'"

The "kurgaru" (castrated ones) are very much in demand in the temples of Anat, the sister and lover of Baal. If this were only about money, Machir's decision would be simple.

He settled on a plan to create a situation that would have Zerah stoned to death at the hands of his own people with Abiel and his family witnessing the brutality. If Zerah behaved as a good boy, Machir might favor him and have his body burned in the valley of Toph so he could be close to his god. Machir was masterful at exploiting people and he used Anan's greed to his advantage. It escaped him how she knew so much about Zerah, but evidently, everything she said was true. If so, Pharez's jealousy could turn him into Zerah's executioner!

Pharez knew enough on Zerah to have him sentenced to death, if the authorities should happen to find out. The biggest challenge would be to entice one of Zerah's kinsmen to report him. No one would pay attention to or believe anything that a liar like Machir had to say. A small amount of silver was all it took, and Anan plotted to approach an unsuspecting Naarah in the marketplace. Machir remembered how easy it had been for him to control Naarah, playing her insecurity against her. Something told him that she would be the key to getting to Pharez.

Naarah failed at mothering, but was skilled in overseeing the preparation of meals. She often went to the open markets for spices and vegetables. It was a brief but powerful encounter. Naarah felt a gentle tap on her shoulder. She turned, expecting that one of the servants who accompanied her had need of her. Instead, she faced a small-framed woman robed in black. The dark circles under her unusual eyes defined an otherwise light-skinned face. Naarah wanted to look away, but succumbed to the stare of one brown eye that veered away and the other sharp green eye that danced as it pierced into her soul.

Anan was at her best. "Woman, I am sent from the netherworld to speak wisdom to you."

Naarah's voice quivered, "Who are you? What do you have to do with me?"

The woman seemed not to hear her. "You have lived in disgrace for years, but your time has come. You see things clearly, things that others of your master's house cannot tell. G-d has granted you favor with his favored son. You must protect him at all cost or you will be judged severely. The house of Abiel will cast you out and you know where that leads!" With that, Anan turned and ran away.

Naarah yelled at the top of her voice, hoping to overpower the noise of the market, "Wait. I said wait…come back. Come back here." She chased after the black robe, but in vain. Her mysterious visitor disappeared into the press of people, leaving Naarah weak in her knees and faint of heart.

Watching Pharez come in from work all tired and dirty, knowing that Zerah was off somewhere amusing himself, angered Naarah. If it were not for Pharez working untiringly with his father, there would not be any wealth for Zerah to waste. Her temper went over the edge the day Zerah had the audacity to show up at his father's house wearing a piece of dark red rope around his neck. Its meaning was not lost on anyone, especially Pharez. Naarah pressed her point, "He stays gone for days at a time, won't tell anyone where he has been, neglects his schooling and everything else that he is asked to do. It is plain to see that the only reason that he bothers coming home at all is to get more silver from

Abiel and to see Egla. She is the only one that he even cares to talk to and that is if she doesn't press him too hard."

She worked on Pharez for years, preparing him for the confrontation that was inevitable. Her speech took on an air of urgency after her encounter with the strange eyed, black robed woman. Pharez politely listened to what she had to say, but usually dismissed her words as talk that offended his father. This time, her fervency got through to him in a way that she never had. Anger flashed in his eyes at the mention of his brother's name, so she was not altogether surprised when Pharez came to her early one evening asking, "What are we going to do about Zerah? I hoped that one day he would leave and never come back, but every time he comes home, he seems seven times worse than before. And now he wears a red rope necklace as a challenge to me."

"I know. I saw it, too. I am sure that your father must have seen it by now."

"Naarah, you know that I will never intentionally disrespect my father, but I fear he loves Zerah so much, that he will never do anything to stop him from destroying us all. Many of father's most faithful friends are talking about us and how father allows Zerah to ruin our family's name."

This kind of talk from Pharez made Naarah lick her lips. "Pharez, I have made it clear to you for a long time now how I feel about this situation. The time for talking has passed, and it falls upon you to do something. I have been thinking and I believe there is a way to get rid of Zerah and your father will never know how it happened."

"I'm listening."

"Do you remember the statute of a half man, half bull; the one that you and Zerah fight about?"

"How could I forget?"

"It is a graven image to Baal."

"I know the name well. The rabbis often teach against the worship of Baal. It is an abomination to G-d."

"The reason that your father doesn't want us to tell anyone about Zerah having an idol or much less that he talks to it, is if certain people knew; your brother would be put to death."

"Yes, I know and as much as I despise my brother and what he is doing to our family, I will not be the one responsible for his death. Father would hate me forever."

"I understand your feelings and I respect you for it. I'm not suggesting that you tell anyone, but you asked me what to do and I have a plan."

"What is it?"

"Well, you don't have to tell anyone about Baal. All that you have to do is threaten to. Tell Zerah that you will no longer stand by and watch him break your father's heart, rob this family of its wealth, and disgrace the family name. Let him know that you will not oppose him getting his share of the family inheritance as long as he agrees to leave home and never come back."

"But father will never agree to Zerah going away."

"There is something that you do not know, Pharez. Our law tells us that a father is to punish a child who inappropriately demands an inheritance by stoning him to death. You know that your father would never stone one of his sons. So given the choice of executing judgment on Zerah or seeing him go away for some time, Abiel will surely choose the latter. He will justify his action in that he spared his son's life and he will trust that Zerah will come home once his inheritance is spent. You and I know that thieves or one of their kind will do G-d's work for us. Your evil brother will never make it home."

"G-d's work. Hummm. I hadn't thought of it that way. You are right. G-d surely hates Zerah as much as we do."

"You will grow in understanding of why G-d allowed you to be born first. Your family has always feared G-d. He knew you and your brother while you were in your mother's womb. G-d gave you the strength to be born first. He knew your heart. Imagine what would happen to this family if Zerah was the firstborn."

The conspiratorial web woven by Machir, Anan, and Narrah was complete with the addition of Pharez's righteous indignation. Now to snare its victim in its sticky plot.

CHAPTER 22

Confrontation & Chaos

Pharez pretended to be sick, excusing himself from work so that he could stay home on a day he knew Zerah would come by to get silver from Abiel. His heart pounded with anticipation as he heard Zerah greeting the servants on his way into the house. Pharez wasted no time in getting to Zerah, knowing that once he learned that Abiel was not at home, he would not stay long. Besides, Pharez was on the verge of changing his mind about what he intended to do. The plot was deceitful and dishonest. "If father ever found out about any of this, there is no telling what might happen." But the decision became easy when he saw Zerah's face.

"Zerah, I, IIII have to to to tallllkkklk to to to yooouuu," he stuttered.

"Not today. I'm in a hurry and it takes you forever to say anything with your cursed stuttering. Where is father? I know that he can't be far away or else I wouldn't be seeing you," he said with more than just a hint of sarcasm.

"Enough of th-aaat, Zerah. Yooour da-da-days of playyyying are done. I ha-aave de-decided to ta-aakkkke matters into mm-myy own haaands. Yooou continue to ha-aarm this family with no-no-nooo regard for an-nn-yoone but-tt yourself. Youuu are fortunate tooo have a father like mine. Mooosst fathers would havvve thrown yooou ou ou out into thhee street aaaa long time ago. But no on-nne had to throw you out. Yo-oou chose to go out oo-on your own. You are nu-numbered with the transgressors, thei-thieves, blasphemers, and pros-prostitutes, and these are only the thin-nngs that we hear about. Only G-d knows what else you do-ooo under the co-co-cover of darkness."

"You speak of darkness; my friends know me as 'prince of the night'. You have no friends. All you know about life is following your father around. No wonder he never remarried. He has you."

Pharez could not take any more. He would not allow anyone to speak so disrespectfully of the father he revered. Without a thought, he grabbed Zerah by his necklace and gave it a forceful twist, causing them both to fall on the floor. Pharez landed on top.

"No-now-w you lisss-ten to-to-to me. I shou-uuld kill yo-oou right now. It is only because yo-uuuuu are someone that my fa-fa-father loves that I-I-I don't, but if I ever hear you saaa-ayy anything against Abiel again, I wii-ill choke the life ooo-out of you. Do yoo-ouu want to be the firstborn ba-aadd enough to b-be-be the first to die?"

Zerah could not have answered if he wanted to. Pharez's grip on the necklace was much tighter than intended. The constriction broke the skin and some small veins in Zerah's neck. This had nothing to do with innocent child's play; it was life and death. Pharez glared down into his brother's reddened face. It was not until he asked, "Do you understand me?" that he realized Zerah could not breathe, much less talk. He rolled off Zerah's chest and loosened his grip on the necklace. For a moment, he feared Zerah was dead. The sound of Zerah gasping for air brought relief. Now that he had his brother's full attention, the time was right to proceed with his and Naarah's plan.

"I know you-uu can hear me-me-mee, sooo hear me-ee wel-well. Yo-ou mu-must leave and I do-do n-n-not just mean ho-home. Yo-ou must leave Jerusalem f-for g-oo-ood. Yo-ou will require pro-provisions so-oo I-I-I will no-ttt object if yo-ou g-g-go tooo father and ask fo-for yo-your share of o-o-our inheritance. Dooo n-n-not think of taking the inheritance and-and staying he-he-here. If yo-you doooo, I wi-will gooo tooo the authorities and report yo-youu f-f-for worshiping idols. I k-kn-know whooo the half-bull man is, and I-I-I to-took him f-fr-from your room. I-I am keep-keeping it as evidence of-of yo-yo-your blasphemy. If-if yo-you dooo n-not o-obey tooo what I-I-I tell yo-you tooo dooo, I-I-I will gladly cast t-t-the first stone o-on yo-you myself. Doo w-w-we have an agree-agreement?"

"Yeess, yes. I agree, but hear me. We are no longer brothers. You are a bastard who regards me as a stranger."

Pharez lunged toward Zerah, but thought better of it. If they fought again, it would be to the death.

"I will happily leave this place forever. My friend Machir told me this day would come, and I am glad it is here. I should thank you. If you think taking the image of Baal away from me will change me, you are wrong. Baal is in my mind and heart and you or no one else can do anything about it. I warn you that Baal is a god of vengeance and the person who tries to keep him from me will be punished."

"Z-zerah, yo-you have lost yo-your mind. After the way f-f-father brought us up and the teach-teachings of-of o-o-our religion, ho-how can yo-you b-believe t-t-that a molded p-piece ooof b-b-brass harms or-or h-h-helps anyone?"

"You will see. Trust me, you will see. Remember the story of Joseph in your schooling texts. His brothers did not believe in his dreams. He was a prince in disguise. His brothers hated the color of his coat and his dreams. You take exception to me being "the prince of darkness." You, like them, will cast me away. I too am destined to become a ruler in a strange land, just as your Joseph did in Egypt."

"Z-zerah, yo-you are n-not the patriarch J-j-joseph. Besides, h-he did no-not worship i-idols. Yo-you are hope-hopeless. F-f-father will beee ho-ho-home before lo-long, and we-we can settle this m-matter o-once and f-f-for all."

Abiel could see by the looks on their faces that something was terribly wrong. Although his intuition warned of impending disaster, he mustered courage to say, "All right my sons, I can tell something is troubling the both of you; so come on, out with it. It can't be that bad."

His speech clearing considerably in the presence of his father, Pharez spoke first. "F-father, Zerah tells mee that hee wishes too leave home f-for good. Yo-you of all people know t-that hee and I n-never got along but he-he is still my b-brother."

Zerah defiantly wagged his head in disagreement of being a brother to Pharez.

"In one way, I-I will hate to seee him leave, but on t-the other hand, h-he does have a-a lot of growing up t-to doo and being on h-his own may b-be best for him. T-that is all I-I will say. I will abide by whatever decision t-that yo-you and Zerah make."

Abiel felt hot tears well up in his eyes as he turned to look at Zerah. "Zerah, is this true?"

"Yes, it is."

"But why, what is it you lack that you cannot find here with me?"

"Sir, I know that you try, but try as you may, you can no longer hide the fact that Pharez is the son you prefer. The answer to your question is no. I need more than food, clothing, and shelter. I want things that your beliefs will not allow you to give. I need things that are mine and mine alone, not shared unequally with him." He stuck his finger close to Pharez's face. "Mostly I seem to get the lesser part of your affection. It is little more than pity or sympathy. Truthfully, it is not enough for me. This is shameful. Your servant Egla is more my mother than you are my father. I will never fit in your and Pharez's world."

"Why haven't you said these things to me before? Maybe…"

"The days of maybe are passed. I am determined to leave. I do have one request of you."

"What is it, my son?"

"I want you to give me my inheritance. It is not good that I go away from here empty. If I go into a far country with nothing, I will be disrespected and will have to work for another."

Abiel was taken aback. "I am not prepared to answer a question that you should not be asking. I hope that you ask this out of ignorance, for you put yourself in serious violation of our law."

"There, you just gave an example of something I need you can't provide, like unconditional love. Let me see; it must be wrong for me to ask for what is mine because it is not wholly mine. Most of it must belong to my brother Pharez who stole it from me at birth."

Abiel lifted his hand to slap Zerah on his mouth for such talk. As he did, he saw blood running down Zerah's neck. Seeing his son injured made his heart sink lower than his angered right hand was raised. He lowered his voice and his hand. "You will never again call your brother a thief, not in this house."

Zerah responded, "Good then, it is settled; I will leave."

Abiel searched for the right words to say. He wondered, "What would a mother say?" The remark about Egla demanded his attention. "Maybe, I have failed as a father."

"Come here, son; what happened to your neck?"

Without moving, Zerah coldly and calmly replied, "I was in a fight."

Abiel asked, "With whom? Someone nearly killed you."

"It should be of no concern to you or Pharez. I am a man, and I can take care of myself."

"You don't look like you did a very good job of it. Go with Pharez and let Egla dress your wound."

"I'm not going anywhere until you answer me. Will you give me my inheritance?"

"Son, please go and take your rest. You look terrible. I will give you my decision in the morning."

"All right, but regardless of your decision, I will be leaving."

As he followed behind Pharez, he complained, "The morning, always the morning in this house. No wonder I love the night."

Abiel hoped a night's rest would ease the tension, but the chaos was just beginning.

Zerah fell asleep soon after Egla finished dressing the wound on his neck. Once Abiel was certain that he was asleep, he summoned Pharez for a talk. Tonight, neither of them would sleep. Abiel suspicioned there were secrets Pharez kept from him. Pharez never lied to his father. The thought of starting now made him dread this night more than any he remembered. It bothered him, knowing he let Naarah talk him into getting involved in this debacle. Yet in his heart, he had to admit he wanted Zerah to leave more so than anyone else.

"Pharez, I don't care what you promised your brother. If you know anything at all about what is happening to Zerah, you must tell me."

"Father, I haven't promised anything to Zerah. He told you his reasons for wanting to leave. What else is there to know?"

"I believe he is in trouble. Perhaps his life is in danger. He has a terrible injury to his neck, and I intend to find out who did this to him, regardless of what it takes. Do you know any of his friends or enemies? Has he ever confided in you?"

"Surely you know Zerah never confides in me. I am the last person he tells anything. Wait, I just remembered; as we were talking earlier, he did mention someone that he called a friend."

"Who was it, son?"

"He said his friend's name is Machir."

Abiel turned pale and looked like he was about to vomit. Pharez did not realize the significance of what that name meant to his father. Abiel jumped to his feet and ran toward the well in the courtyard to splash some water on his face. Pharez was right on his heels, pleading, "Father, what is wrong? Are you all right?"

Abiel could do nothing but nod his head.

Pharez could not figure what happened. "What did I say? Do you know this person?"

It took forever for Abiel to collect himself enough to answer. He continued splashing cold water all over his head.

"Do I know Machir? I not only know him; he is one of the few men I have met that I should have killed with my own hands. He is a common thief who preys upon the misery of others. In my opinion, he is capable of doing almost anything, including persuading Zerah to leave home and stealing his inheritance."

"Zerah said his friend Machir told him the day would come when he would leave home."

"I warned Machir that I would bring him down if he ever bothered me or my family. Now it is time to remind him I am a man of my word."

"What are you thinking about doing, father?"

"I am past thinking. I want you to go with me to the house of my friend Eli."

"You mean Nasi, the High Priest?"

"Exactly, Machir is about to have some uninvited visitors down on Crook Street."

In no time, Abiel and Pharez knocked on the door of Eli's house. One of the servants opened the door and asked them whom they wished to see. Hearing Abiel's familiar voice, Eli called out from his room, "My friend Abiel, to what do I owe the honor of your visit? Come on back here."

The servant ushered them to Eli. He looked tired, sitting in his big chair with his feet propped up. He only allowed his best of friends to see him like this.

"Thank you for allowing us to come here unannounced. I wouldn't bother you if it wasn't so important."

"Out with it, Abiel. You are in the company of a friend, and you know I will do whatever I can to help."

"It is my son."

Eli looked at Pharez.

"No Nasi, I'm sorry. I do not mean Pharez. It is Zerah that needs our help."

"Ah yes, I have heard rumors. Does this have anything to do with the fact that he has been seen at night in parts of the city not fit for a young man to be in?"

"Nasi, have you heard of a man by the name Machir? He owns a bazaar on Crook Street."

"Heard of him? I should say I have. We have suspected for years that he is involved in prostitution, drugs, theft, witchcraft, and many other crimes against G-d. Our problem is we can never find anyone to come forward and witness against him. Everybody must be afraid of him. I cannot say that I blame them. He is dangerous."

"I am not afraid of him. I will witness against him, and my son Pharez will be a second witness to establish our word. If necessary, I have a third witness by the name of Naarah. She will come forward."

"What will you accuse him of?"

"Zerah is seriously injured, and he is asking for money so that he can leave home. It is apparent someone is pressuring him. I believe he is a victim of extortion at the hands of Machir. Some years ago, I had a personal encounter with this man. He all but admitted he is involved in prostitution, stealing, and selling people into slavery. I dealt harshly with him, and he may be looking to get even with me through my son. Will this be enough for you to order a search of his property? I will risk my reputation; we will find much more than we expect if we catch him off guard."

"I admire the courage you and Pharez show to defend your family from this predator. I am with you all the way. I can have the temple guards assembled on short notice. When do we go?"

"We prefer to go tonight if at all possible. Zerah is home asleep. I hope this will be over before he awakens tomorrow morning. He must be kept out of this at all costs."

Machir was pouring his second cup of "spirit drink" when the front doors of his shop came crashing down. Twenty-four "temple guards" stormed in with Eli, Abiel, and Pharez following behind them.

Machir bellowed out, "Whhaattt, what the hell, what is going on here? What right do you have to break in here? This is a place of business and you have no..."

A crashing blow from the right hand of one of the guards landed squarely on his chin, cutting his sentence short. Machir was already under the influence of "spirit drink," so the punch didn't hurt. However, it quieted him long enough for Eli to inform him he would be wise to remain speechless unless asked to talk. His days of ruling the nights on Crook Street were over. In fact, his "subjects" ran like rats as word spread over the darkened streets of inner-city Jerusalem that Eli and his guards were inside GUWR's Bazaar.

Eli's voice rang with conviction as he declared, "Machir, you stand accused of horrible crimes against humanity and violating the laws of God. We come in search of evidence to support the testimony of numerous witnesses. Guards, consider this man under arrest while the investigation is under way."

It did not take long to uncover poorly concealed evidence. The guards were anything but respectful or timid when it came to searching a suspect's property. They discovered a large book containing the names of prostitutes and large sums of money that they were forced to pay to Machir. Sadly, the book bore record of many women sold into slavery. The search also netted numerous items commonly used in the practice of divination and sorcery; this included potions containing drugs that induce hallucinations. The drugs and sorcery tools were sufficient to condemn Machir. However, the most significant find came when one of the guards kicked at a rug. It slid across the room, exposing a trapdoor leading down into a darkened cellar. When several of the guards tightly clutching oil lamps descended into the cellar, a massive, glittering object came into view. It was "the god of the stranger," GUWR-BAAL.

Excitedly, one of the guards ran to get Nasi.

"Nasi, sir please come quickly. You must see what we have found in the cellar."

Eli, not being one given to excitement, calmly motioned for Abiel and Pharez to follow him as he made his way to the cellar's entrance.

"Abiel, would you go down in front of me? I need to lean on your shoulder. My steps are not as steady as they once were."

The guard at the bottom of the steps busily trimmed his lamp.

"Careful, sirs," he cautioned.

Abiel and Eli recognized what and who the bulky bull-like figure was. Impulsively, Eli cried out against the idol, "Anathema, be upon Baal and his worshipers. Blasphemy, cursed be those who call upon the name of false gods." He almost knocked Abiel down in his effort to get back up the steps. Eli did not care to defile himself by touching anything unclean. It surprised Pharez and Abiel to see a Nasi get so riled. This went beyond religion as his voice rang hot with personal anger. It made Abiel fear that the trap he set for his enemy would inadvertently snare his son. He hated himself for tolerating the bull-man in Zerah's room. At least Machir was in deep trouble and Baal stood rigid, unwilling, no, unable to come to his aid. The guard holding the lamp backed away a few steps. As he did, other items came into view.

"Nasi, sir, look over here."

Eli recognized the heap of utensils as tools that belonged to the temple. They were "holy things" used in worship, gone missing from the temple. There they were, censers of brass, gold candlesticks, and the like. It is a serious criminal act to steal from G-d, but to bring contraband and put it at the feet of an idol is unforgivable. Eli's "rile" converted to revile.

"Machir will be punished for this. He will die a death that is befitting his crime. Even as adulterers are stoned, let it be so for the one who went whoring after other gods. He forsook the worship of the highest G-d, and stole the "holy things" pertaining unto His worship. He defiled them in the presence of a heathen deity. Guards, secure this place until I return."

They returned to the room where the guards held Machir. Abiel queried, "Nasi, what do we do now?"

"Abiel, you and Pharez return home for now, but I will need for you both to appear before the council tomorrow morning at the third hour of the day. Meantime, I will take Machir for interrogation. I fear there are many more involved in this matter, and I will see to it that they all meet with the same fate. If we do not stop this now, we could see a revival of idol worship. It brought death to our people over our history."

Abiel choked back the sickness simmering in his stomach that rose toward his throat. Daringly, he tested the limits of his friendship with Eli as he reached out and caught the shoulder of the High Priest.

"Nasi, I respect you too much to insult your character by asking you to be a respecter of persons. Nevertheless, I fear for the life of my son, if he is involved in this. If you show him mercy, considering his age and the circumstances of his life, I will be in your debt forever. If you cannot grant my request, then hold me responsible for his actions and let me die with the transgressors. I will die anyway if anything happens to my son. It will break my heart, but as I told you earlier, Zerah has requested to leave home."

Abiel tried to read the face of his friend, but Eli was a stone.

He pled on, "If I send him away, surely that will be enough punishment for all of us. Please sir, by your mercies, let my request be acceptable unto you. I vow to you, I will bring a fattened calf to you once a year, so you may offer atonement for my sins and the sins of my son."

"Abiel, I cannot promise you what you ask. The decision is not altogether mine. I can advise you to see to it that Zerah is gone before it is too late. If we cannot find him, one can come to all kinds of conclusions. I will do everything in my power to keep him out of this, but none of us can guess what Machir will say before the council. Give him this much. He is shrewd and will stop at nothing to save himself."

CHAPTER 23

Convicted by the Council

The early evening hours wore on over into the lateness of the midnight watch. Machir was correct in telling Anan that no one, not even Zerah, could usurp his title as "prince of darkness." The later the night, the harder his heart and the stronger his will to resist interrogation became. Assuming "the salesman" would give up would be a big mistake. Although, Machir erred in imagining he could outsmart, outtalk, and wear down Eli's moral resolve. His conceit made him uncooperative and unresponsive to his questioners. He waited for Eli to weaken. If that moment came, he planned to seize the opportunity to negotiate his way out of trouble. His street savvy told him that Eli was a friend to Abiel. Their camaraderie was a weapon he could wield against them.

He plotted, "I will threaten to implicate Zerah in theft and idolatry. As much as I hate the self-righteous priests, this Eli is stupidly fair. He will not punish me and let Zerah go free. His council would not go along with it. I may get a beating, but at least I will live to leave this cursed place."

Machir gained respect for one aspect of Hebrew law, that being the equality of its judgments. Fairness never worked well in his world, but this time, he was glad for it.

Coming back to the reality of his situation, he lectured himself, "What am I doing? I hate laws and customs and they are my enemy. I need to think about what I know best—people, priests, fathers, and sons. One of them will get me out of this."

Behind his mask of arrogance, an uneasy sense of finality nagged at him. It wore away at his confidence.

He jumped awake in a cold sweat after nodding off long enough to dream of a priest putting his hand upon the head of one goat and then another. For no apparent reason, the priest let one goat go and cut the throat of the other. The dream was troubling. It was like something out of Machir's world, devoid of equality or justice. "Maybe the council will condemn me and let Abiel's son go unpunished." Machir gathered his nerve to make his case.

He slurred through a busted lip, "Nasi, as you are called, I am ready to speak to you."

One of the guards standing nearby raised his fist, believing Machir spoke disrespectfully.

Eli stopped him. "No, don't hit him again. Save his face for the stones. Besides, we want to hear him repent and renounce Baal when he feels the wrath of true believers executing the judgments of the one true G-d."

"Come now, Nasi; you haven't heard my defense and your council hasn't convicted me of any crime. There is still time for us to reason together so no harm comes to an innocent person. You seem awfully close to Abiel and his family. You see, we have a lot in common, you and me. Actually, Abiel's son Zerah thinks of me as a second father, and I would hate to see the boy dragged into a misunderstanding like this. Abiel is angry with me because he feels rejected by his son. Surely, you know enough about this family to be aware that serious jealousy exists between Zerah and Pharez. It is so bad that Abiel worries they will harm each other. You as a scholar of your Scriptures know they say 'Jealousy is as cruel as the grave.'"

Eli grimaced. It pained him to hear Scriptures quoted by a vile heathen. Nonetheless, he allowed Machir to continue.

"I am not a learned man, but in my language, that reading means, if someone is jealous of another, the jealous one is capable of murdering the other. Don't you see this is what is happening here? Years passed and Abiel had no interest in witnessing against me until his son came to me. I did nothing to harm the boy or turn him against his family. I often tell him to go home and make things right with his family. I even told him how I lost my family in a similar way and how it pains me until this very day. He should do everything in his power to make things right before it is too late. As far as the idol and the stolen items in the cellar, I had no idea those things were down there. Many people come and go from my shop, and sometimes I am away for days at a time. How can I be aware of everything that goes on in my absence?"

Eli clapped his hands in mock applause. "That was quite a performance. I must admit I now have a clear understanding of how the serpent deceived Eve.

However, I am not an impressionable girl and not at all taken by your lies. Today is not the first time I heard the hissing of a snake. Now, tell me your next tale and when you get through with it, you might try the truth. I don't know why I bother, because I don't believe that the truth is in you."

"All right, I see that you are wise and onto me, so let me start over. Here it is straight from one man to another. If you take me before your council and condemn me to death, I will tell them about your friend Abiel's son. I didn't lead him into idolatry. I don't even believe in Baal or any other god. I bought the idol of Baal at a bargain price so that I could resell it to some fool that believes in him. I am not afraid of you or much less, the powers of your god, but you and Abiel should fear me. I hold the power to take his beloved Zerah with me to your stone pile. Is that what you want?"

"Well at least we got somewhat closer to the truth that time, but I have real bad news for you. Last night, Zerah approached his father and demanded to leave Jerusalem. He has left, and there is no word of where he has gone. As you know, we have no jurisdiction or authority beyond our borders. You are right, I am a friend of this family, and as such, I have no passion or intention to pursue Zerah. You led many young girls and boys into your godless trap of sexual transgression for your own gain. It is time for you to pay for your crimes. I will sleep better knowing you are dead and your den of iniquity destroyed."

Machir never met a man he couldn't persuade. Something told him this Nasi wasn't about to be swayed. He studied Eli's face. It looked as rigid as the brass idol that he hid in his cellar. His countenance showed no anger, sorrow, pity, or hate—nothing but brass resolve. For the first time in Machir's life, he feared another man. Abiel caused Machir embarrassment, but this was different. This man called Eli was dangerous.

Tired and angry, Eli had enough. He waved his hand in a way that demonstrated his disgust and turned to leave the room. The cruel jealousy Machir lectured Eli about stirred in "the salesman's" heart. He was doomed, but determined to take someone dear to Abiel with him. If Zerah escaped judgment, so be it. Naarah might even be a better prize. It would take the best performance of his life, cunning enough to deceive the judicious Eli.

"Nasi, wait, before you leave. I have always been able to persuade men with my speech. I confess, I have not always used it for the good of others. I said I do not believe in any god, but I see something in you, stronger than anything I know. Perchance this is god speaking to me through you in my last hours. If the last thing I do on earth is good, maybe there will be hope for me in the next world. You asked me for names of people who participated in blasphemy with me. The truth is that there is no one else."

"You tell me to wait and for what, to hear more of the same from you?" Eli moved toward the door.

Machir yelled in panic, "You must let me finish!"

Eli stopped but did not turn around. He listened.

"I told you that I don't believe in idol gods, and I have been truthful about that. Prostitutes and slaves, yes that part is true, and I deserve any punishment that you mete out to me for that. Drugs and witchcraft were just games to me. The drugs were a way to make my miserable life bearable for a few hours. I don't expect you to understand, but hear me out. I will help you and Abiel to rid yourselves of one that is evil, that being his servant Naarah."

Eli spun around on his heels. "How do you know of her?"

"At one time she was my concubine. She volunteered as a wet-nurse for hire for Abiel's sons when their mother died. Naarah bore a child for me, but the child died. Believing it would comfort her, I allowed her to go to Abiel. He desired her, so he threatened to expose my involvement in prostitution if I didn't give her to him. She never stopped loving me and often came in secret to see me. She and I conspired together many times over the years as to how we might gain Abiel's fortune. Naarah planned to marry him. Then she and I would have him killed by some people that we know who do that sort of thing for money. She was my spy in his house and vowed to help me get even with him. I am not a man accustomed to losing."

Machir heartened as he detected an ever so slight change in Eli's demeanor. Ignoring his onrushing fate, he celebrated, "I will win. Death will give me property back, and I will have my revenge on Abiel. Stupid priest. He is a decrepit old fool. No match for me!"

Being a salesman, he smelled blood, and it was the time to close the deal.

"Sir, I tell you this silly woman is like clay in my hands. She believes in Baal, and I use it to control her. She taught Zerah to love the bull-man. If you don't believe me, go to Abiel's house before the morning breaks. If Zerah left in haste, you should find an idol of Baal somewhere inside the house. My guess is Naarah's room. If she is not a danger to you, she certainly represents danger to your friend Abiel. Ask Abiel if Naarah caused trouble between his sons. Ask him why he hasn't taken her as his wife. Ask him if he threatened to banish her from his house. Most of all, you should ask yourself the question, how did Zerah find me and end up under my care? Naarah is my confidant and my conspirator. I love Naarah in my own way and selfishly want her to die with me. If my selfishness can do some good, then so be it."

Eli was not about to give the impression he believed anything Machir said. Without one word, he turned and left the room. He did believe part of Machir's story. Eli sorted Machir's words. "The part about selfishness is true, but doing good to find redemption; that was spoken strictly for my benefit. His words are like Abiel's twins, so alike and yet so different. It is difficult to tell Machir's lies from the truth, albeit, in Abiel's interest, I have to investigate."

Eli called for several guards to accompany him to Abiel's house.

Abiel was still awake and stirring as Eli and his men approached in the early morning hours. There was much for Abiel to do. After conferring with Pharez, he decided to give Zerah his part of the inheritance. Abiel was surprised but gladdened by the attitude that Pharez had shown. He expected Pharez to be angry, but instead, he agreed that his brother should not be sent away empty-handed. One of Abiel's servants ran to advise him that there were soldiers approaching. Abiel, believing that something had drastically changed since he had left Eli, told Pharez to go get in the bed with his brother and lie so closely to him that it would appear to be one person sleeping. Abiel did not wait for a knock on the door. Instead, he went to the courtyard, hoping to deflect any trouble and not raise unnecessary questions among the servants.

Abiel called out into the dark of night, "Hail, who is it that comes at this hour of the morning?"

All that he could see was the glow of torches.

"Abiel, it is Eli. I come on business of the council."

The warm friendliness left Abiel's voice. "What do you require of me?"

Eli appeared out of the shadows looking more imposing than Abiel had ever seen him.

"I mean no harm to you or any of your family." Eli calmly said.

"You are always welcome at my house, but if this is not about my family, tell me sir, why do you come with guards at this hour?"

"Abiel, please invite me inside so we don't rouse the entire neighborhood, and I will tell you why I am here."

Once inside, Abiel ordered his servants outside.

"Abiel, I must ask you a few questions."

"You know that I will answer."

"Earlier, you said you had a problem with Machir some years ago. True?"

"Yes, I did."

Eli pressed, "Did this involve Naarah?"

"Yes, but..."

"Please, let me finish. Has Naarah caused problems between your sons?"

"Truthfully, yes, she has," Abiel admitted.

"Is this why you have not taken her as a wife or a concubine?"

"Partially true sir, but that is not the only reason."

"Have you ever threatened to banish her?"

"Yes, but..."

"I asked you to let me finish. Remember, I am here as a friend, but I also represent the council and I have a job to do. Believe me, when I finish, you assuredly will know I am your friend. Now, this is the hard part. I promise not to use this against you. Have you ever seen an idol that resembles Baal in this house?"

Abiel took several deep breaths before he could answer. He knew he would be confessing something that could cause his son's death!

"Yes, but Zerah said he found it by his mother's grave, and he never considered it a god nor did he attempt to worship it."

"Be calm, Abiel. You have no idea of the meaning of my questions. I told you I mean no harm to you or your sons. Although, what I am about to say will shock you."

Abiel dropped his head, doubting if he was still capable of being shocked, "What is it? After today I don't know what else can happen."

"I strongly suspicion that you have an enemy living in your house. Have you wondered how Zerah became involved with Machir? It seems like more than coincidence."

It shamed Abiel to admit he did not know more about his son's life. "I just found out yesterday."

"Machir told us the whole story. Naarah has spied on you and conspired with Machir to take your money and have you killed. Fortunate for you that you never married her or you would be dead. She is the one who wrecked your family and enticed your son into idolatry. I am sorry, but I must search her quarters. We should find evidence to support Machir's story. If this is true, the consequences will be dire."

This time the guards were much more respectful of property than they were at the bazaar. As they moved Naarah's bedding, they found two concealed bundles.

"Nasi, we discovered these hidden in Naarah's room."

Abiel was more than a bit curious to see the contents of the bundles. Never before had there been the need to hide anything in his house. Apparently,

Naarah did not honor Abiel's trust. He could not believe his eyes. The necklace he gave Ammah for their wedding lay in the palm of Eli's hand along with a nose ring, which he did not recognize.

"Let me see that." He held it close, hoping to be wrong. "We have looked for this for years. I never suspected that Naarah would steal something so precious to me."

"What about this ring?"

"I have never seen it before."

Eli quickly undid the second bundle. Before he finished, it became clear what its contents were. Eli threw the unclean cloth across the room and the small idol fell out spinning across the floor. Eli punctuated the moment with long drawn-out sounds of affirmation.

"Ahhhahhhhh, the liar from Crook Street does have some truth in him."

Abiel's mind spun as madly as the idol on the floor.

"I know the idol belongs to Zerah. Why did Naarah have it and why did she hide it? If I don't tell Eli what I know, terrible things will happen to her, but if I do tell…" His decision came easy when he thought of the one sleeping just down the hall. Zerah was not supposed to be in Jerusalem. If found, he would be arrested.

He reasoned, "I know Eli promised to protect us as much as he could, but even he cannot overrule the council. I have to get the soldiers away from here."

Eli noticed Abiel's nervousness. He sensed that Zerah had not left yet, so he began making good on his promise of protection. He did not need to search any more of the house. He had more than enough evidence to bring Naarah before the council.

"Abiel, go with the guards to your courtyard and identify Naarah so that they can arrest her."

"Nasi, I don't mean to be disobedient, but I don't believe that I have the strength."

"All right, I understand. Guards, go to the courtyard and call out Naarah's name. When she responds, arrest her. Ask the other servants to identify her. We don't want her to get away."

Eli whispered to Abiel, "I will leave you now. I know you have much to attend to. Please do not ignore my advice concerning Zerah. I do have influence, but the council is going to come down hard in this matter. Our fathers learned a deadly lesson about tolerance to idolatry. G-d will judge us if we do not judge those who forsake his laws. He will not have any other gods before him! Remember the story of Achan and his stolen goods that belonged to the heathen. Whatever you do, make sure that you and Pharez come before the council at the appointed time."

"Eli, before you go, I implore you to grant me one more request."

"Abiel, I am tired and I really…"

"Sir, I understand, but the council only requires two witnesses. You are a witness, and I will stand by my word to be a witness. That will be sufficient to satisfy the law. I beg of you not to call Pharez as a witness. Even if Naarah did do wrong, she has been with Pharez since the day he was born. I know she caused strife, but I was blind to her other sins. I confess I have always loved her and I know Pharez does as well. If she is found guilty and worthy of death, I, as her accuser, am required to cast the first stone. I am losing one of my sons as it is. Forcing Pharez to do the same will cause me to lose him, too. What crime have I committed that I am required to lose both of my sons?"

The ever stoic Eli hung his head for a few moments and as he turned to leave he said, "I will see you at the third hour of this morning."

"You do mean just me?"

"Yes, just you."

Abiel stepped out into the courtyard and dismissed the servants. Everybody needed rest. There was not much more that anyone could do until daylight came. Although Abiel had to see what happened when Pharez went to Zerah's room. He paused long enough to put his ear to the door. It relieved him not to hear anything, no quarreling, no fighting, nothing. He eased the door open and peeked in to find his sons sleeping peacefully next to each other. Pharez's arm draped over his brother as if to protect him from harm. "Why can't life be this way?" Abiel could not answer his own question, at least not tonight. It prompted him to ask a second question that he could not answer. "Why do we even bother to ask ourselves questions that we know that we can't answer?"

It did Abiel absolutely no good to go to bed. His main concern was to inventory his camels, asses, sheep, cattle, and goats. His flocks and herds were so large that even one-third of them would be too many for Zerah to manage on a long journey. Zerah and those who would travel with him would require livestock for food, camels to ride, and the asses to carry furnishings and clothing. Zerah knew nothing of shepherding, caring for animals, finding his way through unfamiliar territory, or much about any other skills that he needed to survive. The roads and hills were full of thieves who lived off inadequately protected caravans. Earlier, Abiel sent Ebed out to hire men skilled with weapons that were willing to accompany the caravan to its destination. Fortunately, Hiphil served in the military and he knew some good men who would likely go on such a mission. Abiel hoped that Ebed remembered to ask Hiphil for their names.

Abiel needed to talk to Pharez, but it behooved him to be gone before Pharez woke up. He might not be able to dissuade Pharez from going before the council. Abiel needed someone wise to explain to Pharez what happened during the night. "Who else but dependable Egla?"

Abiel was not the only one suffering through the night. He neared Egla's room hearing the sound of someone softly crying. He whispered, "Egla, it is me, Abiel."

She muffled her voice.

He repeated, "Egla, I need to talk to you. Please come out and talk to me." He showed a lot of respect by his asking please of a servant. She stepped out into the hall. Abiel motioned for her to follow. They stood in the fading darkness as morning approached. The few remaining stars brightened and hung near the earth as if they wished to hear the conversation.

"Abiel, what in heavens name happened? I watched as the temple guards led Naarah away. Then, Ebed said Zerah is leaving and to make ready his departure. None of this can be good."

"Egla, if I fully understood, I would try to explain. Everything happened so fast. All that I know for now is I must appear before the council in a few hours to give testimony against Machir and Naarah. I am trying my best to protect all of us. Pharez and Zerah are my main concern. I desperately need you to help me with them."

"You know that I will, but what will happen to Naarah? Remember, I brought her to you. She is so helpless. I am like a mother to her."

"All that I can tell you is she is in G-d's hands now, and he will do with her according to his will. When Pharez awakens, I need you to be waiting and to tell him it was not necessary for him to go with me today. He will know what I mean. Tell him not to try to come where I am. I need him to stay here and help arrange for his brother's departure. I have a list of the livestock I need for him to gather for me. Please give this to him."

"Do you mean it is true? My child, I mean your son; I'm sorry Abiel, you know how I feel about Zerah. He is going away?"

"It's all right; I know how you feel about Zerah and it makes me glad. You see, I must ask you to leave Jerusalem and go with Zerah. I cannot bear the thought of him being alone without someone who truly cares for and understands him. The other thing I need you to do is to make sure that Pharez gets busy and does not notice that Naarah is missing. I know he will ask you why the temple guards came here last night. Tell him that they came to ask me some more questions. Instruct all of the other servants not to mention one word about the guards taking Naarah. I will explain everything to him when I return. Tell the menservants to make sure Zerah does not leave the house. He may not like it, but it is my order. He is not to leave the house."

"Abiel, are you sure that you will be all right? This is frightening me."

"Dry your eyes; our faith is in G-d and everything will work out for our good."

With these words, Abiel headed out toward the inner city. By walking fast, he got there just after daylight. He had time to see what, if anything, was happening on Crook Street and still be on time to witness before the council. He arrived just in time to see a number of burly men struggling to load the bulky idol of Baal onto a cart drawn by a pair of oxen. The idol looked much more impressive in the glistening morning light than it did by lamplight in Machir's cellar. It is a good thing that the oxen were accustomed to the noisy streets of Jerusalem. Otherwise, they might have bolted when a pack of street dogs surrounded the cart, barking and showing their teeth at the sight of Baal. Other men stood by, propping themselves up on all sorts of tools, apparently waiting for orders. Just then, a priest stepped forward and gave the signal that the workers awaited, "Tear it down and carry it off. Load the carts and do not leave one stone standing."

Abiel saw several other carts coming down the street. The priest shouted, "Get busy. This is G-d's work and G-d abhors a sluggard."

The men moved like ants gathering winters harvest. GUWR's Bazaar would soon be nothing more than rubble. It became clear to Abiel that the meeting of the Council would be a mere formality. Nothing he did or said would affect the outcome! Abiel walked toward the Temple Mount as reluctantly as someone being led to his own execution. The city began to wake up and stir. Abiel heard voices of children making their way out to play. His nostrils caught the smell of smoke from morning fires stoked up, for the purpose of preparing for the day. The markets started to open as their vendors pulled back blankets revealing all kind of fruits, nuts, and other sumptuous fare. Life was so deceptively normal. Abiel wondered if he was the only one whose life was turned upside down. In less than one hour, he walked past everything about life that was good, to journey into the fearsome jaws of justice. As he neared his destination, he began to sing the song of the prophet David, "Yea though I walk through the valley of the shadow of death, I will fear no evil."

Abiel never took anyone's life. He was not sure that he could even kill a vermin like Machir, much less participate in the death of someone he loved. Nor had he witnessed against anyone, anywhere, especially before the council. He had no idea what to expect, but he knew one thing for sure. He would not lie regardless of the consequences.

Judging by the sneer on Machir's face, no one would suspect that he stood before those who held the power of life and death. It was evident; he savored his sadistic reasoning that a second chance to get even with Abiel was worth dying over. In contrast, Naarah cowered as if she were a terrified child cast into a pit with a wild beast. For the past few hours, Machir unrelentingly tormented her.

"I always knew that you would come back to me. You just couldn't stay away, could you? What is the matter? Was Abiel not man enough for you? You chose a real bad time to come running back. Look at the mess that you got us into, you and your bull god." His ranting stopped just long enough for a rabid laugh, only to continue abusing her without mercy.

Machir was oblivious to the council, as the guards led him into the chamber. He hawkishly spotted Abiel standing as far away from the proceedings as he possibly could and still be considered present. Machir wasted no time mocking his nemesis. "Why master Abiel, you are up and about early this morning. What brings you here? Did you lose something valuable?"

"Quiet," insisted Eli.

Machir replied defiantly, "You have no authority over me. I will say what I..."

Those were the last words that Machir would ever utter and perhaps it was fitting that his last word was "I," in that he lived his entire life selfishly for himself. The shaft of a guard's spear caught Machir flush on his jaw, breaking it in several places, rendering him unable to speak. Unbelievably, a look of treachery remained on his grotesque face.

Eli began by saying, "Yesterday I and my guards entered the property owned by the accused. There we found evidence of this man's involvement in prostitution, illegal slave trade, drugs, theft of holy objects, and worst of all, idolatry. We went there on the word of a well-respected witness. We know Abiel as a man of honor, and he is here in our chamber to bear witness. He has knowledge of the crimes of the accused."

Eli motioned his hand toward the door and four guards pushed a cart into the council chamber. Its cargo was the image of Baal taken from GUWR. The thing was impressive even though it was lying on its side. Eli refused to allow it to enter the chamber standing erect. Eli's G-d overthrew idols, and no image of Baal would enter a court of his laws with dignity.

Naarah's weakened voice drew everyone's attention as she begged, "Abiel, do something. You must get me out of here. Tell them. Tell them, Abiel…"

Eli cut short her plea, emphatically telling her, "Quiet, woman." He did not have to tell her twice. The guard standing near her lifted his spear to a threatening position. Another of the guards entered the room carrying a large book and several other items wrapped in sackcloth. He placed them on the table in front of the council members. A second guard carrying some of the holy things stolen from the temple followed closely behind him. He likewise placed his items on the table.

Eli was not in a mood to tolerate disruptions, so he had one of the guards put a gag in Naarah's mouth. Eli scrutinized Abiel closely as the guard pulled a wrapped cloth tightly around the back of her head and tied it off. Judging from Abiel's reaction, it would be asking too much of Abiel to witness against the woman for whom he held deep feelings. Eli anticipated that this might happen. Acting as a friend would, he found a way to avoid it. He decided to take Abiel's place as a witness against Naarah. In his deserved distrust of Machir, Eli had taken precaution and made him write out his testimony of Naarah's involvement in the conspiracy. It was a good thing he got the confessions in writing, now that Machir's jaw was broken. Otherwise, Eli would have no choice but to call Abiel as a witness. Eli tried Naarah first because it is illegal to have a condemned person testify against another. If he tried Machir first and convicted him, then he could not use his testimony against Naarah.

Eli began by reading Machir's statement. Then he added, "I verified the prepared statement by questioning Abiel. Abiel confirmed the things spoken by Machir were true and upon searching Naarah's quarters, we found an idol of Baal in her possession along with other stolen items belonging to Abiel. I bear witness against her. She stole from her master and committed the unpardonable sin of blasphemy. Members of the council, what is your judgment concerning these charges?"

"Gedeliah, what say you?"

"Guilty."

"Uphaz, what say you?"

"Guilty."

"Ithran, what say you?"

"Guilty."

"Lehabim, what say you?"

"Guilty."
"Thebez, what say you?"
"Guilty."
"Yacob, what say you?"
"Guilty."

"The finding of this council is that you, Naarah, are guilty of the crimes of theft and blasphemy. I condemn you to the punishment of having your right hand cut from your body and then stoned until you are dead. Never again will you bring reproach upon yourself, your people, or G-d.

Eli reluctantly had agreed to allow Machir to cast the first stone in exchange for his testimony against Naarah. It repulsed Eli to grant any wish this evil man had, but better Machir kill Naarah than forcing Abiel to do it. Several guards took Naarah up by her arms and led her out of the chamber. Abiel could not bring himself to look up until the doors opened and he heard the clamor of the self-righteous crowd gathering in the street. They lustily anticipated participating in stoning the blasphemers. He glowered at them in disgust, wondering how they got word of an execution hours before the trial began.

Eli instructed the guards to remove the gag from Naarah's mouth. "We want to hear her renounce the name of Baal when he does not come to help her." It was common for the most hardened criminal to weaken when facing the certainty of death. Eli moved close to Naarah so she could hear him over the noise. He admonished her, "Woman, save yourself from eternal damnation. Confess your belief in the G-d of your fathers and recant the worship of idols." The only savior that she hoped for was on his knees just inside the chamber of judgment. At this moment, Abiel was every bit as powerless to help her, as was Baal was to help Machir. He prayed for mercy to the G-d of the priests, knowing that G-d always hears the prayers of righteous men. Although, he despaired in knowing that mercy was scarce among those who represented themselves as the administrators of his justice. He put his hands over his ears to keep from hearing Naarah incessantly calling for him, "Abiel…, where are you? Abiel…, Abiel…, why have you forsaken me?"

Abiel could not cover his ears tight enough to block out Naarah's bloodcurdling screams brought on from the pain inflicted by the indignance of the guard's sword. Her severed right hand fell to the street, tellingly staying open reaching for help. She fainted but revived all too quickly from the chilling effect of the bucket of cool water poured on her at Eli's request. Nasi doggedly insisted she be awake during her stoning, demanding she repent. Her eyes clearing to see Machir standing over her worsened her horror. He stomped his foot on the bloody stub of her wrist to stop the gush of her blood. He made sure she didn't bleed to death before he satisfied himself by crushing her with the first stone. Mercifully, for her, Machir couldn't speak with his jaw shattered and swollen, but he pushed past his pain to grin at her with his teeth seeping blood. Keeping his foot firmly in place on her wrist, he stooped down and picked up a large stone. With one motion, he raised it high above his head and moved to bring it down on Naarah's head. Tauntingly, he stopped short of letting it fly. Seeing Naarah recoil in fear made Machir's broken jaw quiver as he strained to laugh. The spectacle was so disgusting that Eli ran up to him and demanded he throw his stone, but he wasn't inclined to take orders from anyone, not even a holy man. He scowled at Eli and dropped the stone off to the side of Naarah. Then he stooped once again and wrote in the dirt with his finger. His action aroused Eli's curiosity enough to make him lean over to read the writing. "Abiel."

"A-b-i-e-l? You wrote Abiel's name. What do you want with him?"

Machir could not answer. He kicked his free foot toward the name written in the dust.

"Where is Abiel? Guards find Abiel and get him over here now," Eli shouted.

He respected everyone's feelings, but this was G-d's work and his patience wore thin.

A guard took Abiel by the arm and led him into the street. Machir agonized to say aloud, but could only think, "I said I would win. Look who obeys who."

As Abiel neared, Machir rose from his haunches to face his enemy with the swagger of a conquering hero.

Allowing a crazed criminal to take charge enraged Eli, but he needed to end this farce.

Machir motioned for Abiel to come closer.

The time for praying was over. An angered Abiel pushed his way through the press of people, attempting to keep his eyes on Machir, but he disappeared from view. Once Abiel got to him, he saw that Machir stooped to get the huge stone, it now firmly in his grip. Next, he saw Naarah lying, bleeding underfoot of her self-appointed executioner. Machir looked at Abiel, at Naarah, back at Abiel, again at Naarah. Without warning, he slammed the stone into her flinching face. The onset of violence cajoled the crowd to join in.

Machir made no effort to move out from under the hail of stones as they rained down on him and Narrah. His plot to deprive Abiel opportunity to witness against him and deny the council their day of judgment worked flawlessly. The one thing he overlooked was the rage that he aroused in Abiel. A large stone fell short of its intended victim, landing close to where Abiel stood. Abiel went as blank as he did the day that he walked out of Kidron after burying Ammah. Grabbing the rock in both hands, he lurched at Machir who looked wild-eyed at his attacker. This was not to end with an unidentified stranger indiscriminately casting stones from a throng of faceless people. Abiel drew last blood, bringing the stone down, splitting Machir's skull with one vicious blow. Eli frantically waved the frenzied crowd off to prevent them from throwing any more stones. He and Abiel were both slightly injured, but nothing hurt as much as the lingering vision of Naarah, with her battered and bruised body lying under the vilest of men. Maybe Machir didn't misjudge. He certainly controlled the outcome of the council. He outsmarted the spiritual judges of Jerusalem by using their legal system against them. Before the council could use Abiel's testimony to convict him of a crime, he angered Abiel into behaving as if he were the criminal.

The temple guards backed off, momentarily permitting the mob to strip the clothing off Machir's body, only to rush back in to scare the scavengers off. The law dictated that male criminals hang naked on a tree for a few hours, and the soldiers were impatient to get this done. Later, he and Narrah would burn in Tophet, but for now, he had to serve as an example of what befalls blasphemers.

CHAPTER 24

No Consolation

Abiel's feet felt heavy as iron to him as he headed for home. For the first time in his life, he was hesitant to go there. Home had always been his haven, the place where he escaped from the cares of life. When his children were born, he loved home more than ever. When Ammah died, he longed to be at home. Being near her mother and father, seeing and touching her possessions, and holding his and her children afforded him comfort. Today, going home meant more heartbreak, if it is possible to break something already shattered. His reluctance to face his family also arose from a feeling that was new to him. Feeling guilty, he mumbled, "I took the life of another man. My hands, look at my hands. I need to find a place to wash them before I get home." He attempted to console himself by reasoning, "Machir was not a man. He was a wild animal that attacked me, and anyone would have done the same as I did."

Abiel stopped at a small pool of water and washed away Machir's blood, but water and reason did not remove his feeling of guilt. "I didn't say one thing to Naarah. I should have at least held her one last time or told her I loved her."

Abiel thought more and more about Naarah as he walked, but thinking only made matters worse. "I should not have been so angry at Naarah for taking Ammah's necklace. She likely wanted it, so she could have something of mine, knowing she would never have me. And the nose ring? Now, I remember. The first time I saw her, she wore it. Machir forced her to wear it as his slave, but once with me, she pulled it off. I know she loved me, not as a spy for a plot devised by Machir. No one will ever convince me that Naarah tried to hurt my sons or me.

"The house will never be the same; no Ammah, no Naarah, no Egla, many of my faithful servants gone, and my beloved son will leave to go only G-d knows where. I still have Pharez, but how can I ever face him and tell him what happened to Naarah?"

After Abiel, Pharez considered Naarah his closest friend. "What will I do if he blames me for not protecting her or leaving him asleep at home, preventing him from standing up for her? He will be hurt and angry." Abiel fought away his fear. "What will I do or say if Pharez is so angered at me that he decides he too should leave home?"

Realizing he was in no condition to face the challenges awaiting him, he turned from making his way home toward a solitary grove of olive trees. He knew the place well. He and Ammah used to go there to sit and talk. It was not that he hoped to find inspiration from her memory. He simply had to get alone and talk to his best friend. The one who ever lives, never dies, and is always there when someone needs him. It did not take long. Abiel listened. His friend spoke the right words. Strength came and Abiel headed home assured, confident, and consoled.

CHAPTER 25

The Caravan

As Abiel neared home, it was evident that Pharez had as always been obedient to his father's wishes. The noise of braying, bleating, and lowing animals that enjoined the voices of servants, shepherds, and curious onlookers alerted Abiel that the hour of Zerah's departure was at hand. Ebed hurried out to meet Abiel.

"Master, thanks be to G-d that you are back. We had a most difficult time keeping Zerah from leaving the house. He demands to see you now. We had to solicit the help of Ormah and Hiphil just to keep him here."

"Where is he?" Abiel asked.

"He is in the courtyard."

Upon entering the courtyard, Abiel heard Zerah shouting threats at the servants.

"All right Zerah, stop it. Leave the servants alone. They are doing what I told them to do."

Zerah was spoiling for a fight. "Aha, I have been made lower than the servants. He pointed to the livestock and asked, "Are these animals mine? If so, give them to me and let me get out of here, then you, your son, your parents, and your servants can be happy."

"Son…"

"Don't call me son. You treat me worse than a servant and call me son?"

"Son, please don't say these things. You are beguiled into believing I do not love you. My main concern is your safety."

"My safety, what do you mean, my safety? I am not in danger from anyone but you and my brother."

Abiel tried to ignore Zerah's remark. "There is a lot you don't know. Machir is dead and his dwelling destroyed. The authorities sought to accuse you of the same crimes of which they convicted him. You too would be dead if it were not for my friendship with Eli. If you do not leave Jerusalem within the hour, no one, not even I will be able to protect you."

Zerah thought of calling his father a liar. Fortunately, enough reason remained in him that he accepted the fact Abiel would never stoop to untruth, even if his cause were justifiable.

"You say that Machir is dead. How do you know of Machir?"

"Son, we don't have time for explanations. You really must go. We own far too many animals for you to take your share, so I will pay you for the ones that rightfully belong to you that you cannot take. I must hurriedly go and count out your silver and gold. It will be loaded in bags. Keep them close to you. I am sending hired men with you, who will protect you from murderers and thieves. They are good men known to your grandfather as men you can trust. I asked Egla to go with you. She loves you as a mother loves her own child. I beg of you, listen to her. You will have plenty of animals to feed yourself and your caravan for many days until you reach your destination. Do not stop until you are well beyond the jurisdiction of our council. If you can, please send one of your hired men back to me, so that I might know where it is that you have gone. I will escort you to the gate of the city. If anyone tries to stop you, just keep on going and leave them to me. Do you understand?"

Obedience came hard for him. He stubbornly nodded his head. However, Abiel's report bothered him. He was not nearly as brash and brazen without Machir around to support him. He looked like a disgruntled child, squatting under the courtyard's lone sycamore, rubbing the ground with a stick.

Abiel reappeared with several servants at his side. Each of them carried four extremely heavy bags. The men were stout, but they strained so hard that their blood vessels bulged in their arms and necks as they hoisted the bags over the backs of several she-asses. Abiel surveyed the situation with his keen eye, not wanting to miss one detail. Everything appeared ready, except for one thing missing. He sat under a tree while everyone else did the hard work of preparation. Abiel yelled out, "Zerah, get over here; you need to see what we are doing."

Hiphil and Ormah stood in the door of the house. They heard Abiel raise his voice. Hiphil, accustomed to military discipline, could not resist a remark,

"Too little, too late. If only Abiel would have corrected that boy years ago." He and Ormah strenuously disagreed with Abiel's handling of Zerah, but were guilty of saying as little to Abiel, as Abiel was of spoiling Zerah. As always, Ormah accepted the blame, "It is my fault. I should have talked to Abiel. Now look what this has come to!"

It stunned Zerah to see what awaited him in the street. He had no idea of the size of his father's business. He saw what seemed to be several hundred animals kept together by dogs running in circles around them, gnarling their teeth at would-be strays. There were a few shepherds moving about waving their herding staves, in turn shouting at the stock and the dogs that herded the animals. Forty other well-armed men joined them, and as it was with the shepherds and their staves, one could tell this was not the first time they handled weapons. Abiel called the names of ten servants, including Egla's name, and as they stepped forward, he warmly embraced, spoke blessings, and handed each of them a small bag. The scene disgusted Zerah. "Tender words and tears for servants. What next?" he exclaimed as he watched his father and his wretched servants wipe their eyes. He was right; "Abiel thinks more of his hired servants than he does of his own flesh and blood son."

It was time. Abiel was as ready as he would ever be. "Ebed, position four soldiers next to the she-asses that Pharez is holding with his rope. Station others at the head and the rear of the caravan." Turning to Zerah, he said, "Son, I have done all that I can do for you. It is time that you take control of your life and this caravan."

Zerah took up the challenge, "Pharez, give me that rope. Men, stay behind me with these asses. Someone help me up on my camel, and, oh yes, bring a camel forward for Egla. Let's move out."

Without as much as one thank-you or any other word of consideration, Zerah was atop his beast and kicking at its shoulders to get it moving. Only the efforts of the shepherds kept the caravan together. Soldiers know fighting, servants know serving, and Zerah knew nothing of being in charge. He might be able to choose sides in a popular game, but this was not child's play. He did not seem to notice anything happening behind him. All he needed was a fresh camel under him and to head in a direction away from Jerusalem with eight bags of gold and silver. This was much more than Machir had to start with and look what he accomplished. Zerah would not even glance at Egla. He wanted nothing to dampen his enthusiasm for the freedom that awaited him just outside the walls of Jerusalem. No frown that would condemn him, no smile that might convict him, nothing, nothing at all.

Abiel did not know what direction Zerah would choose to go in, but he hoped as he left the city, that he would avoid the main gates. It would not be advisable for the caravan to attract any unnecessary attention. Abiel commandeered one of the caravans' straggling donkeys and rode behind the soldiers who walked as rear guards for the caravan. He breathed a sigh of relief as they turned toward the Dung Gate. It was sparsely populated and the least visited of all of the gates of the city.

Zerah did not think of discretion; there were other motives turning him toward the Dung Gate. He intended to go through Tophet, the place where he first experienced Baal. He had to swear to Baal that he was not forsaking him, but he was on his way to the city of Gubla in the land of the Canaanites. Machir assured Zerah if he went to Gubla, he would be free to worship Baal without fear of reprisal. His other reason for going through Hinnom was so he could stop at his mother's grave.

The guard stationed at the Dung Gate was surprised to see such a large troop of people and animals departing Jerusalem through his gate. All he ever saw was funerals, garbage collectors, and soldiers with carts carrying the bodies of criminals out to be burned in Tophet. In fact, he likely would have been sleeping if it were not for the temple guards who passed by with the bodies and possessions of some blasphemers less than one hour ago. Abiel, taking full advantage of the slowed procession, furiously spurred the small donkey he rode into a lope toward the front of the caravan. He was not about to let his son leave home without hearing he was loved and he had a father who would never stop praying that someday he would return home. The sight of Abiel, riding a donkey up alongside of Zerah's camel, illustrated the meaning of the ancient proverb, "I have seen a mystery in the land; paupers riding horses, and princes walking." Zerah sat high above the caravan on the back of his imposing camel, looking princely, his shoulders cloaked with a brightly colored shawl. His kingly father resembled a peasant with his long legs nearly dragging the ground as he struggled to wrap them around the belly of the small beast to keep from falling off its back. Once the guard recognized Abiel, he knew that all was well. As he turned to walk away, he lazily motioned for the caravan to proceed. Abiel reached up and grabbed Zerah's leg in an attempt to get his attention. Zerah suspected one of the soldiers might be bothering him with a detail, but as he lurched far to his right, he looked down into his father's tearful face.

Zerah derisively asked, "Don't you think it is a little late for this?"

"I don't know how late it is for you, but it will never be to late for me to tell you I love you more than ever, and I want you to know that wherever you go and whatever you do, nothing will ever change my feelings."

Zerah leaned away from his father.

"Son, I am sorry to anger you, but I want you to look at me."

He looked because he wanted to leave and needed to be done with this. He did not expect to see a smile.

"I want you to see me smile at you. I cannot have you leave thinking I am angry. Someday you may find yourself in difficulty, with no friends or family to help. If this happens, I want you to remember this moment."

"Right, just what I need from you, some money, a few animals, and a smile."

With that, he pulled his leg out of Abiel's grasp and with one swift kick of his foot; the caravan moved out. Abiel dismounted and slapped the donkey on its rear to encourage it to rejoin the other animals in the caravan. He was such a just and fair man that he preferred to walk home rather than defraud his son of even one donkey. The last of the hired soldiers passed through the gate, marching into the haze kicked up by the animals. Abiel stood and watched until the dust settled and he no longer heard the sound of animals or men. His son was gone!

Zerah eyed activity just ahead from his lofty perch atop his camel. Tophet was not a place that anyone visited unless coming on specific business. As always when he needed an answer, he turned to Egla. "Temple guards! What are they doing here?"

She knew the answer, but didn't know how to answer except to wave her hand high as a signal for the caravan to halt. Zerah strained on the rope that looped through his camel's mouth, bringing the mighty beast to a stop.

She attempted an explanation. "Your father did not lie to you about Machir. There was something else he didn't tell you. "Naarah…"

He stopped her, "Don't ever mention her name in my presence again. She is the reason my friend Machir is dead and I wish she was."

With that said, he told Egla to keep everyone back. He slacked off the halter rope and urged his camel forward, risking recognition that would result in the guards arresting him. The awful smell of burning flesh was familiar to him. It brought back memories of his other trips to Toph. Now he knew what the stench was. He wisely stopped in a spot where tree shade partially covered his face. Sneaking past soldiers was at least one thing he was good at.

"Who are these criminals whose bodies are being burned?" Zerah questioned in a deepened voice.

"It is the blasphemers, Machir and his concubine Naarah."

The guards turned their attention away from Zerah, giving him a chance to move past the ghastly scene. He tried to take it all in, but there was more there than he could comprehend.

"Did the guard say, Machir and his concubine Naarah?"

Zerah got close enough to see two bodies. The smaller of the two corpses was missing its right hand, but in what would have been its left hand he saw his Baal that Pharez stole from him. A hot fire had melted the brass off Machir's charred wooden bull idol, which lay as smoldering testimony to the truth that Machir was dead. Two bodies next to two burned out gods. He looked back to see the guards staring at him. It was time to leave and with haste. His curiosity was beginning to arouse their suspicion. Anyone brought here was someone society wished to forget. Tellingly, Tophet's landscape was not dotted with markers or memorials as Kidron was.

The camel grunted its displeasure when Zerah whipped it to a lanky trot. He hurried to the safety of his caravan.

Once assured that no one chased after him, he foolishly wanted to make camp. His soldiers were secretly under orders from Abiel that they should ride for two days without stopping. Zerah was impatient to sit with Egla. He was sure that she knew everything that happened to Naarah and Machir. His questions burned hotter in him than the midday sun or the fires of Tophet. The soldiers eventually persuaded him to press on, but at his insistence, they agreed to stop at Ammah's tomb before departing Kidron. Even though he bragged to Pharez that he would return as a prince, he had no intention to come back to this forsaken place. This would be his final goodbye to his mother. He stopped the caravan a ways off, once he was within sight of Ammah's tomb. He rode ahead alone, dismounting at a safe distance so his camel would not desecrate the family gravesite, even though sheep frequently pastured there. Unlike the camel, Hebrew law considered sheep clean and besides, they helped the gardeners keep up the grounds. Zerah berated himself for disrespecting his camel. Precepts taught to children are lasting. Here he was on his way to religious freedom and foolishly, he respected his father's faith. "All of these clean, unclean rules, who can possibly keep up with them?"

He made excuses by pretending his respect was for his mother's sake and had nothing to do with Abiel.

All quibbling over religion ceased, as he laid his body up against the massive boulder that served as a door to the tomb. He spread his arms and embraced the stone as warmly as he would have if it were Ammah. He did not move until he deemed their unspoken conversation to be finished. He could have spoken to her, but he did not; she could not speak aloud to him, but she did. "What did she mean? She said we would speak again someday!"

He was back atop his ride and on his way to the "land of the red people."

CHAPTER 26

The Far Country

Zerah summoned several of the shepherds to the head of the caravan. They were men well-acquainted with the roads and paths leading from Jerusalem. He made it known that his destination was the Canaanite city of Gubla. They knew of the place and the direction in which it lay, but asked for some time to decide on a route. It was about a two-hour journey to Hammath where there were refreshing hot springs. It would be a good place to rest while determining how to proceed. They could see how everyone fared, and repack the goods and gear. After Hammath, there would only be one other hard climb to reach Ludda near the valley of Sharon. The caravan circled west to get out of Kidron, picking up the road to Hammath and heading toward the great sea. Yes, Hammath as a first stop made a lot of sense. Day one of the journey was grueling until they reached the plains of Japho. Their troubles eased as they put the hills behind them and started downhill to the flat lands of the coast. The soldiers hoped to persuade Zerah to go to Japho and then turn north to Tyre. The coast made for easier travel, not to mention safety. If he chose to follow the Jordan River to Samaria, they would be vulnerable. The big forests provided cover to thieves. The shepherds agreed. They understood the perils of Mount Gilboa. If they managed to get through Gilboa, then they would have to reckon with the seemingly insurmountable heights at Golan. Roads of any kind were rare in this rugged country and chancing less-traveled trails to the east would be dangerous. East and north went into the jaws of the Ammonites and the notably cruel Assyrians, whereas peaceful Phoinike people inhabited the coastline. Being merchants, they built roads to facilitate trade. Merchants traveling with their goods and foreigners looking to purchase some, used the byways. Most wealthy merchants hired mercenaries to protect them, as Abiel did for Zerah. The presence of professional soldiers discouraged would-be robbers.

Zerah's navigators were unanimous in their agreement. The caravan should go to Japho and then turn north, staying near the coast. The youthful and untested leader had opportunity to show his maturity by allowing others to do their job without his interference. However, he falsely assumed that respect comes with position. His soldiers were accustomed to working under men that earned their authority on fields of battle. Fighting men cannot afford the luxury of diplomacy. So, one of the shepherds who spent his life convincing stubborn sheep to go to greener pastures wisely intervened, "It is rumored that Zerah worships the idol god Baal. This is why he wants to go to Gubla."

One of the mercenaries confirmed, "I have been to several of the coastal cities and the worship of Baal is openly practiced."

The shepherd continued, "Good, we can use this to convince Zerah that this is the reason why we go as planned."

A house servant, knowing of Zerah's rebellion against his father's faith, added, "We should tell him that if we turn north now, it will take us to Bethel, a city known as a stronghold of the Hebrew religion. He will avoid it as he would a leper."

Their strategy worked like a charm and they were on the way to Ludda. Word spread around the convoy that upon reaching Ludda, there would be all manner of fruits, nuts, and melons available for purchase. Ludda is near the fertile vale of Sharon. This reminded the servants to open the small bags that Abiel handed them as they left home. His kindness overwhelmed them. He had advanced one year's wages to them all. Ludda's market would be the perfect place to spend some of their unexpected prosperity. This place was a vitally important crossroad. The road from Jerusalem to Japho intersected with the thoroughfare caravans used to travel between Babylon and Egypt.

With the labor of setting up camp for the evening all done, everyone except the guards on duty anxiously departed for the markets. Plenty of fresh water, good wine, delicious nuts, all manners of fruit, and enlightening conversation with strangers from diverse places put everyone in a good frame of mind. Zerah was the one exception. They returned to camp with the spoils from their shopping, sharing their food and stories with each other. However, their joy subsided when confronted by the sullen, brooding mood that possessed Zerah. The small bags containing Abiel's love gift also held the poisonous scorpion of Zerah's envy. He mistakenly thought he left his jealousy behind the walls of

Jerusalem. Its sting was as painful as ever. He was yet to learn that jealousy is not a place. It is a condition of the heart.

"Father does not want me to succeed. Without being here, he challenges my manhood and makes me look weak to the servants. Damned be his bags of silver. I will show him who is weak."

Come dawn, he would have them all up and on the move. "Let them all drink, dance, and laugh the night away. If too much celebrating makes them feel terrible come morning, all the better. Their job is to provide for my needs and protect me, not to indulge in pleasure, at least not by getting part of my inheritance. Abiel did not even trust that I would pay them."

The next morning he was up early and feeling vengeful. He decided to enjoy himself every bit as much as the caravan did the previous night.

"Everyone up, up this very moment. Come on, you slothful slaves, up! You are wasting my time. Get up, I said."

Two guards assigned to keep watch over the gold and silver had succumbed to sleep, but leapt to their feet, feigning to have been awake the entire time. Zerah shouted so loudly that the animals joined in braying, bleating, and bellowing their displeasure at the early start to the morning. The ruckus startled the slumbering soldiers, sending them scurrying for their weapons, assuming they were under attack. They were right about an assault, not about its source.

"Line up one by one and do it now," he demanded.

Surprisingly, he included Egla in the lineup.

"Listen and hear me well. Abiel gave you to me as part of my inheritance and you are my property. My father acted inappropriately by giving you silver. It was not a ransom to set you free. Some of you are not my property; I pay the rest of you to assist me. Abiel paying you for work that you have yet to perform was a big mistake. I know you will run away, leaving me unprotected if trouble comes. None of you act as though you understand your duty. I have decided to take matters into my own hands. Everyone return to your tents immediately and fetch your silver. Bring it to me and lay it at my feet. If any of you are not willing to do as I say, then you are free to return to Jerusalem, but not with my inheritance. Bring me that which is left of my silver and you will be released from your obligation."

The servants, accustomed to obeying orders from their masters, ran to comply with Zerah's order. Contrarily, the soldiers, to a man, decided to leave the caravan before venturing any further from home. In spite of their loyalty to Hiphil, they could not follow a reckless wimp like Zerah. He would get them all killed. "Too bad, he is not half the man that his grandfather is." Out of pride, they did give Zerah their silver.

The desertion of the soldiers did not alarm Zerah. Mercenaries were easy to find in Ludda. He got them for a lot less than Abiel paid Hiphil's friends. Besides, Zerah heard rumors that once he reached the port city Japho, he could find ships and sailors for hire. From there, he could sail up the coast to Tyre, then to Zidon and on to Gubla. He had never been to sea and it would be faster, more exciting, and safer than traveling by land.

Egla was so upset at Zerah that she refused to ride alongside him when they departed for Japho. She was the only one allowed to keep Abiel's silver, but she graciously gave her share to the departing soldiers so they had provision for their return to Jerusalem. The caravan made good progress in the coolness of the early spring day and before the sun outraced them to its western setting, they espied a lone rounded hill. Surrounded by flat land on all its sides except for the seaside caused it to stand out. The hill was dotted with the outline of buildings up to six stories in height, towering above the walls of the city. Set against the hazy blue horizon of the sea, this made for a most impressive sight. The lofty peaks of Mt. Carmel were visible off to the north of the city. One of the newly hired soldiers who himself was a worshiper of idols, informed Zerah that many of the Baru prophets of Baal lived up in the mountains of Carmel. Drawing near the city, he saw huge flocks of sheep, goats, and cattle herded by nomads heading north toward the foothills of Carmel. The spring grasses were abundant and the hills made perfect pastureland for fattening the animals. Come summer, the markets would fill with fresh meat. Zerah entertained the idea of bypassing Japho and following the flocks up the mountain. Not that he had a longing to be a shepherd; he just envied the animals for their privilege of pasturing near the Baru. He calmed down when his guide told him that the prophets were difficult to locate in the mountains. Most of the true seers were reclusive and besides there would be plenty for him to see once inside the walls of Japho. Soon they cleared inspection by the guards at the eastern gate of the city and began preparing for the night. This night was to be very different from the last one in Ludda. No laughter, no dancing, no joy; it was all business and besides everyone was extremely tired, not having fully recuperated from the previous evening or morning. As was the case the night before, Zerah could hardly wait for the dawn, but this time for a different reason.

Japho held a fresh fascination for him. For one, the further from Jerusalem he traveled, distanced him from the constraints of his old life. Second, the vastness and openness of the sea spoke of his freedom to explore anything and everything that his heart desired. Early the next morning he summoned Egla to accompany him down to the port. He wanted her to go with him so that he could mend up the trouble between them. In spite of his attempt at leadership, the role was strange to him and he could use some assurance. His behavior was typical of a boy on the verge of manhood; one moment wanting a mother, the next, disdaining any suggestion that he ever needed mothering.

He began, "Are you still angry with me? I know that I made you stand up with the others, but I did not want to show favoritism. Besides, I did give you all of your silver, didn't I?"

"Is this what you and I have come to? Am I about the silver? You have the power to sell me, but you will never be able to buy what I feel for you. I gave your silver away."

"What? You did what?"

"I gave the silver to the soldiers so that they would not return to their families empty-handed."

"You had no right to do something like that."

"Why? You just said that the silver was mine and now you say I have no right to do with it as I please. Your father was always kind and generous to me, and you would do well to treat people as he did."

"Treat people as he did? How did he treat Naarah? She came to us the same day that you did. Whose testimony convicted her as a criminal and burned her like rubbish? I don't need that sort of kindness."

"How can you speak disrespectfully of the one who gave you a sumptuous inheritance, when according to the law he could have sent you away with nothing or punished you with the same death that Naarah suffered?"

"It wasn't out of kindness that he gave me anything. It was more like a bribe to get rid of me. Do you see these scabs on my neck? Pharez nearly choked me to death the night before I left home. He told me if I did not leave, he would kill me. He and father proved that they were capable of murder. My closest friend Machir and your friend Naarah are dead. I am sure that I would have been next if I hadn't left home."

"That is serious talk and full of assumption on your part. There are many things that you aren't aware of."

"I am aware that Machir is dead and the pain in my neck doesn't lie. Father claims that he loves me, and you say that you do, too. What I need is for someone to show me. I do not expect you to understand or believe in everything that I do, but if you do not love me enough to stand up for me, you are free to return to Jerusalem. I am going to sell most of the animals and send the shepherds and servants back home. I believe that there is a slave market here in Japho, and I intend to sell everything and everyone that reminds me of the past."

Egla fell deftly quiet; not for lack of further argument, but rather her need to think about what she heard and how love demanded she react. Zerah's planned actions angered her, but she was determined to honor her commitment to Abiel and stay close to his son.

Japho was everything and more than Zerah imagined. For one, he found out that a king, queen, and their court of wealthy merchants controlled Japho. The men of the court were self-made men, unlike Jerusalem's fanatic priests who usurped their inherited power over the helpless masses. Men from all corners of the world inhabited Japho. The continuity of commerce and trade was amazing, given the diversity of cultures and languages. Zerah had no problem selling and bartering his animals. Abiel's stock was some of the finest. The marketplace of this city was unlike anything that he or Egla had ever seen. Not only did the merchants trade in goats, sheep, camels, cattle, and horses; they bought and sold all kinds of birds—doves, pigeons, falcons, peacocks, and even eggs from ostriches. There was another section where one could purchase precious stones, gold, silver, ivory, ebony, copper, tin, and iron. The availability of building materials such as oak, pine, cypress, and especially cedar wood was truly astounding. Artisans extracted oil from the cedars and exported it to Egypt for use in embalming their dead. This was of special interest to Zerah. Before today, he knew nothing of embalming and its significance in the Egyptian religion.

Egla wandered away from Zerah, her interest being the selection of food and clothing. It was to be expected that in a port city fish would be plentiful, but along with the fish there was an abundance of salt, all kinds of grains such as wheat and barley, honey, walnuts, almonds, and pistachios. The varieties of fruit found here were unheard of in Jerusalem. There were dates, figs, apricots, pomegranates, pears, peaches, and many other delicacies, not to leave out the finest olive oil, wines, and many, many spices of which she was unfamiliar. To tempt a woman's vanity, the sprawling market had vendors selling cosmetics, perfumed oils, and incense. Perhaps the most alluring of all were the textiles. There were fine linens from Egypt, wool spun locally in Japho, and even some silk from the Far East.

Zerah noticing that Egla had strayed off hurried to catch up to her. He too was anxious to see the cloths of which he had heard so much. He wasn't disappointed. The deep blues made from African indigo, were beautiful, although the crimson-colored cloths, for which this part of the world was famous, stood out as his favorite. He now understood why Machir called the Phoinike's "the red people." Clutching the cloth in both hands, he thought of Machir. He thought of the necklace that Pharez ripped off his neck. He was close to his destiny. Egla walked away disheartened. She did not have any thing to trade or barter with and was much too proud to beg from Zerah. He must have read her mind. He handed over silver in exchange for a sufficient amount of scarlet-dyed linen material for Egla to make herself a kuttoneth. He also gave her several other gifts that he purchased while she was distracted looking around the market. She loved the impressive pair of gold earrings and the cosmetics.

"Here, please accept these gifts and don't be angry with me."

"Zerah, you shouldn't have done this. You will need your silver when you get to Gubla."

"You do mean, when we get to Gubla, don't you?"

"Why yes, you know that I am going with you. I have been with you since the first day of your life, and I will be with you until the day you no longer want me to be."

As the two of them walked from the market toward the port, Egla's euphoria went away like a receding tide of the sea. The ancient words of Jeremiah, a renowned Hebrew prophet, flooded her mind. The clarity and exactness of his words rang in her ears, drowning out the din of the marketplace. "What are you doing, O devastated one? Why dress yourself in scarlet and put on jewels of gold? Why shade your eyes with paint? You adorn yourself in vain. Your lovers despise you; they seek your life. I hear a cry as of a woman in labor, a groan as of one bearing her first child—the cry of the daughter of Zion gasping for breath, stretching out her hands and saying, 'Alas! I am fainting; my life is given over to murderers.'"

She had no idea that a prophecy given for a nation would touch her life in such a personal and fatal way. Never has she worn the color scarlet, gold jewelry, or paint on her eyes. Dressing like that identified her as a harlot by Jerusalem's standards, but this might be her last chance to get closer to Zerah. Nothing within reason would stop her from trying. Egla gained her wisdom from experience, but this was her first encounter with the futility of compromise and the lesson would be costly.

They walked in the direction of the port, and they happened up on the yards where the massive sea-going vessels were being built. The skeletons of the ships were more impressive than the finished product. To see the massive hewn timbers coerced into contours of beauty was an awesome sight, especially to someone seeing it for the first time.

"What craftsmen these Canaanites are," Zerah said in awe.

Machir tried to tell Zerah, but words did not suffice to describe what unfolded right in front of him. Machir told him that the Canaanite builders erected the great temple of Solomon in Jerusalem.

"What an advanced society the 'crimson people' are. Instead of killing people who disagree with their gods, they help them prepare a place to worship their own. The day will never come when the Hebrew people are that tolerant or understanding."

He did not know that the worshipers of Baal considered the Hebrew Elohim to be their beloved El, the father of all gods. Secretly, the Canaanites laughed at King Solomon as they constructed a temple to their god El in the Hebrew capital.

Zerah and Egla were close enough to the sea that they smelled the salty air and caught occasional glimpses of gentle waves breaking against the rocky shore. Egla noticed a large crowd of people gathering down close to the water's edge.

She asked another woman who scurried by, "What is happening, just over there?"

"A ship just arrived from Egypt carrying slaves. There will be a sale today."

Zerah overheard the words "slave" and "sale" and got in on the conversation. "A sale? Where? When?"

"Over there," she pointed, "where the crowd is gathering, and it should start any time now. I saw the judge go by shortly ago. He will be there to sign the purchase agreements and to oversee the branding. He was once a slave himself."

"What do you mean? He was a slave and now he is a judge."

"Where are you from, young man? Do you not know our laws? We believe that every man has the right to be free if he or she is willing to work for it. Not only do our slaves gain their freedom, we respect them for their efforts and oftentimes they are promoted to positions of power."

Egla saw an opportunity to emphasize the freedom of women as well as slaves, so she smartly seized control of the conversation. "Where were you going when I stopped you?"

The woman replied, "I am on my way to the sale. I am in need of labor for one of my businesses. I intend to buy some of the slaves if they are hearty and not diseased. My physician is meeting me there so he can look them over for me."

This took Zerah back. "A woman involved in trade, commerce, and owning her own slaves."

Her attire attracted his attention. "This is the way that I want Egla to dress. This woman is a person of means and she looks it." She robed herself with silk and expensive jewelry and colored her face with the soft hew of a sunrise.

Zerah told her he had a number of slaves he needed to sell. He assured her they were well cared for and fit. If she could arrange for a ship to carry him to Gubla, he preferred to barter for the slaves. Anyway, he invited her back to his camp to talk. It gladdened him that Egla went along. If she and the woman made friends, that could facilitate their doing business.

The women warmed to each other, though they were a contrast in culture.

Egla cordially inquired, "May I ask your name?"

"My name has been changed to a title, so for now you may call me Naditu. What is your name?"

"My name is Egla."

"Ah! Egla is one of the few Hebrew names that I know well. If I am not mistaken, your name means 'the calf'. When you arrive in Gubla, you will soon learn that the god we worship is Baal. He appears as a bull and his sister Anat is often in his company. She appears as a heifer. Together they produce calves to sustain us during our times of need. Anyway, enough of that; I know it is not polite to talk religion unless asked. Besides, we came here to talk business."

Egla was not offended, but she was astonished that a smart woman like Naditu believed in the idea of a god having a sister. Having sex with ones sister was immoral and a god no better than a bull was absurd. Naditu spoke of Baal with the demeanor of a storyteller, not with the passion of a believer. Egla answered, "I agree, but first may I ask you, is there a meaning to your title?"

"Well, it is sort of personal, but I am not able to produce children. I am married, yet I hold the position of priestess in the worship of Baal. Our society does not scorn infertile women, as do many other cultures. People honor us. Baal loves that we serve him, not our children or our husbands."

"Naditu, I must tell you, where I come from, your speech would be cause for divorce. Shouldn't you be careful?"

"Not here. My husband will never divorce me. I am held in higher regard than he, and if he did attempt to put me away, he would have to return my dowry."

Zerah listened intently. It made him uncomfortable that women and slaves had rights. "Good thing I took back my silver from the slaves. They could have bought their freedom, robbing me of the money I can get for them."

Naditu proved to be a perfect trading partner for Zerah. Within one week, she secured a ship for Zerah's travel and helped him sell his animals for a good price. Zerah paid off the servants, shepherds, and soldiers for their days of service and sent them on their way. His last instruction to them was they were not to speak one word to his father concerning his whereabouts. Naditu took possession of the slaves and the once grand caravan was down to six—Zerah, Egla, two soldiers retained to guard the gold and silver and two sheep for food to hold them until their next stop.

CHAPTER 27

Casting off the Coast

Sailors are a different breed of men from anyone Zerah ever met. He came to think of them as cousins to the fish with whom they share the sea. They all would surely die if forced to stay on dry land, but amazingly revived once back in the water. Zerah could not tell if it was the water, or wine mixed with seawater that cheered them. Never in Zerah's entire life did he hear so much grumbling and cursing as when the sailors loaded the ship with goods and stores. Curiously, as soon as they untied the last rope, hoisted the anchor, and dipped their oars in the water, the grumblers broke into spirited singing. Straining in one accord to the beat of a drum and the chant of the head oarsman, they slowly moved the ship away from shore. Once out of the port, they could store their oars and hoist the sails, but first they must exercise extreme caution, making their way safely out of the chaotic harbor. Aside from larger ships, hundreds of small fishing boats came and went, but an untold number of cedar logs floating down from Tyre posed a real threat. The timbers were so thick in the water, the loggers walked on them as if they were dry land. The ship finally escaped the harbor, land soon disappeared into an ever-expanding horizon of blues and greens, as a favorable wind filled the sails. All color disappeared into a night so dark that Zerah imagined he could feel it. It discomfited him not seeing where he was at or where he was going.

He whispered to Egla, "Do you think we can trust these sailors? I feel uneasy. They could easily overpower us and our guards."

She wanted to say, "Now you think about it," but decided it would not help. She tried to soothe him by calmly saying, "Naditu knows who these men are, and she would not put us in danger." Still, confined quarters with men he did not know, and devoid of a way of escape, chained him to the ship as prisoner to the sailors' prerogative.

Unpacking his personal effects helped him stow away his negative thoughts, at least for awhile. Comfort was in short supply aboard the ship and the ever-increasing sea swells increased his distress. He slipped out of his quarters to go up on the deck. He did not want Egla to know. She showed no sign of illness, and he was close to being violently sick. The small ladder leading up to the main deck provided the perfect perch from which to see the shining road map that some god put in place as guidance for seafarers. The stars lined up the same as over Jerusalem, but out here, over the water, they bowed low, making it easy for the mariners to read them. Once on the deck, he made his way to the bow of the ship so the spray of sea would wash over him. It helped to quell the queasiness in his belly.

Zerah did not expect company up on the bow, but he was sure he saw someone's face in a splash of misty spray. Staring hard, he could barely make out a carved effigy of the faces of two men. "Are they twins?" He leaned as far over the bow as he dared without falling, running his hands over their faces, frantically feeling for differences. He made out the word *Om* on one side and *Ot* on the other.

"Who are these men?" he demanded. "Pharez? Me and my cursed brother. It has to be him." His queasiness had subsided, but it rushed at him again with the vengeance of an angry vomit.

"Surely, Pharez will not follow me to the ends of the earth."

It may have been a lot easier to leave home, than to get home to leave him.

Unashamedly, Zerah called out to Baal, "Your prophetess Anan broke the power of Pharez. Stop him. Stop my brother from intruding into my life."

He listened, thinking that Baal answered him, but it turned out to be the voices of sailors coming from the stern of the ship. They sounded happy, and he reasoned that to join in might rid him of his troubling thoughts of home.

One of the most seasoned seafarers, seeing him step out of the shadow of the sails said, "Ah, master Zerah, to what do we owe the honor of you presence?"

"Actually, I was feeling uneasy down in the belly of the ship. This is the first time that I have ever been aboard a ship."

The seamen enjoyed entertaining themselves at the expense of an inexperienced patron.

Zerah was curious how these men knew the direction to steer the ship in at night, not having any point of reference, so he asked about navigation. The helmsman was disappointed that the conversation took a serious turn. He preferred having some fun.

"Why don't you have some wine with us and I will explain it to you. Besides, my guides are getting brighter by the minute."

"Your guides?" Zerah asked.

"Yes, the great twins of the heavens. I do not know if you saw the bow of our ship, but if you did, you saw *OmOt*. They are the twins that appear in the heavens and guide us to our destination. Look, up there. Here they come, just as they have since the beginning of time. They are always faithful to point the way for us. Only the storms can hinder them."

Zerah walked behind the helmsman so he could see where the man pointed. "I see two very bright stars near to each other."

The helmsman instructed, "That is them. Now follow up this way to the north and you will see the rest. Though twins, they are opposites. Om drinks wine and is full of revelry like we sailors. Ot is the serious-minded brother, as we are during storms. Every man has both in him, and this is what makes us complete."

Zerah could not restrain himself. He blurted out, "It is a lie. I am nothing like my brother."

Not all seafaring men were unlearned, and this helmsman had seen it all—the merchants in search of fortune, criminals running from law, thrill-seekers looking for adventure, explorers hoping to find new lands, people trying to find themselves, and others who had no idea where they were going. From the sound of Zerah's voice, this might be fun after all. He knew he was on to something, so he continued, "The people of the Far East call them Ying Yang, but we know them as Om and Ot. Even the Babylonians who are the best at reading the heavens acknowledge them. They call them Mastabbagalgal or the great twins. If the twins ever part ways, our ships will be useless. Our trade, our travel, and our lives would be ruined."

The seafarer did not know what he said that stirred such emotion, but it must have something to do with a brother. He went with his gut and asked, "You Hebrews have a history of fighting with your family members. We know the fable of your earliest brothers. You know, the ones you called Cain and Abel. Your story goes that Cain was chased his entire life by a supernatural voice of his murdered brother's blood, and it caused him to run and hide upon the face of the earth. Are you running, master Zerah?"

"I don't believe in the fables of my people, and I'm not running from anybody or anything. I go to Gubla of my own choosing and it is of no concern to you."

"Perhaps you would do well to believe in the stories of your people. Some of the stories involve our history as sailors. Did you not see the statue of the great fish back in Japho?"

"No I didn't see any statue of a fish, but why would that be unusual in a city on the sea?"

"This is why you and the reason you are aboard this ship concerns us. One day a Hebrew man by the name of Jonas arrived in Japho seeking to hire a ship to go to Tarshish. No one questioned him, although it was strange for a follower of the Hebrew God YHWH to want to sail to a city renowned for its worship of many goddesses and gods. Once the ship was out in the deep sea, a mighty wind arose and the vessel was in peril of sinking. The sailors knew this was not an ordinary storm, but rather one produced by an act of a god. They drew lots to see whom it was that god was angry with, and the lot fell on Jonas. He confessed he was a holy man, and he was running away from his family and his god. They had to toss him into the sea to quell the wind. The sailors thought they had seen the last of Jonas until their ship returned to Japho. Many of the villagers witnessed a big fish rolling around and vomiting in the midst of the shallow water and rocks just off the coast of Japho. Then the most unbelievable thing happened; the holy man appeared from the sea. He went into the city and was seen by a multitude of people."

Zerah explained, "I know the story, but as I told you, I don't believe in these fables."

"Fact or fable; it doesn't matter to us. The safety of our ship and our lives are what we care about and as long as there are no strange storms, you will be all right. Almost all of those who hire us are merchants looking to buy or sell goods. I find it unusual that you sold your possessions and came to us with nothing but silver, gold, a few soldiers, and a woman that you don't even sleep with."

For a moment, the serious talk gave way to laughter. One of the sailors, enjoying the effect of his wine, suggested, "If you don't care for her, I will gladly help you out."

His remark encouraged the others to join in, "I'll take her."

"No she is mine."

"I spoke first."

"Maybe we should fight for her."

"I know, let's cast lots for her, and see which one of us god will favor."

The laughter became uncontrollable, to the point that Zerah contemplated calling his soldiers who were below deck guarding his gold and silver.

The captain of the ship showed up on deck just in time. His appearance brought calm to the commotion.

"What is all the laughter about?" he queried.

"Sir, we welcomed the young master aboard with a few stories and some good humor."

Zerah did not agree it was a welcome or good humor, but he figured that he should not anger these men by making trouble for them with their captain.

He told the captain, "It's all right. Everything was all in good fun and besides, it's been a long day, and we all need some sleep."

Zerah doubted that sleep would come easy. His mind swayed worse than the ship did. Nothing went as well as he hoped. First, he hated the caravan. He despised dealing with stinky animals and shepherds who did not smell much better. He resented the insubordination of stubborn soldiers. They of all men were supposed to take orders. He liked the servants the most, but imagined that once they got home, they would try to get in good with Abiel. "I commanded them not to tell Abiel anything about me, but my ears are ringing with the stories that they tell." Getting rid of them should have solved my problems, but I am stuck aboard a floating prison with stupid sailors pretending to be poets or pirates. I cannot tell. This is worse than the caravan. At least I was in charge before boarding this ship. I hope that all the Canaanite people are not as well versed in Hebrew lore as these sailors are."

CHAPTER 28

Carnival in Canaan

One Week Later

Zerah managed to survive the remainder of his journey aboard *OmOt*. Even after assuring his safety by hiring six more soldiers in Tyre, he could not have been happier to see the sails come down and hear the sound of oars splashing in the waters of the bay of Gubla. A welcome breeze blowing inland rocked the narrow wooden ships at anchor. Their rectangular sails hung loosely, drooping from their masts as relaxed as Zerah would find the people of Gubla to be. Looking ashore with great anticipation, he saw pale-skinned, gray-eyed men in loin cloths rubbing shoulders with shaven-headed, dark golden-skinned men in sheer white linen robes. Joining them were numerous bare-chested men adorned with tattoos commemorating their pilgrimages to holy sites. It was easy to identify the masters of the port. They were mostly dark-haired and bearded men with intense and proud eyes. Even in the afternoon heat, they remained wrapped in richly textured and patterned garments of red, blue, green, yellow, and purple, their feet shod in delicate leather shoes, earrings dangling from their ears, and their thick wavy hair secured by bright ribbons.

As Zerah stepped off the ship, the smell of animals commingled with the richly seductive odors of cinnamon and cedar, frankincense and myrrh, acacia and many other spices accosted his nostrils. Nearly naked slaves with stringy, sweaty muscles bulging under heavy weights walked up and down the swaying gangplanks, unloading materials and loading finished goods onto the ships. Women draped in brightly embroidered and woven robes passed by. Their fragrantly oiled long hair gave off a seductive smell. Zerah could not believe the openness this society provided for women. These were the prettiest women that he had ever seen, and the jingling of their large golden earrings sounding in unison with arm bracelets and neck chains dangling with amulets of silver, gold, and engraved gemstones beckoned to his manliness.

Looking up an impressive hill, Zerah got his first glimpse of the city. It looked compact within its enclosing wall, but one could see stucco-faced stone buildings glistening in the sun; most of them were two or three stories high with some reaching up to six stories. Farther to the east were the rolling foothills of the distant mountain ranges that ran north and south, paralleling the coast, still green from the winter and early spring rains. The slopes and ridges were highlighted with a darker green color of cedar and cypress, pine and oak, considered sacred to the deities.

It was late afternoon and Zerah was anxious to get into the city so he could find lodging. After staying on the ship for many days, most anything would seem nice. As he and Egla walked toward the gate to the city, they heard the high pitch of horns. Looking up toward the wall, they saw priests and priestesses in white robes silhouetted against the darkening sky. They stood on the temple walls waving fiery torches in the deepening dusk. They both felt awkward as the men and women around them began to sing a farewell to Shapash, goddess of the sun, as she descended into the netherworld. As the mournful notes began to fade, the people sang again, this time joyously, some beating hand drums, clanging cymbals, to welcome Yarikh, the moon god. All around, the Canaanites danced on their sacred eve. If Japho, Tyre, and Zidon were bazaars for commerce, Gubla was the open market for spiritual things.

Zerah could not have planned his arrival any better, even if he would have known about the "day of rites" to take place on the morrow. No wonder the harbor was so laden with ships. Of course, the port was busy with everyday commerce, but hundreds of foreigners were coming to Gubla for something for which the Phoinike were famous. In a feast of collective pleasure lasting many days, the people venerated what they considered the divine nature of sexual joy. The Canaanite carnival was about stirring the senses, thus the participants bathed and anointed their skin with herbs and essences. They darkened their eyelids, painted their faces, and decorated themselves with jewelry. Their dark hair was set in curls with scented lotions. Arrayed in all their finery, they toasted the goddess and her lover with wine, and performed serpentine, circling dances to the haunting music of lyres, flutes, and drums. Sacrifices and libations perfumed the air with the heady scents of cinnamon, aloes, and myrrh. At the peak of the lavish carnival, the king approached the temple, bearing offerings of oil, precious spices, and tempting foods to offer Anat. The crowds thronged the temple precincts chanting sacred erotic poems, creating a highly charged atmosphere of sensual anticipation and mystical participation. In these poems, the priestess who embodied the goddess prepared herself with great care, often quoting, "When for the bull, for the lord, I shall have bathed, when with amber my mouth I shall have coated, when with kohl my eyes I shall have painted. I shall go in to him to lie with him."

In addition to the activities of the sacred temple prostitutes, there were sacramental sexual initiations that demanded that every woman of the land once in her life had to sit in the temple of love and have intercourse with a stranger. The men passed in front of the women and made their choice. The man offered a sum of money, which the woman never refused. It was sinful to reject any offer. The money, once tendered, became sacred. After having intercourse, the woman became holy in the sight of the goddess and thus was free to return to her home. Thereafter, it was unlikely that she would ever be unfaithful again. Men chose the tall women with fair skin first. The dutiful were then free to go home, but the uncomely ones often had a long wait because they had not fulfilled the law. It was not uncommon for some of them to remain for three or four years. Upon hearing of this Zerah reasoned, "It makes much more sense to sell something of pleasure in the name of religion than the useless sacrifice of innocent animals just to feed the bellies of spoiled priests."

Unending sounds of drumming and chanting throughout the night was the traditional way of ushering out the old year. Things would not soon calm down, as the New Year's festivities continued for seven days. The next seven days were every bit as fateful for Zerah as the first seven days of his life had been. The past week aboard a ship was so hectic that he had not thought about his approaching birthday. Egla awakened him with a jest, "Wake up, Zerah; the entire city stayed awake all night celebrating your birthday." She placed a basket filled to overflowing with fresh fruit on the foot of his bed. "This is all I could afford, but I give it to you with love on your special day."

He rubbed his eyes in disbelief. "You must not have slept at all. Where did you get all of this?"

"There is a market just down the street from here. Did you plan this, that you would arrive at our new home on the first day of the new year of these people and your birth date?"

"No, I didn't. For one, I did not remember that it was my birth date, and I certainly was not aware that today was New Year's Day. Nevertheless, this is wonderful. I can't wait to get out into the street and join the celebration."

"I hope that you won't be upset with me if I don't join you. I am tired after seven days aboard that ship and besides, I would like to unpack and put up our belongings. Please promise me that if we ever leave here, it won't be on a ship."

Laughingly he promised, "We are never leaving here. I have found my home. Just think, today is the day of my first birth. It is in the plan of the gods that I arrived here on this date. I am born a second time and will start a new life. I may even change my name."

It bothered Egla, hearing Zerah speak so foolishly. She started to correct him, but instead prayed silently for G-d to consider the frivolity of youth and continue to show mercy to him. She excused herself from the room. Zerah hurriedly ate pieces of his fruit, the last one as he went out the door into the street. Heaviness came over Egla. So much so that she ran to the door, hoping to find him before he disappeared into the crowded street. It was too late. He was gone. Even though she was not his birth mother, she had the soulful connection that mothers do with their children. Angels whisper in their ears when something is wrong. She had no idea of the depths of demonic activity in this city, but as she stood in the doorway, an undeniable presence surrounded her. From that moment, Egla knew that she, as Zerah said, would never leave Gubla. Only now, she understood she would never leave here alive. She hurried into her room, collapsed on the floor, and prayed with such passion that her words became unintelligible groans.

Zerah's guards happened by the door to her room and couldn't help but overhear her. For a moment, it alarmed them, until they realized she was drunk.

"We were wrong about the woman. We saw her come and go in the early morning hours. She must have stayed out all night drinking wine. All this time we thought that she was a holy woman."

Egla never experienced a vision before, but as she prayed, she saw Abiel running past Jerusalem's Dung Gate. He smiled and stretched his arms for an anticipated embrace. She heard him shout, "The one thought dead is alive."

Then he said to her, "Egla, you are with my son, but he is not with you and you feel all alone. Please know that I am with you and G-d is present with you. G-d hears you pray, just as he heard the prophetess Hanna cry for her son, the prophet Samuel. She too travailed until no one but G-d understood her. G-d understands the language of your heart. Do not despair; your prayer will bring Zerah home."

Next, she saw a man running toward Abiel. It had to be Zerah. He cried, "My father, my father." But he was so thin and nearly naked.

The vision lifted Egla to her feet, and she danced to G-d for helping during her hour of distress by sending his word. She wiped her eyes, seeing that Zerah would make it back home one day!

CHAPTER 29

The Convert

Zerah pushed his way past the revelers, stopping only once to ask directions to the Temple of Baal. The temple would not have been hard to find, even without directions. There were hoards of people making their way there; most of them carried a special oblation. It dawned on Zerah that he was on his way to worship and had nothing in his hand to offer. Everything he knew of Baal he learned from Machir, but crime cut their time together short. He needed a teacher to show him the ways of the crimson people. As he neared the temple complex, he heard a compelling rhythmic chant. He followed its hypnotic sound to a place where a crowd surrounded Zammaru, the psalmist and sacred poet, the chanter of the myths. Canaanite gods loved reminders of their abilities. Usually, when someone asked for help, Zammaru recited stories; otherwise the god would not intervene. He was the person who knew best how to flatter the gods into doing favors. There was no reason for a man so important to the gods to be interested in the young man standing in front of him, except for the fact that he was undeniably Hebrew. It was unheard of for a Hebrew to risk curiosity or dare to convert. This made Zammaru leery, but at the same time irresistibly intrigued. He singled Zerah out of the crowd.

"Ibriy, what are you doing in Gubla?"

No one expected his answer. "I am a true worshiper of Baal, and I have come to pay homage at his altar."

Zammaru tested him. "Has YHWH, the son of EL, and his priests given you permission to come here?"

"Please sir, do not mock me. I forsook everything to come here. I came because my allegiance to Baal is strong, and it cost my best friend his life because he attempted to help me get here."

Still wary, Zammaru questioned, "And why would your friend want you to be here?"

"My friend Machir frequently visited here, and he told me of the wonders of this place. Ever since the first time I heard of Gubla, I lived for the day I could see it for myself."

"Machir, did you say Machir?"

"Yes, I did."

"Machir the Ibriy? You say he is dead?"

"Yes, killed by the priests because of his faith in Baal."

"Machir was well known and respected here in Gubla. The news of his death will sadden many people. If you wish to meet some of his friends, I will take you to them."

"Oh sir, I can think of nothing I would love more than to meet anyone who knew Machir."

"Meet me here tomorrow morning and I will take you through the temple. Afterward, I will introduce you to Machir's friends."

Zerah did not want to wait until morning. He was anxious to see everything and furthermore, mornings never treated him well. His wait was short to begin his orientation to life in Gubla. As a stranger in town, he was entitled to a night of sexual adventure inside the temple, and Baal's party planners were happy to have someone young, rich, and willing to invite to the orgy. Zerah learned where the recipe for Machir's strong drink came from.

After a full night of drinking wine mixed with an elixir of drugs and unrestricted sexual encounters with women of his choice, Zerah woke up to a throbbing pain in the upper part of his right arm. He looked to see the source of his pain, not remembering getting the image of a bull tattooed on his right arm. He tried to rise up for a better look, but a weight on his left arm held him down. The soft voice of a woman greeted him good morning as she lifted her head off his arm. A rush of blood sent feeling into his useless limb. He responded sheepishly to her greeting, as he struggled to regain use of his arms and memory of the past night. "I'm sorry; I had so much to drink last night. I really don't remember very much."

"It's all right, Zerah. You told me about your family, your journey to get here, and everything you have been going through. You deserved to have a night of enjoyment and if you have any questions, I will be happy to help you remember. Do you know my name?"

"Of course I; no, I'm so sorry. My mind. My head."

"I told you, it is all right. Let us start at the beginning. I was out in the street with some friends of mine. We were celebrating our holiday. We were near the great temple, and we met you as you were leaving there. As you know by now, strangers are most welcome here, especially at this time of year. I was immediately attracted to you."

Zerah said, "Now that my eyes are working again, I see why I am attracted to you and to your gods."

"I am glad that you like me. You were drunk last night. You told me that you were to meet with Zammaru today. He must like you, too. For him to offer to meet with you is unheard of. People know him as 'the recluse of the temple.' He talks to the gods and stays to himself."

"He knew my friend Machir. That is why he shows me favor."

The young woman unabashedly got up out of the bed, showing her nakedness without demure. She turned to silhouette herself between the early sun coming through the window and the bed where Zerah lay. She tantalizingly said, "My name is Sahar. In my language, my name means "rising of the morning." She posed and asked, "How is this for your first sunrise in our city?"

Zerah was breathless. She was beautiful and bold, but his infatuation subsided when the meaning of her name overtook his lust. "Sahar" clanged like a loud cymbal in his hurting head. "Did she say Sahar means rising of the morning?"

She stepped out of the room, and he hurriedly availed himself of her absence to get dressed. He did not want Sahar to see him naked, at least not while they were sober. He quietly slipped over to the door she went out of and put his ear up close. Sahar was singing:

> My lover is radiant and ruddy,
> outstanding among ten thousand.
> His head is purest gold;
> his hair is wavy and black as a raven.
> His eyes are like doves by the water streams, washed in milk,
>   mounted like jewels.
> His cheeks are like beds of spice yielding perfume.
> His lips are like lilies dripping with myrrh.

> His arms are rods of gold. His body is as polished ivory decorated with sapphires.
> His legs are pillars of marble set on bases of pure gold.
> His appearance is like Lebanon, choice as its cedars.
> His mouth is sweetness itself; he is altogether lovely.
> This is my lover, this is my friend.

The song was unlike any he ever heard. It made him wonder if Sahar sang the words about him or if it was a song known to many people. He never thought of himself as a lover, but he loved the thought of someone thinking of him as one.

Soon they were out in the crowded streets, making their way toward the temple. There were so many things that Zerah wanted to see that he could hardly walk for turning one way then another. Sahar urged him, "You have the rest of you life to look. We best hurry. Zammaru is not someone you want to keep waiting." He turned around, stumbling into the path of a herd of swine that came grunting and rumbling past him. He tripped and fell back on his buttocks, instinctively, trying to avoid contact with the pigs.

"Where are they taking those filthy things?" he complained while dusting himself off.

Sahar could not resist a giggle. His religion put him on his seat and she knew it.

"They are being taken to the temple to be offered as sacrifices."

"Oh, forgive me. It is just that back in Jerusalem, pigs are unclean and forbidden for sacrifice or to even be touched."

"Come, Zerah. You managed to get your body out of Jerusalem; now we have to get your mind out of there. I know that Zammaru can help you."

Zammaru was punctual and fully prepared to pastor the prodigal Ibriy in the ways and worship of Baal. Sahar waved as she walked away, stopping just long enough to tell Zerah she would be back later to meet up with him. Zammaru cleared his throat to regain Zerah's undivided attention.

"Sir, I apologize. I didn't mean to be disrespectful."

"Young man, I understand; she is a beautiful girl. Anyway, sit down for awhile and I will tell you about us, and then I will take you through our temple. I hear that you spent the night there."

It embarrassed Zerah, but Zammaru intervened, "Never be ashamed of the consecration of one of our women. This is the will of our goddess Anat. She is the sister and lover of Baal. You see, we do not believe that marriage is important when it comes to sexuality. Anat's name implies, "spouse of no one." I tell you about her because she is inseparable from Baal. In times of need, she is his heifer. Her fertility and the power of Baal the bull, breaks famines and spares us from pestilence. Today you will see many of their sons serving as priests here in the temple. We call them the *Assinnu*. They, like their mother, never marry and from birth, they are different from many males. They love only among themselves. We appoint a special woman to serve as the priestess Qadashu or "the holy one." She is sacred to Baal. You will have no trouble recognizing the Qadashu when you see her. She is the only person in the temple allowed to wear a beautiful scarlet-colored robe colored with the dyes that we make here in our homeland. She will be attended by many others, mainly ones that we call *sinnshat zikrum*."

Zerah cautiously complained, "Once again, I apologize, but I am a bit lost and confused. I am tired and dull after a long night of uh, consecration. Please don't think I'm being too bold, but I believe it would help if I could see these things as you explain them to me."

"Perhaps you are right. I forget how new all of this is for you. Come on, follow me."

Zerah had no idea how massive and sprawling the temple was. It literally was a city within a city. It had its own economy. It was the center of commerce as well as a place of worship. He and Zammaru were on the outer perimeter of the temple. It served as a staging area for hundreds of animals brought to the temple for sacrifice. Tellingly, Zerah did not complain or comment about the sacrifice of animals to Baal, the god who let him do anything he wanted. However he was altogether critical of similar sacrifices made to his father's G-d, who sought to restrict wanton behavior.

Zerah could not help but cast a furtive glance at the swine. Religion aside, he had a hard time seeing any redemptive purpose for a pig. Maybe sacrifice was the answer. Kill them all. All they are good for is to attract flies. Zerah resisted the temptation to hold his nose. Mercifully, he and Zammaru moved past the area quickly, taking them to something that was far more familiar to Zerah. He was accustomed to seeing merchants congregate in a holy place to conduct business. With an abundance of wealth flowing into the temple, the money mongers were not far away. Zammaru pointed in the direction of a group of men and women who appeared to be working with some interesting looking tools.

"The *mare ummani*; I'm sure that you will want to see them." Zammaru was right about that. He explained, "The *ummani* are artists that made statues for the worshipers." Zerah saw an icon identical to the one that he found in Toph.

"You seem attracted to the image of Baal."

Zammaru listened carefully as Zerah began his story, "I found one like this when I was a small boy. I kept it all through my childhood even though my father hated that I had it. Just before I came here, my brother and his servant stole it from me. It became a curse to them and the woman died with it in her hand. Now you know why I am here. I came in search of the very thing in front of us."

"But how did you survive? I know that the Ibriy religion forbids anyone to have an image of Baal."

"My father thought it to be nothing more that a toy for his child to play with. Because my father is wealthy, he is influential with the priests. They all were fools and didn't suspect that I was wise enough, as a youth, to recognize a true god."

Zammaru was touched. "Here, take this as a gift from me. Anyone who has been loyal to Baal as you have been deserves to have his image nearby."

Zerah kissed the image and pulled it closely to his breast. "You will never understand how much this means to me."

"I do understand. My entire life is devoted to worshiping Anat and Baal. I spend my days saying prayers and poems that give glory and honor to my gods."

"Would you repeat one of your favorite poems for me now?"

"Yes, I will be glad to say one for you. It depicts a conversation between Lord Baal and the supreme god El. It goes as follows:

> My wives, O El, have given birth,
> Oh, What babies they produced!
> Two have been born,
> Shaharu and Shalemu,
> Dawn and Dusk!

Zerah grimaced at the words, "Two have been born." Zammaru paused from his prose, wondering what he said that so adversely affected his convert. Possibly, he was taking Zerah too far, too fast.

"You have had enough for one day. Why do you not go now and rest? We will continue another day."

"I waited for years to be here and if it is all right with you, I would like to see more."

"Of course we can. It is just that I saw the look on your face as I recited the poem. Did I offend you in some way?"

"You did nothing to offend me; it is just that I lived in my brother's shadow most of my life, and it seems he follows me everywhere I go."

The poet-philosopher in Zammaru could not pass up his opportunity to help Zerah think differently about the poem and its meaning for him and his twin. "You had no control or choice concerning your conception or your birth. Therefore, you were born a twin. Did you choose to share your mother's womb with anyone? Now you are a man, and you chose to come to Canaan and convert to our religion. You do not have to share that with anyone. If you hear the entire poem, you will see that Shaharu and Shalemu are opposites. They are dawn and dusk, light and darkness. When I look at you, I see dawn and light. Light and darkness cannot inhabit the same space, even though they come from the same source. You and your brother were born of the same mother, but from that day you were set on a different course. When you think of your brother, think of him as the darkness that enhances the light you live in."

Zerah was impressed. These were the most sensible words he ever heard. The temple recluse might be able to answer his hardest questions. "Why is there day and night? Why are people so different, like my brother and me? Most of all, why are religions so different? Are they not supposed to lead us to G-d? All I remember about my father's religion is it starts with, "Thou shall not."

Zammaru answered in the manner of a philosopher by answering a question with a question. "Is there more than one road that leads to Jerusalem?"

"Yes, of course there is."

"There, you see. You answered your own question. There is more than one path to truth."

"I don't believe I have. Your and my father's roads do not go in the same direction. Baal is tolerant; my father's G-d is judgmental. Why would G-d create a thing and forbid us to have it? Why did he make anything evil? These questions have turned me to Baal."

"Tell me Zammaru, is there anything forbidden in your culture?"

"That will require a long discussion and I will gladly teach you the law of our land, but to answer you with a few words, I believe that everything can be good or it can be evil. There is some of both in all of us. The gods made us this way, like them. We encourage our people to experience life and find what is good for them. We eschew evil, but nothing is evil of itself. Mainly, our laws forbid harming another person or stealing their property, but aside from that..."

The rattling of tambourines and piping of flutes prevented any further discussion. Qadashu and her court were about to make a rare appearance. The rhythmic music sounded sensual, but did not compare to the visual effect of the most beautiful people Zerah ever saw. Everyone in the procession robed themselves in white. It made for a startling contrast to the colors on the lips, cheeks, and eyes of the musicians and cantors who joined them. People came running from all over the temple complex, gathering in hopes of catching a glimpse of Qadashu. Zerah had to rise up on the ball of his feet and toes to see over the heads of the frenzied crowd. Next, a large group of women, flawlessly made up and wonderfully adorned with an assortment of precious jewels, came walking. They carried huge baskets laden with brightly colored flower petals. The women tossed them high into the air and as the petals fluttered and fell to the ground, they formed a gentle covering for the feet of those who were to follow, that being women bearing burning censers filled with powerfully perfumed incense. In a matter of moments, the air that Zerah breathed wafted with a sweet scent as a gentle breeze softly stirred, swirling the smoke of the offerings. Zerah discreetly waved his hand in front of his face, not in offense to the savor of the smoke, but because he could not wait to see what was next. The emotion of the crowd told him that something spectacular was about to happen. His first glimpse of the *sinnshat zikrum* was something that he would never forget.

Zammaru leaned over and whispered in his ear, "*Sinnshat zikrum*; remember, I was about to tell you of them earlier, but we got off on another subject." As he pointed, he informed, "These are who they are."

Zerah indulged himself with a long hard look. The *sinnshat zikrum* possessed the physical features of women, but purposefully made themselves look like men.

Zammaru informed him, "They were born as women, but forsook sexuality to serve the wishes of Qadashu. She is so appealing that men who desire women must be trusted to guard her."

Zerah forgave himself for feeling attracted to them. Zammaru was watching Zerah closely and he saw the look.

"Which one of the women do you like the most?"

Zerah turned to look again, resisting the temptation to give a quick answer. He was learning that Zammaru had a motive for everything that he did or said.

"That one right there, the one with the long black curly hair."
Zerah chose her because she was extremely feminine looking.
"Are you sure?"
"Ye...Yesss, I'm sure. Why do you ask?"
"Please don't think I'm playing games with you, but I must tell you that the one that you have chosen is not *sinnshat zikrum*. You remember I told you about *assinnu*, the sons of Anat and Baal."
"Yes, I remember."
"Qadashu's sons are intermingled with the *sinnshat zikrum* and the one that you would love is *assinnu*. These men and women are the answer to your question. What is good and what is evil? Who is male and who is female? Does it matter as long as they serve the gods? If you are to live in Gubla, you must change the way you think. I will help."
"I will change. With your help, I will change my ways," Zerah pledged.

The music stopped and Qadashu stepped out of the smoke of incense that parted like a curtain. The high priestess of Anat, the lover of her brother Baal, arrayed in scarlet clothing, adorned with all manner of precious jewels, walked in procession with the rest of her court. She held a glittering gold cup in her right hand. One person, male or female, only G-d knows, walked alongside of her performing a solitary act—refilling the golden cup with wine. Qadashu stopped every few steps and poured out her wine as an offering to her lover. She eyed Zammaru and came to where he and Zerah stood. She emptied the golden goblet of its contents as she recited the same poem that Zammaru did earlier.

The poem was about her. It was customary to quote it during the New Year celebration.

> My wives, O' El, have given birth,
> O' what babies have been born!
> Two have been born,
> Shaharu and Shalemu,
> Dawn and Dusk!

She and Zerah stared at one another until Zerah became uncomfortable and looked away. Her face burned an image on his brain to the extent that she visited his dreams for many nights to come. The dreams were too bizarre for him to repeat. "Even if I were not a stranger here, and a Hebrew at that, how could I ever tell anyone that Qadashu, the queen of heaven, bowed down before me?" He dared not to tell anyone that Qadashu bowed to him, not even in a dream.

CHAPTER 30

Collapse of the Canaanite Civilization (and Zerah's Conscience)

SIX YEARS LATER

It took six years of uncontrolled and riotous living to exhaust the inheritance that Zerah's father so graciously gave him. The parasite prostitutes and priests of Baal feasted sumptuously off his possessions and property. Like civilizations before them, the Canaanites failed to realize that while devouring their citizenry, they in fact consumed themselves. Their culture and religion became one of the weakest, most decadent, and immoral in the known world. Their enemies were emboldened and on the move against them, their economy faltered, crops failed, and sickness was rampant. Venereal diseases ravaged a large part of the population. As conditions of daily life deteriorated and circumstances steadily worsened, the theocratic leaders of Canaan intensified their efforts to tighten their grip on the necks of the population. They used a concoction of rituals, magic, astrology, divination, and theology to convince, or better said, compel the people to thinking that the only way out of their troubles was to appease the gods. Exorcists, healers, and purifiers deceived the public as they roamed the streets of Gubla plying their trade for pay. Even the prophets of Baal who dwelt in the mountains came down into the city. They too were nothing more than hirelings. None spoke the truth about the impending disaster descending on Gubla. The oracles went house to house ranting and tearing at their clothes, convincing multitudes to offer their children as sacrifices to Baal. Profane altars normally reserved for swine and other animals now ran warm with human blood, as firstborns shared a common fate with the pigs. Baal's murderous crew used the rumbling noise of drums to drown out the screams of children getting their throats cut just before thrown into ovens and burned like rubbish.

Zerah was out of money and out of morals. The practices of the "red people" did not bother him, nor did the truths he learned as a youth come to mind. He mistook promiscuousness for development. Sahar was his personal emissary of evil, leading him farther and farther into decadence. She taught him to worship multiple gods while they shared multiple sex partners. The deeper his sin, the higher her praise of him. Sahar's name may have meant brightness of the morning, but she was midnight to Zerah's morals.

The only shining light still flickering in the midst of this madness was Egla's unfaltering faith. True to her promise to Abiel, she continued to watch over Zerah, in spite of his considering her mothering a nuisance, if not a festering thorn in his flesh that never healed up. Some time ago, she realized that talking to Zerah made matters worse. Her only recourse was prayer. Frequency and fervency of prayer cloaked Egla in the beauty of holiness. Zerah hated to look at her. Her face was a mirror to him and what he saw in her convicted him. Conviction had no place in Canaan!

Her sacrosanct beauty not only convicted Zerah, it convinced the temple authorities she was a danger. They were not about to allow an Ibriy who refused to accept their culture, their gods, to be acknowledged as the most beautiful woman in Gubla.

Zerah did not expect the visit from the personal emissary of Qadashu or the invitation he bore, requesting Zerah to meet with her. However, as he followed Qadashu's messenger out into the street, he remembered his oft-recurring dream, the one in which Qadashu bowed down to him. His heart pounded as they walked into an intersanctum that Zerah knew very few mortals had the privilege to visit. Nearing two massive golden doors, the messenger abruptly turned and ordered Zerah to wait there. Shortly thereafter, several people he recognized to be *sinnshat zikrum* came for him and escorted him through the gold laden doors to a vast chamber. His greeters explained that they had to cleanse him before taking him to Qadashu. They disrobed him and led him down into a large pool of water, washing him from the top of his head down to the soles of his feet. He had long since forgotten his modesty that embarrassed him that first morning with Sahar. Once they finished bathing him, others came with vials of oil and spiced perfumes and they anointed him, massaging the mixture into his skin. Lastly, they dressed him in a white robe and put a wreathed laurel on his head.

"Now you are ready," one of the attendants announced.

Up until now, Zerah had not spoken one word. He supposed he knew what would happen next.

"Yes, I am ready," he confidently replied.

The man who summoned him from his house reappeared and motioned for him to follow. They stopped at a heavily guarded set of doors. From the moment that he stepped through this second set of doors, he began to live out the dream that filled up so many of his nights since the first time he saw Qadashu.

He walked past a number of chanters. Some of what they said made no sense to him, but he was aware their prayers concerned him. They mentioned his name in their liturgy. It unnerved him until he saw his mentor and friend Zammaru sitting among the chanters. The prayer ended, followed by silence that hung as heavy in the room as the profuse smoke from pungent incense. The sound of soft footsteps was the only announcement of Qadashu's arrival.

Zerah was about to bow before Qadashu, but she stopped him simply by extending her hand with her palm facing him. It put him in suspense. "What does she mean for me to do?"

His anticipation intensified. She closed her hand except for her index finger, which she used to point at him. "Naguodea, are you prepared to fulfill our ancient prophecy?"

He recognized the word *Naguodea* as their word for "deliverer."

He wondered, "What will she think of me? I don't know what the ancient prophecy is."

He covered his ignorance.

"We have many wonderful prophecies. To which one do you refer, my queen?"

"The one that brought you to us. Our seers knew you from the first day you arrived in Gubla. They recognized that you are the deliverer to come before the day of trouble. Did you not think of yourself as you read the prophetic words?" Naguodea will come to you from a far country;

> The country of those that you count as your enemy.
> He will hunger and thirst for knowledge of your Lord Baal.
> As a sign that I, El, have called him out of his land from the day of his birth,

He shall come wearing scarlet around his neck as a symbol of his strength. He shall bring with him one whose name means "a calf" and she shall be a sacrifice for the salvation of my people.
My lord Baal, the bull, shall lie with her, then sacrifice her as an oblation for deliverance from our enemies, and rest from the famine.
She will not give birth from the seed of Baal in that she will not be a believer. Thus we will not be her sons or her daughters, but by her sacrifice she will be as a mother giving life to our people, just as the Naguodea is her son, even though she is not his mother.

After a long pause, punctuated by everyone in the room looking at him, Zerah confessed, "I knew nothing of the existence of this prophecy. I would be a fool to deny its accuracy. Why has no one told me about this before now?"

"We hoped the day of trouble would never come and none of the drastic things called for in the prophecy would be necessary. We know that you love the woman Egla who has been with you from the day you were born. How could we ask you for her? Yet you watch as we sacrifice and burn our children, so again I ask, are you ready to fulfill your destiny?"

Curiously, one pious woman, whose only crime was praying for G-d to change one man's heart, threatened a city, a creed, a culture, and the Canaanites as a people. She prayed in the manner of the prophet Daniel, remembering his exile and the window facing east that he opened to offer daily supplication. The time neared when she would face her den of lions, in the person of a purple-robed priestess of Baal. Zerah cast a quick glance in the direction of Zammaru, looking for some sign of affirmation. An ever so slight nod of Zammaru's head was all it took to prod him to answer.

"I will. Yes. Yes, I will do anything for my lord Baal and his sister, for you Qadashu."

Qadashu clapped her hands in feigned excitement. "You truly are Naguodea. You are our savior. People will mention your name with the names of the gods."

Her flattery intoxicated him. Since the day of his first birthday in Gubla, the day he boasted of a second birth, he vowed to change his name. Qadashu gave him much more than a new name. She bestowed him the title of "savior."

He suggested, "I will take leave of you now and go to Egla. I will explain the prophecy to her. She is a spiritual woman and if she knows her sacrifice will save thousands of people, she will agree."

He would not need to talk Egla into anything. For when he turned to leave, the big golden doors opened, not for his departure, but for Egla to enter. He did not recognize her with her head shaved and her face painted. Her black clothing stood out in stark contrast to the white robes of the *sinnshat zikrum* that held her by both of her arms. There stood Egla facing Qadashu. Qadashu turned her around in Zerah's direction. He still did not recognize her face. The woman's lips moved slowly, but not to ask Zerah for anything. She began quoting a Psalm written by the Ibriy King David, the one about the valley of the shadow of death. He recognized her sweet voice and knew that she was the only one present who would know the hymn of David.

Zerah's lips moved, but no sound came out of his mouth. He choked on the name that he called ten thousand times as a child. Finally he managed to say, "Egla, is it you?"

Her answer was, "I will fear no evil. You are with me. I take comfort in your rod of correction. Prepare me a feast here in the presence of our enemy."

Zerah did not see Qadashu slip out of her scarlet attire. She placed her crimson red robe over Egla's head and shoulders, allowing it to drape as a loose covering.

She spoke to Egla, "I relinquish my position as Qadashu for one night. I stand naked before you O' El, divesting myself of my powers, and I bestow them upon the one before me who wears my robe. May she take my place as the lover of Qadasha, the high priest of Baal? Grant unto Qadasha the potency of the bull and accept our offering of the calf. Accept the sacrifice of something so innocent and lovely and break the curses that have come upon us! Bring prosperity and peace to our people. Grant favor to Naguodea for he is the one who brought the calf to you."

When she finished her exhortation, Qadasha, the high priest of Baal, entered the room. In all Zerah's years in Gubla, this was his first time to see Qadasha, and quite a sight it was. His appearance was unlike anyone Zerah ever remembered seeing. Dark curly hair covered most of his tall muscular frame, making it to hard to tell his body from his garment made from the hide of a black bull. His headpiece supported the long sharp pointed horns of a bull. He walked in an unusual way, lifting his legs high and bringing them down full force, as trying to demonstrate his strength. Servants followed closely behind him rolling a life-sized molded gold idol of a calf. Qadasha went directly up to Egla, lifted her up into his arms, placing her on the back of the calf. Without a word, he turned and left the room. The chanters simultaneously picked up their chorus as he, Egla, and the golden calf disappeared behind the doors.

Zerah noticed that Egla stopped praying when Qadasha picked her up, but just as the doors closed, he heard her cry out, "*Benoni, Benoni*. Why have you forsaken me, *Benoni*?"

CHAPTER 31

Joined to the Certain Citizen

At first Zerah had mixed emotions about the sacrifice of his longtime surrogate mother, but after all, the prophecy was so accurate, and it was unprecedented for Qadashu to relinquish her power to anyone. He felt honored that the gods deemed Egla worthy to save the Canaanites from certain destruction. She always loved children and Zerah convinced himself that she willingly gave her life to spare them suffering and starvation. All of Gubla heard about what happened; subsequently Zerah became a hero. People looked upon him as a lord of the gods. As Naguodea, he was entitled to their worship as well as their wealth. The one thing he disliked about his position was he no longer could be with Sahar. She was considered a commoner and not worthy of the company of a lord. One of the remaining prominent citizens of Gubla, a man named Dryhus, requested to befriend Zerah. Prosperity deserted the land and an elite few controlled what remained of its resources. The rest of the population groveled in abject poverty. Dryhus owned and controlled the swineherds in the Gubla region of Canaan. Control was the one word Dryhus lived by.

He was short, obese, and most unappealing to look upon, mainly because of his eyes. They were large, round, and protruding. Their dark color set against the reddish hue of the part that should have been white, warned of his temperament that many men his height have; forever trying to be five cubits tall. Early in life, he was one of the *Assinnu*, but managed to leave temple life to pursue a related business. The leadership of Gubla gladly let him leave temple life because he did not look the part. Most of the *Assinnu* were pretty as women, but it did not take a second look to tell Dryhus's gender. Unlike many of the citizens of Gubla, Dryhus was not bisexual. His desire was for young men, and he was accustomed to having anyone he wanted. He was reputed to be easily bored and disinterested in his partners, but the thought of being with a Naguodea intrigued him.

Qadashu and Qadasha never intended to share their glory with some upstart foreigner. Just because Zerah adopted their gods did not mean they or their gods accepted him. They welcomed his wealth while his wasteful living lined their coffers; but that gone, he was expendable. They used Zerah to rid themselves of Egla. Dryhus, the ruthless sadist with insatiable desires, would rid them of Zerah. Many of his lovers unexplainably vanished. Their disappearance probably had something to do with his well-fed fat hogs. He called his pigs '*dowd bariy*' or "lovers fat."

Dryhus wasted no time taking control. Using his cleverness, he urged Zerah to confide in him. Zerah unearthed his long since buried story of his life back in Jerusalem. Mournful agreement from Dryhus accompanied every painful detail.

"I know how you feel. That is awful. It should not be that way. I would never have done that to you. They do not love you. You did right to leave home; I would have, too."

Then they cried together as Zerah recounted the death of his mentor, Machir.

Dryhus had the information that he needed and he almost laughed aloud, "He thinks he needs a father. This will be easy. I have seen it so many times."

His devious plan began with, "I love you for what you did for me and my people. The impending famine would ruin my business, but you are Naguodea, my savior. It is Canaan's blessing that your family rejected you."

"You are too kind to me."

"Your father didn't believe in you, but I do. I want you to join me as a partner in my business. You gave Egla as an offering and our troubles are at an end. The people will be sacrificing more than ever. I must greatly increase the size of my herd. I know you have used much of your wealth, if not all of it, just to stay in Canaan. I will secure your future. El is an eternal god and as such he will always be worshiped, so will our business last forever."

Zerah was elated. "Are you sure about this? No one except Machir ever treated me so. You remind me a lot of him."

Naguodea, the savior, at last felt saved and it was as simple as the affirmation of an older man. Sadly, Dryhus was insincere and had no lasting interest in Zerah's welfare. He wanted more than a partnership or friendship. It was a conquest: his chance to be with a god.

It was not that Zerah had not been with a man, but up until now his encounters had always included women. The biggest concern he had was that he desired the company of women, and he did not know how Dryhus would feel about that. Unfortunately, his need for security and approval from a father overrode his qualms about committing to a man. He was caught in a snare.

Zerah soon discovered he was not the only house guest under Dryhus's roof. Men of all ages and walks of life came and went, and there wasn't any distinction between friends, lovers, servants, and slaves.

Dryhus treated his friends like slaves and rewarded his slaves as lovers. Loyalty meant less to Dryhus than one of his hogs. He traded trust for satiation of his lust and brutality.

Zerah's mistreatment was mild at first, not much more than harsh words. When he asked questions about the business, the answer was, "Before you can run a business, you must learn to be obedient in other ways." Zerah soon learned the meaning of "other ways." Judging from the distressful sounds coming from Dryhus's room, there were worse things than verbal abuse going on in this house. Zerah was not about to be obedient to most of the "other things" that Dryhus suggested they do. This infuriated Dryhus and he berated Zerah. Even worse, he persuaded everyone he could to join in the mocking.

"Naguodea, ha! Some savior you are! Our savior's purpose for coming is to make us glad. But you; you regard yourself as being better than Baal, too holy to bring pleasure to your servants. You must be the Ibriy Lord 'Yasha', lord of austerity."

Dryhus forbid his servants or his friends to use the title Naguodea or the name Zerah. Yasha was Zerah's new name. This was especially hurtful to Zerah, for he felt he sacrificed everything to serve Baal.

He tried to defend himself, "I have proven myself to Baal and his servants. I have given to him until I have nothing else to give. You have no right to treat me as you do."

Dryhus disagreed. Yasha was just beginning to give. Zerah had not yet given the one thing that Dryhus insisted on having, being in control—control of Zerah's mind, his body, and his life itself. "You eat my bread and drink wine in my house and say to me that I have no rights over you. We will see. We will see who has rights!"

Zerah wondered, "What happened to the man who said he loved me, understood me, and would never treat me as my father did? Dryhus was right; my father never treated me so badly."

The title "savior" became bitter gall to him. It finally came to him. Hearing the word *Yasha* reminded him of when he was a young boy in schooling, a rabbi teaching him a saying of the prophet Yesha yahuw. It went, "He was despised and rejected by men, a man of sorrows, and familiar with suffering." Some believed these words were prophetic of their savior who was yet to come. Zerah couldn't help but feel that he really did not want to be Naguodea or Yasha! Regardless, his suffering continued, even when he closed his eyes to sleep. He repeatedly dreamed of his childhood. Zerah saw Pharez bury his face in his hands and cry as he and his friends shouted, "Chamor rosh, Yasha, Chamor rosh, Yasha, Chamor rosh." The faces of his childhood friends all looked like Dryhus. Pharez would turn and run to Abiel as Zerah awoke in cold sweat, words of torment ringing in his ears. The dream forced him to feel Pharez's pain and for the first time he was sorry.

Dryhus, not accustomed to waiting for anything, planned a party with the intention that one way or another he would have his way with Yasha. He and his companions commenced consuming wine and strong drink in excess. Zerah, still under the influence of his bad dreams, was in no mood for a party. His sullen disposition was all the excuse Dryhus needed to go into a tirade. Zerah had enough of the abuse and retaliated, unleashing his pent-up frustrations. "Little wonder you turn to men. You likely cannot find a woman who will have you. If you continue to treat everyone the way you treat me, the day will soon come when all you will have left to sleep with will be your sow pigs." Zerah underestimated the violence that this confrontation would unleash.

Dryhus scowled, "My fellows, what should we do about the insolence of this Ibriy bitch? He comes under my care, eats my food, shares my wealth, and insults me in the presence of my companions?"

It was obvious that Dryhus planned the outcome of this evening. The men attacked Zerah like a pack of wolves on a lost lamb, abusing him without leniency. Dryhus shouted to them, "Show him who is lord here. Show him. Show him!" He took up a shepherd's staff and beat the men as if he were herding animals into a stall. The last words Zerah heard before he passed out were, "Who is it that sleeps with pigs?"

He awakened to the noise of grunting swine as they rolled him over in smelly mud, using their snouts, turning him like a scrap of food. He knew he was near death and feared the hogs would help themselves to his carcass if he passed out again. He barely had strength to stand up, but he pushed through his pain, realizing that he had to get out of the pen or else perish there. His eyes were full of mud and wiping them made matters worse. He decided to stumble in one direction until hopefully; he would reach a rail post or something to lift himself up. He heard the sound of hundreds of biting flies swarming around him. It made him thankful for the muck that covered his body. It gave him protection from the bloodsuckers that live off the pigs. After what seemed like a lifetime, he escaped the confines of the pen and found some grass with which to wipe his eyes. Before he finished, he heard laughter as several men approached him. His first instinct was to get back in the pen with the pigs. He feared those who abused him more than the pigs. He just managed to get back in the hog pen, when he recognized Dryhus.

"Yasha, I see you are up early. I appreciate a partner who rises early in the morning to tend to my business, although I am jealous that you got to sleep with my sows."

His companions snickered.

"You Ibriy people have a great reputation as shepherds; you even make kings of them. You are no longer Naguodea or Yasha, the savior; you are a 'shepherd of the swine'. Tend to our 'flock', or I will personally fatten them with your flesh."

They walked away leaving Zerah alone, abandoned without friends, family, fortune, future, and faith.

Zerah found a small stream of water and washed as best he could. He could hear the pigs squealing for something to eat. He had no idea what to feed them, and he soon learned that pigs are voracious eaters. He had to feed them or become food for them. He spent his first morning feeling sorry for himself and fighting flies. Only once did he afford himself the luxury of crying. Tears did him good. They cleared his eyes and his mind, and it came to him. "I don't know how to survive out here, but I must. I have no one who can teach me." He stopped for a moment remembering, "Most pigs are fat even though many are not penned up and fed by men. The pigs can teach me."

Watching them root and grovel for food, he realized that if he managed to get one of the pigs out of the pen, it would lead him to whatever it was that they were supposed to eat. The hard part would be getting just one or two out of the pen. "And if I do, how will I ever get them back in? Ah, like the shepherds do. Dryhus said that we are great shepherds. I hope that he was right because I am about to find out."

His jealousy of Pharez returned, but for a different reason. Not over the inheritance, but, "Pharez would know what to do."

He sat down and watched the pigs. He noticed when something came near the pens; the pigs ran to see if it was edible. A grin showed on his face, revealing a trace of his boyishness that Dryhus failed to steal. Zerah got an idea from Dryhus's mention of shepherds that became kings. He gathered up a few stones, just as David did to use against the giant. Zerah's foe was not nearly as formidable. Well, maybe. He flung the first rock way across the pen, and the pigs went thundering toward the rock as it splashed into the mud.

"That worked pretty well," he proudly declared.

He tossed a second rock, which landed near a gate where Zerah hastened to position himself. The greedy animals scurried toward the prospect of something to eat. Zerah reached through the gate and grabbed the leg of the smallest pig he possibly could as he threw the rocks in his free hand across the pen. The pigs had not caught on to his wily trick and away they ran to fight over the rocks. All of them ran except the one that Zerah struggled to drag through the gate. Zerah feared it was going to tear a hole in the fence, allowing the rest of the herd escape. He would be a dead man for sure! However, to his relief, his prey settled down and ambled off across an open field toward an expansive stand of kharub trees. Zerah was too weak to keep pace as the pig broke into a fast trot once it neared the trees. When he finally caught up, the pig busily fed on pods of kharub fruit that had ripened and fallen to the ground. Zerah waited to see if the pods were poisonous before he mustered courage to join in. Not knowing pigs' habits gave him an anxious moment when the pig stopped eating and laid down as if dead. Zerah breathed a sigh of relief when he poked the animal with a stick, and it jumped and grunted an aggravated complaint to protest the interruption of its nap.

It was his turn and much to his surprise, the kharub pods contained a sweet gelatin-like nectar. They tasted much better than he expected. Zerah had his answer for feeding the pigs, and a bigger answer about himself. He was not ready to lie down and die. He had more fight in him than he realized.

The next few months were nothing short of torturous for "the shepherd of the swine." He learned to hate flies worse than the pigs. At least the pigs occasionally shut up and slept, unlike the relentless flies. Zerah resembled one big sore from the accumulation of bites, until he took time to learn more about the pigs than what they ate. Aside from the shade of the kharub trees, he had no relief from the sun until he studied why pigs wallow in mud. The pigs were not filthy. The mud was cool and made a good coat to keep their skin from burning in the heat of the day. Their earthy covering also provided protection from the annoying flies. Too bad nothing could prevent or soothe the biting sarcasm of Dryhus and his sex slaves. Their mocking stung worse than the fly bites. Even though Zerah's faith in Baal faded, he had no one else to call on. The mockers heard him and it earned him yet another name. He did not know the meaning of Baal-Zebub until he heard Dryhus say, "King of the flies. It all fits; the shepherd of the swine has become the king of the flies." It seemed as though Dryhus would never tire of coming up with new ways to taunt Zerah.

Zerah recalled the rabbis' saying Baal-Zebub is the name of the devil and he certainly looked the part. His blood red eyes and the red cord around his neck was all that showed from beneath his matted hair and malnourished body completely covered with maggot-infested mud.

CHAPTER 32

Coming to

The forlorn sound of the *yowbel* awakened the city of Jerusalem at dawn on the tenth day of the seventh month. It signaled the start of the long awaited Day of Atonement at the beginning of the fiftieth year since the last "year of jubilee." This was the day slaves became free men, property returned to rightful owners, inheritances were reinstated, and, in general, all civil wrongdoings made right. The coming year would be one of rest and respite for the people and the land. Abiel did not wait to hear a yowbel; he was up long before the sun showed its face over the eastern horizon. The ceremonies planned for the day epitomized the heart of this benevolent man. Doing good came natural to him, thus his reputation for kindness and generosity was renowned among his peers. But Zerah had more on his mind than servants, slaves, and reinstatement of property rights. His faith told him this year of jubilee signified the time of Zerah's return, and he believed in putting legs under his faith. A sabbatical from working his vineyards for one year would free him to do nothing else but watch and pray. Reports of famine hitting hard in the land of the Canaanites bolstered his faith. Abiel was certain Zerah was somewhere in Canaan, and if it took tragedy to get him home, so be it. Hiphil's soldier friends reported to Abiel that his son had gone to Gubla.

Abiel vowed to visit the Dung Gate three times a day to wait for his son's return. The Dung Gate was not a logical place to watch from if you expected to see someone approaching from the east, but it was the last place that Abiel saw Zerah, and he believed it was from there he would see his son returning. Abiel's family and friends were concerned that losing Zerah drove him to madness.

His prayers were anything but quiet requiems. He prayed to get somebody's attention, anticipating it to be G-d's! This early morning he petitioned, "Oh G-d of mercies, this day, please let Zerah see my face. Just as I looked at him and smiled when he was leaving and I told him that if he ever wondered about my loving him, he could close his eyes and he would see me smiling at him."

Zerah had no idea what day of the week it was or what sacred traditions anyone observed back in Jerusalem. Nor did he know if life went on as usual with his family or if they missed or thought of him. His life was worse than the hell that he did not believe in. He spent his days toiling to feed pigs with unending appetites, fighting flies, rolling in mud, and using sticks to scrape scabs off sores that refused to heal. The first few months in the fields he worried that he would become too weak to work and Dryhus would kill him. Gradually, weakness turned into sickness, and he slowly was losing his will to live. Dread of living replaced his fear of Dryhus killing him. As he weakened, he lapsed into deep sleep; so much so, he often lodged himself in a tree to rest, in hopes of keeping the hogs from eating him.

By midmorning, he was exhausted and made his way to the tree. Once up to the limbs fork where he lodged, he closed his tired eyes; however, a vision came in the place of sleep, and the face he hoped never to see again appeared to him. True to his father's parting words, Abiel smiled while repeating his promise that he forever loved his son and wanted him to come home. Hot tears of loneliness filled Zerah's eyes and unexplainably, he cried out, "Abba, Abba, Abba." Zerah did not know it, but he was praying, and there is no greater one-word prayer than the word, "Father." Abiel's prayer found its way to the tree next to the hog pen, and Zerah's unintended prayer knew the way to the Dung Gate.

He hugged the tree and slid from the limb to the ground, but his confidence continued sliding even after his feet reached the ground. "I must be delirious. It is not possible that father wants me back after all that I have done. What could I possibly bring him? He has riches. He has a son. He has hired servants. He has bread enough and to spare, and I am dying of hunger! My only hope is to arise and go to my father, and say unto him, I have sinned against heaven, and before you, and am not worthy to be called your son; let me be one of your servants."

Abiel's smile restored Zerah's desire to go home, but Zerah's physical condition would make the journey home every bit as difficult as desiring to be home had been. He lacked strength, sustenance, and the protection of soldiers. Uncannily, his body healed quickly now that his mind settled on going home.

Without money, there was nothing he could do about hiring someone to protect him, but he had to procure food or else he would never make it.

It came to him, "The pigs, my answer—phuuwee—right under my nose."

He took six piglets just after their weaning and hand-fed them, making sure their sow mothers got sold off quickly. Naturally, the piglets bonded with Zerah and before long, they followed him everywhere he went. It was not nearly as impressive as his caravan that left Jerusalem, but nonetheless, he and six pigs were ready to move.

It was the first day of the ninth month, and the Canaanites struggling to find anything to celebrate during these lean times were anxious to commemorate their annual feast of their twin gods, Shaharu and Shalemu. It was a sign to him that his day of departure had come. The day passed quickly and as the stars appeared, signaling the end of another day, Zerah watched the Gemini constellation rise up in all of its glory. He thought of Om and Ot, the twins carved on the bow of the ship, and of Zammaru's poem. Before the dawn of another day, the twins would walk together on a familiar path over the horizon. He lay awake for hours watching the twins march across the night sky and wondered if Pharez would welcome him home.

Zerah was up well before daylight. He needed to be gone before the unfed pigs started making excess noises that might bring notice. Although during these days of celebration, it was unlikely that anyone would rise up early. The timing was perfect for an unnoticed exodus. Everyone was intoxicated with false hopes of deaf, dumb, and dead deities delivering them from famine. Heading out, he went to the stand of kharub trees to gather enough pods to keep himself and his followers fed until he could become desperate enough to kill one of them. As he hastily grabbed handfuls of the kharub fruit, he noticed "scarlet worms" crawling down the side of the trunks of the trees. He knew the worms to be the source of the special dyes that the Kinakhnu people used to make their world famous fabrics. The sight of the worms prompted Zerah to reach up to his neck and remove his red rope necklace. As risky as it was, he chanced running back to the pen. The hogs were awake and nosily anticipating their morning meal. A proverb came to his mind, "Do not cast your pearls before the swine." He answered it, "What would be wrong with casting your curse to the swine?" He tossed his bitterness and his muddy necklace over the fence. As the hogs hurried to eat it, Zerah headed south, his entourage not far behind. It amazed him how the hogs ate most anything. He, like them, had eaten the slop of every ideology thrown to him, and now for the first time in his life he would resort to eating the most despicable animal in his forsaken culture.

On the third night, he gave in to gnawing hunger. After months of eating kharub pods, he craved something with a different taste and his reasoning told him he needed meat for strength. He had to share the meal with his companions or else. Zerah felt guilty eating something that loyally followed him around. When darkness completely enveloped Zerah and he could no longer see the hogs, he listened to them well into the night. They sounded contented as they used their powerful jaws to break the bones and finish off any part left to fight over from the flesh of one of their own.

Living and dying with the hogs was teaching Zerah many lessons.

"I did the same thing to my family that these lowly swine do to each other." He started to cry in repentance. The sound of breaking bones broke his heart. "I know I broke father's heart and would have destroyed my brother for my own gain. How could they ever forgive me?"

CHAPTER 33

Coming Home

Abiel remained vigilant in his visits to the Dung Gate, divergent to all human reasoning. He sat through many uneventful days, staring with a look of anticipation that things would change in the next moment. Occasionally, the gate guards saw Abiel leap to his feet, assuming that he saw his son approaching. Abiel's burning heart, mingled with the swirling smoke of Toph, made him see things that were not there. The elders congregated at the Damascus Gate heard rumors that Abiel lost his mind. He was a man possessed!

Meanwhile, Zerah was well on his way into the wilderness to the east of the Phoinike coast. There was nothing left for him in Canaan. He planned to make his way down to Capernaum where he would circle the sea of the Galileans to find the head waters of the Jordan River and follow them to the south. Then he could turn west and make it to Jerusalem. Paradoxically, Om and Ot, the twins of the constellation Gemini, were the ones guiding him home. He wisely chose to travel at night. It was much safer to travel under the cover of darkness, avoiding unwanted attention. Further, the pigs, nocturnal by nature, followed better at night.

After some days, he made his way around the sea of the Galileans and came to the river Jordan. His four remaining pigs ran headlong toward the boggy banks of mud to indulge themselves in miry madness. Zerah stood back watching them enjoy themselves and wondered if there was anything on earth that could make him feel as good. "Strange, I tried everything only to feel nothing." The numbness of nothingness was better than the excruciating pain of feeling dirty, depraved, and disowned. Zerah walked to the bank of the river and looked at the muddy water. "Maybe there is something. Death could not be any worse." Drowning would solve many problems, stop the embarrassment of returning home empty-handed, and end the pain of being empty-hearted. Without realizing that he took a step, he stood at the water's edge. A chilling fear gripped him to realize just how close to death he was. Out of shear fright, he screamed out, "Oh G-d of my fathers, you spoke to me when I was dying in slavery to evil men in the land of Canaan. You called me to return unto my father's house in Jerusalem so I can be a servant to him. Did you bring me to this river that I should perish or will you allow me to see the face of my father yet one more time?"

Zerah spun around thinking that someone behind him spoke, "Naaman."

"Who's there? Come out from hiding and show yourself."

A sensation quite different to anything that he ever felt came over him.

The boy who left G-d to go and search for a god was conversing with G-d. Startled, he blurted out, "Who are you, and why do you call me Naaman?"

A soft, calming voice spoke again, "Be still and know!" Zerah fell backwards away from the water into a sitting position and repeated the word *Naaman*, searching his soul for its meaning. He was exhausted after a long night of walking, so as the hogs stretched out for their morning rest, he too went into a deep sleep. Once there, he witnessed a prideful captain of the Syrian army wade out into the Jordan River to dip himself seven times, as the Hebrew prophet Elisha had commanded. The leprous soldier went up and down in the water six times without any change in his condition, but as Naaman broke from beneath his watery grave for the seventh time, his rotting flesh was like that of a child.

Barely awake, he answered the mystery of the calm voice, "I know now. I know who Naaman is and what I have to do." He plunged into the water with abandon, stopping only when the water reached his shoulders. He looked back toward the bank of the river, wondering if the voice would speak again. All he saw or heard were four disinterested, undisturbed pigs. Slowly, down he went for the first time and then a second. Some caked mud loosened and fell from his face. Under he went for the third, fourth, and fifth time. He took a deep breath and ducked his head for the sixth time. The decisive moment had come and he worried. "Whatever will I do when I dip again, if nothing happens?" Still there were no more words from the calming voice. Just as he got the courage to go under for the seventh time, the hair bristled on the backs of the hogs as they ran close to one another. They sensed danger. Zerah had to go under now or lose his nerve. Buckling his knees, he lowered his head beneath the water, but something powerful grabbed him and pulled him all the way down.

Zerah pushed against the soft bottom of the river, vainly attempting to raise himself up. A voice very different from the soft voice defiantly said, "We will not let you go."

What followed made Zerah believe he had died and gone to the netherworld. His head reeled with the same feeling he often got from drugs and drink. Out of the blackness of death, life as he had known it flashed before him. A young boy ran past him, mocking and cursing as he disappeared into the mouth of a massive brazen idol. The idol regurgitated and out came a multitude of tormented men and women. The cycle was unending, for as the women gave birth, they turned and offered their children back into the same hell they experienced in the belly of the idol. Zerah watched in horror as demons reached into the wombs of those still pregnant, stealing their fetuses, only to throw the unborn away as if they were nothing more than rubbish. The tormented ones marched across the land murdering for money, envy, jealousy, pettiness, and even for religion. He saw masses of people practicing lewdness as a religion. Myriads of rebellious angels sat by watching and applauding their fallen comrades who helped them thwart their hated creator's plan. He was seeing the spirits in residence of his soul, and his trespassers planned to fight their eviction. Using his last breath of air he pled, "Please G-d, set me free from these evil spirits or let me die." He breathed in, expecting to inhale water and die, but to his amazement, his head was out of the water and his lungs filled with fresh morning air. When he exhaled, he literally watched the exodus of the evil spirits from his mouth. Unfortunately, for the frenzied swine, demons are not choosy tenants, and they moved in on the helpless hogs, causing them to gnash at one another as they ran into the river squealing in torment until they suffocated and drowned. It shamed Zerah that a smelly pig ran to water to wash away the stench of Satan, knowing he lived with those same spirits for years, tolerating their repugnance.

He looked at his skin and his garments; the water washed them clean. Even better, Zerah felt spotless, but it had nothing to do with water. A torrent of joy, swifter than the streams of Jordan, flooded over him. He smiled for the first time in months, as he danced, splashed water with both arms, and fell back into the cool currents of the river. "I'm free, I'm free!" he shouted.

He went into the water afraid of living, dying, and everything in between, but came out with newfound faith in his father's forgiveness. "My father called his G-d father. I never understood it, but if G-d has forgiven me, father will do the same."

His self-administered baptism bolstered his resolve to complete his homeward trek, even though his source of food had drowned. Without food to sustain him, impoverished and unprotected, he was unafraid; his money squandered, his innocence stolen, his morals surrendered, and his life shortened, still he was unafraid.

His timing for a return to Jerusalem could not have been better. The law of the year of jubilee required the tillers of the soil and keepers of the vineyards to share the fruits of their labor with strangers. No one passing through the land need go hungry or be thirsty. Unlike the Canaanites who wasted their young women's virtue on the lust of strange men, the Hebrews provided for the necessities of newcomers to their nation without alluring them to commit sin. Zerah had forgotten the graciousness of his people. All along the way, people invited him to eat food from their fields in which he had not sown, sup from vineyards that he did not harvest, and drink from wells that he did not help dig. The contrast was stark. He left Canaan with its children begging for bread, and their parents prostituting themselves just to stay alive, whereas the land of Judah was flowing with milk and honey.

Zerah sobered as he approached the Kidron valley. "This is the place where my problems began," he confessed, "the place where I met and made a covenant with Baal."

As he stood looking down into the valley, he thought back to his mother's last words, "We will meet and speak again some day."

Even though there were hundreds of graves in Kidron, he remembered the location of his mother's tomb and ran as fast as he could toward it. As a boy, he believed his mother spoke to him when he went to her tomb; this time, he would do the talking. He fell on his knees sobbing salty tears of repentance. He dropped to his knees next to the huge stone that sealed her sepulcher.

"Mother, oh my mother. The last time I was here, I did not even speak to you. My soul was empty, and I had nothing to say to you except goodbye. I heard you say you would see me again. Here I am, the real me, not the rebellious boy who passed by so many years ago. I ask you to forgive me; I am the one who put you here."

A peaceful spirit condescended on Zerah, as confession began its healing work. "I blamed Pharez for your death, thinking he killed you while trying to rob me of my birthright. I hated him for what is rightfully his. I am going to him and to father to ask forgiveness and pray they will allow me to be a servant to them."

Zerah waited for an answer, but did not hear anything. The silence worried him. It caused him to wonder if something bad happened. What if Abiel or Pharez were dead and he would never get a chance to make things right?

Zerah eyed the gardener tending to a tomb up on the side of a small hill. "He will know. G-d, please let his answer be no!"

Zerah ran toward him.

The gardener was wary of a unkempt stranger dressed only in a loincloth approaching him. It was common for crazed lunatics to haunt the tombs of Kidron. The keeper came to recognize most of them, but Zerah was unknown to him. Though most of the dispossessed were harmless, the gardener knew to take care and avoid them if possible.

Hoping to stop Zerah from coming near him, the gardener asked from a safe distance, "Whom do you seek? I am the only living among the dead here, and I am a lowly gardener who possesses nothing of value to you."

Zerah responded, "I am Zerah, son of Abiel and Ammah. Have there been any burials here since that of my mother Ammah?"

"I know of none. I have been here for many years," he said, pointing to where Zerah came from, "and that tomb has not been opened."

Zerah let out a whooshing breath of relief and, much to the delight of the gardener, he turned to head for Tophet shouting aloud, "Thank you, thank you, thank you."

The display of courtesy shown by the young maniac took the keeper aback. He did not hear the last "thank you" or he would have understood that Zerah directed his thoughtfulness elsewhere. Zerah concluded, "Thank you, G-d."

Tophet was a tough test; after all, it is a powerful place inhabited by most every damnable spirit imaginable. The stench of burning flesh seared Zerah's nostrils as the smoke of Tophet swirled in his direction. Fears as hot and real as the fires of Tophet threatened to burn away the peace that came to him at Ammah's tomb. Doubt whispered to him, "You cannot make it home without going through Baal's dwelling place, and he will ask you to return to him. What will you do if you still love him as you once did? If the spirit of Machir still lurks here, will you turn away from him? Remember, he was a friend when you needed him. If you do, and Abiel rejects you and your brother hates you, where will you go? You have nothing to offer them except shame and reopening of old wounds. They doubtless will turn you over to the authorities. Pharez threatened to kill you if you did not leave. Turn around and go back to Gubla. Dryhus was not going to leave you with the swine. He was upset with you because he loves you so much. Remember, he promised you partnership, and he was testing you. He misses you now that you have run away. If you stay in Jerusalem, you will surely die; return to Canaan and live."

The whispers were loud enough to slow Zerah's pace. Then he stood still. His moment of truth arrived!

Abiel sat in his customary place, like a soldier on high alert. He was accustomed to disappointment, but undaunted; he remained vigilant, never giving in to discouragement. Abiel understood; disappointment is not getting what you want, whereas discouragement is thinking, you never will.

Like a phantom, one moment there was nothing, and then the next, the form of a young man appeared out of the nothingness. There was no doubt in Abiel's mind who it was. He and his faith acted out this scene many times. He leapt to his feet so abruptly that the startled gate guard clumsily grabbed for his sword before realizing it was Abiel. The inquisitive guard watched Abiel run with abandon down the hill toward Tophet and then he heard him crying out, "Zerah, my son Zerah. You are home. At last you have come home!"

Abiel's response took Zerah off guard as much as it had the gate's guard. Zerah did not have any weapons to reach for and expecting it was a soldier coming toward him, he looked to see if the runner was armed. He was too frightened to run. He heard the runner call his name moments before the collision. In the same moment, he recognized his father's weathered face beaming with the same smile that visited the hogpen. Abiel ran headlong into Zerah, crashing them to the ground. They rolled on the ground, crying, laughing, and kissing. Abiel's affection continued the healing that Zerah's confession started. Zerah knew the lustful kisses of insincere predators that prey upon the emotions of the insecure. He knew the kiss of betrayal from those that use the unsuspecting for gain. This was different. Zerah revisited his childhood, reliving the kiss that tucked him safely to bed. He was a young boy, with a bloody scraped knee, but not too dirty for his father's mouth to kiss the hurt away. He was a defiant young man looking down from the back of a camel upon his father's sad face as it touched his foot with a warm kiss to say, I will miss you. Abruptly, Zerah felt his father's body go stiff and he wondered why Abiel continued lying on top of him, until he heard Abiel say, "I cover my son with my life. If you try and stone him, death must come to me first." Zerah was shocked as he peeked from under his father's robe to see several temple guards with stones in their hands standing over him and his father. They were attracted to the scene of the reunion by the commotion of the celebration.

Out of sheer surprise, Zerah spoke out foolishly, "Father, let me up from here. I am ready to face whatever…"

Abiel did not let him finish. "Whatever your fate may be, will be mine also. I refused to die until I saw you alive. I am ready for whatever happens. Abiel's words persuaded the hardened soldiers to drop their stones and slip harmlessly back into the smoke of Toph. Zerah never dreamed that after all these years, his father was waiting, watching, or even wanting his return. Abiel's warm love demonstrated true religion, not cold unfeeling brass like Baal. It was neither the high of Machir's drink, drugs, and sex, nor the low of Dryhus's drink, drugs, and abuse. Unconditional love embraced and rolled on the ground with him. Users and abusers deserted Zerah in the muck and mire of a hogpen, but real love met him where he was at and happily dirtied itself to demonstrate its power.

It was not that Zerah wanted Abiel to stop; it was just that he felt he would bust open if he did not let out the emotion built up inside him.

"Father, please sir, there is something that I have to say. I have sinned against everything that you stand for and all you ever tried to teach me—our God, our religion, our faith, our people. I did all of this right before your very eyes. I am unfit for you to call me son. My wish is to be one of your servants."

Abiel placed his hand over Zerah's mouth.

"You are never to say those words again. You are my son and you always will be. Come, let us leave this place and go to our house, the place that you rightfully belong."

Abiel was on his feet quicker than his son and took Zerah's hand to help him up off the ground.

"Come on, hurry. There are many who will want to see you. Your grandparents Ormah and Hiphil are still alive and they never ceased praying for your safe return."

The guard from the Dung Gate shared many days with Abiel, not in faith, but in the performance of his duty. Out of respect, he never spoke a disparaging word to his unsolicited companion, but now he happily helped to herald the great news of an answered prayer. When he saw Abiel run down the hill, he abandoned his post and hurried to announce to Abiel's household that they should hurry to the gate if they would see an unbelievable sight. It was unusual to see a gate guard away from his post and running in the street, thus many inquired of him as he went.

"What has happened? Are we under attack from an enemy?"

"No, it is Zerah. Zerah has come home and Abiel has found him."

By the time that he reached Abiel's house, all his running and explaining left him winded. Abiel's servants waited impatiently as the messenger gasped and gathered himself. They were anxious to hear what he had to say.

"What is it sir? Is our lord Abiel all right?"

All he could say was, "Huggh, huggh, huggh, it is, huggh, Zerah. Huggh, Zerah has returned, and huggh, huggh, he is with Abiel at the gate."

Upon hearing these words, the entire courtyard cleared out as the servants scurried out into the street to see which of them would be first to reach the scene. When father and son reached the gate, a huge crowd had already gathered, and they waved their hands, weeping openly at the sight of something believed impossible. Abiel wasted no time dispatching his servants to carry out his wishes, none of them surprising. Abiel often spoke to his servants of his plans for this moment. Speaking of his hopes as reality had been a source of comfort for Abiel. "Return to the house and make ready the first robe and fetch my signet ring from its place. Make them ready for our arrival."

One of Abiel's most faithful servants pulled off his robe and his sandals and gave them to Abiel, "It is not proper that your son should be seen naked as would a slave. Please allow him to wear my clothing until he reaches home."

Zerah felt comfortable in the servant's clothing. "Father told me not to say that I am a servant, but I can't help but feel it is more than I deserve."

Abiel took the sandals and stooped down to place them on Zerah's feet. The long walk home caused his feet to swell and bruise, but oddly, the sight of them brought comfort to Abiel. Zerah did not get the meaning of his father's words. "Alas, my son, your journey was long and likely more difficult than I want to know. But, the worst is over. I rejoice to see your bruised heel, knowing that every step you took to get home crushed the head of the serpent that sought to kill you."

CHAPTER 34

Celebration and Contempt

Every year since the day that Zerah left home, Abiel took the choicest of all of his calves and fed it the first fruits of the grains from his harvest. Once the calf was fat, he brought it to the temple and offered it as a sacrifice. He vowed to continue this custom until such time that he sat and ate a fatted calf with his sons. Abiel believed that if he gave his best as an offering, he could boldly ask G-d to restore his lost son to the family.

One could hear a song in Abiel's voice, "Today is the day we waited for," he told the servants. "Go fetch our choice eglon that is fattening on the first fruits of our grain. Dig the pit and prepare the fire."

Zerah overheard his father calling for the slaughter of the eglon. Suppressed memories of Egla going to her death in Qadasha's arms gored Zerah's conscience just as the bull god did to Egla.

Zerah wondered, "How will I ever tell father what I did to Egla?" The thought of lying came to him. "No one will ever know any different."

It was not audible, but Zerah heard the soft voice say the words, "I will." It was the voice that he would hear often for the rest of his life. Zerah spoke back, "But if I tell the truth, father may never forgive me."

The same voice simply said, "I will."

Zerah's experience of forgiveness was undeniable, but forgiveness is one thing; forgetting is a different matter.

The rest of the walk home took on the air of a festival. Even if most people did not know how to feel about Zerah, they could not help but be exuberant for Abiel after years of sympathizing with him in his pain. Abiel invited everyone along the street to a feast. Before long, the servants had the calf roasting over an enormous pit. They opened the cellars and brought out the finest wines held in reserve. Abiel was saving the wines for use at Pharez's wedding if he should marry, but decided to use them to celebrate the homecoming. With all of the details attended to, Abiel rose to address his guests and get the merrymaking started. It turned out to be a very short but powerful speech. "My family, my friends." He paused to look at Zerah. "My son was dead, and is alive again; he was lost, and is found. Rejoice and be merry." With one quick motion of his hand, he waved for the musicians to play. Without any goading, the guests rose to their feet and began to dance. Abiel waited for the third song to finish, giving everyone time to get into full swing of the party, before stopping the music to tend to some meaningful matters. He wanted everyone to know his forgiveness was unconditional and that Zerah would reclaim all rights of his sonship. With all of the pomp and ceremony of a coronation, Abiel led Zerah to a huge chair out in the courtyard as his servants arrived with the gifts. The first gift actually brought a gasp from the celebrants. They recognized the robe of the firstborn. A few guests went so far as to ask among themselves, "How is it that Abiel gives to Zerah that which belongs to Pharez?" The gift not only shocked the sensibilities of the guests; it utterly confounded Zerah. He could not challenge Abiel's right to do as he pleased with his own property, but he worried that his brother stood somewhere in the shadows looking on. He was relieved at not seeing Pharez. Perhaps he could make some excuse to remove the robe, without offending his father's generosity. He hoped to get it off before Pharez saw it. Zerah was sincere on that day back in Canaan, when he cast his necklace to the swine. If the placing of the first robe on his shoulders was amazing, what happened next seemed insane. Abiel took Zerah's right hand and placed the family's signet ring on his index finger. This effectively entitled him to all remaining family wealth and the authority to exercise power over it. The ring also was symbolic of social rank and its bearer's ability to speak in his father's name.

If the thoughts and under-the-breath mumblings of the crowd were heard, it is doubtful that anyone in attendance would agree with Abiel's decisions.

"What is Abiel thinking?" Some said.

"Does he not remember what Zerah did?"

"Wherein is the wisdom of trusting someone who proved himself unreliable, lazy, and wasteful?"

Even Hiphil and Ormah covered their mouths with their hands! "Abiel would be wise to wait and see," they agreed.

Only Abiel was confident that the Zerah who came home was not the same wasteful person that went away. G-d would not bring someone back from so far and leave him to fail.

Pharez made his way home after working one of his usual dawn-to-dusk days and as he drew near, he heard the sound of music and dancing. There had not been any talk of a celebration, and he was curious to know what was happening. From a distance, he saw the servants lighting torches around the courtyard. It was apparent that something significant was under way. He was not properly dressed for festivities, and the dust and dirt of the fields soiled his clothing, so he sent one of his servants to inquire of the occasion. The smell of roasting meat beckoned his hungry nostrils, but he would rather sleep with the shepherds before shaming his father by showing himself improperly. His respect was in stark contrast to the reckless behavior that portrayed his rebel brother. His servant quickly returned to report, "Master Pharez, it is unbelievable. Your brother Zerah has returned safe and sound. Abiel has killed the fatted calf. Your family and friends are rejoicing. Abiel requested that you come quickly and join in."

Pharez's anger that rode away doubling with Zerah on the back of a camel, returned at the dreaded news of a reunion. The furious firstborn never refused any request that his father made, but this time resentment got the best of him.

"Go to my father and tell him I refuse to break bread or dip in the same bowl with anyone who knowingly profaned the name of G-d, polluted himself with prostitutes, and pulled down the good name of our family. To me, he is worse than an unwelcome stranger."

"But master, I could never use such strong language in the presence of Abiel and I have never heard you…Pardon me sir, I didn't mean…"

"Just go and tell him that I will not come," said Pharez.

Off he went with the message, fearful of how Abiel would receive it. "Master, I told Pharez that you bid him come to the feast, but he refuses."

"I understand." There was a brief pause before he continued, "No, I don't understand, but it is not right to involve you. Take me to him, and we will settle this among ourselves."

Abiel followed behind the servant, his heart full of bewilderment that Pharez refused to delight over deliverance from certain death of a loved one.

"Pharez, my son, there you are. What is troubling you? This is a great day, one that I have earnestly prayed to see for many years. Now that my prayer is answered, you seem angry."

At first, Pharez feared to answer, afraid that what he said would be offensive. It was much easier to speak up when he stated his feelings to a servant. He remembered the hurt Abiel went through when Zerah left home and Naarah died so violently. He also knew his father spent many sleepless nights praying for Zerah; however, his hatred ran every bit as deep as his father's heartbreak. Abiel was not the only one that prayed. Pharez often rolled out of his bed when he heard his father praying in the early morning hours. He foolishly thought to remind G-d that Abiel prayed out of grief and not wisdom. The worse thing that could happen would be for the curse of his brother to come back on the family after G-d delivered them from him.

Abiel, seeing that Pharez was reluctant to speak up, prodded him, "Who is it that you are angry with? Please talk to me. It is hard for me to see you hurting as you are."

"All right, all right, you are right; I am angry. Mainly at you, because you are the one who can do something about this and you choose not to. I have hated my brother since we were children. He constantly made fun of me because he wanted what I had. He was the one who wasted and squandered our wealth while I served you more faithfully than any servant did or slave that you own has. I never went against anything you asked of me. Yet to my memory, you never gave me as much as one kid goat so I could celebrate with my friends, but the moment that your rebellious runaway decides to come home, you slaughter the most valuable calf that we possess so that he can have a party."

"My son, I am surprised and shocked to hear these words come out of your mouth. You have been with me since the day you were born, and I have never knowingly deprived you of anything you desired. Do you not remember the day your brother demanded his inheritance? You encouraged me to give it to him and to let him go. Have you forgotten that when I gave Zerah his inheritance, I also had to give you yours? As my firstborn, you not only got an equal amount as that of your brother; you received a double portion. It included all that was mine. From that moment forward, everything that I possessed legally became yours—all the land, houses, silver, gold, servants, slaves, and livestock. Everything! I divested myself of all my wealth, not just for Zerah's benefit, but also for you. Yet, you challenge me and dare to complain over one calf when you possess hundreds of cattle. You could have had a calf to feast upon every day of your life if you so desired, yet you begrudge your brother one calf when he comes to us nearly starved. You would not treat a beggar so badly. Pharez, I see another side of you that frightens me. Have you served me all these years because you love me or only for your own interest? Go if you will and sleep with the shepherds. Perhaps you will find the answer to the bitterness of your soul under the stars."

Having said these things, he promptly turned his back on Pharez and went back to the party.

CHAPTER 35

The Conclusion

Zerah asked, "Father, where have you been? I've been looking everywhere for you."

"Your brother had need of me, and I had to attend to him."

"Where is Pharez? I have many things I want to say to him. Is he here?"

"No, he is called away for awhile, but enough about him. We will talk about him later. Tonight is a special night, and I don't intend to allow anything to spoil it."

Zerah had an uneasy feeling. Father is not telling me everything. He reached to rub an old scar on his neck that bothered him from time to time. As he touched the raised skin, he remembered Pharez twisting and tightening his scarlet necklace until he could barely breathe.

"After all these years and not even time for a greeting?" Zerah knew there was something wrong with that. "What if he went to the authorities? Maybe he is marshalling a mob to come for me. Some of the servants that serve Pharez are those that I sent home from Canaan. They might be vengeful and hopeful of doing me harm to get even."

Neither Pharez's robe, his father's ring, nor a servant's sandals made him feel safe. He spent his adult life in a world where fidelity was as fleeting as the contrary winds that blew in off the great sea. The sound of music and the noise of dancers feeling the effects of their new wine failed to drown out Zerah's inner voice of concern. For him, the party was over long before it ended. Many guests noticed his behavior. They remarked, "Poor man. He is not yet over what he went through. He seems so distant, so unhappy." They were only half right. True, he had no taste for the roasted calf; it pricked his heart to think of sacrificing Egla. One servant after another offered, "Master Zerah, you must be hungry. Are you sure I cannot offer you some of the roasted meat? Your father has lived for this day." Egla's memory and concern for Pharez's behavior spoiled his appetite. The same guests who excused his demeanor because of his past were quick to accuse him of being the same selfish person they remembered from years ago, when he broke up the party early, saying he had to go to bed. As always, Abiel defended him. "He is exhausted from his journey and will be fine by morning. Please, stay as long as you like; eat and drink to your fill."

It surprised Zerah to find his room exactly the way he left it. Physically worn and mentally drained, he sprawled himself across his bed in hopes that sleep would provide him respite from his troubling thoughts. As the servant blew out the lamp and closed the door behind him, Zerah longed for someone who could comfort him. He lay shuddering in the darkness thinking of Egla. Being back in this room reminded him of times, when like most children, there were nights when shadows frightened him. Egla always came to hold him, sing to him, and pray until his fear left and sleep came. In that moment, Zerah heard a familiar voice from down the hall.

Abiel went into prayer. His was no ordinary praying wrought with pleasantries. He interceded, "G-d I thank you for the miracle that you brought to pass this day. I will spend the rest of my days praising you for the answer to my greatest need. Please do not count me ungrateful that I come so soon to make another request, but I fear that I have gained the son I feared dead, only to lose the one who has ever been with me. You found Zerah in the land of the Canaanites and called him home to me. This night I ask you to find Pharez out among the shepherds and speak to him for his brother and me. You are a G-d of wonders. Change the hearts of my sons and let us be a family again. I give you all the glory and all the honor. Selah."

Zerah heard the truth of what he suspected. "I knew it. Pharez is angry with me, but at least it does not sound like he went to the authorities. Father sent him to the fields with the shepherds."

Zerah surprised himself. He rolled from his bed, landing on his knees and added his prayer to that of Abiel. "Please G-d, answer father's prayer, I mean our prayer. Change my brother's heart as you have mine."

He stood to get back up on his bed, but remembering the ending, he knelt back down. "I give you all the glory and all the honor. Selah."

It was a heartfelt and desperate prayer, and he did not want to take a chance and leave anything out! For the first time in his life, he experienced the power of prayer. Abiel taught him that prayer moved G-d, but tonight he experienced prayer moving him. Soon he was asleep.

G-d often chooses the place where men sleep as the location for divine confrontation. If you want to make a man listen, you have to get him still and alone. Call him to the top of a mountain, the backside of a wilderness, or to a sheep's pasture under the canopy of stars. It may even be a comfortable bed in your father's house that becomes less accommodating than a pig's wallow.

Pharez angrily stomped down the street that led away from his house, heading north toward the sheep's gate, through which he would go to the green pastures where the shepherds fed and fattened their flocks for temple slaughter. As he neared the gate, he heard the groaning of helpless cripples gathered on the porches of the pool of the sheep. Oftentimes, in the past, he paused to give alms to many of the poor congregated there, but this time his rage caused him to resent the infirm beggars who could not do anything for themselves but leach off someone else's living.

"Just like Zerah," he cursed under his breath. "Helpless, hopeless, having wasted what was given to them, and now begging for what is mine."

Those that lay around the pool waited for the "troubling of the water," believing it occurred under the auspices of angelic intervention when in fact, the sheep pool was a natural hot spring that occasionally boiled up. Nevertheless, never rule G-d out of the affairs of men, as all things are under his authority. Just as Pharez passed by, nature responded to its creator's command and pressured the sulfuric waters of Siloam to shake and shimmer with hope of healings. There was a man paralyzed from his birth lying by the pool. His family left him there unwanted and uncared for since he was a child. He had been there for so many years; he knew the names of many who passed by, especially if they were known as "givers." There was just enough light left in the day for the beggar to recognize Pharez and call out to him.

"Pharez, Pharez, over here."

Pharez was in no mood to be bothered with anyone else's troubles; he had plenty of his own. Yet the voice sounded familiar enough that it encouraged him to turn and take a few steps in the direction from which it came. Divine providence had planned this moment down to the exact number of steps that it would take to place him in the path of a destiny driven by desperation. He took several more steps before someone grabbed hold of his leg.

"Whhaaat," he blurted out as he attempted to jerk free. Pharez did not realize how powerful a man's arms could be if that man spent his life using his arms as his legs and his arms. He held Pharez so tightly it hurt.

"How do you know my name and what do you want of me?"

"I know you because I have been here for many years. This pool is my home and you often pass through my house. Would you not know those who pass through your house? You are known here for your kindness, you and your father."

"All right, if it is alms that you want, let go of me and I will give…"

"No sir, it is not silver or bread that I want. Do you not hear the rumble of the waters? I have no one who cares for me who will put me in the healing waters. I beg of you, put me in the pool and I will let you go."

Pharez started to call for the guard at the sheep gate, but decided it might cause him even more inconvenience if he involved others. He would hurriedly handle this bothersome delay and be about his business. Reaching down, he took hold of the man under both of his arms and attempted to lift him up enough to drag him to the pool, but alas, the man would not let go of his leg in fear that as soon as he did, his helper, as well as his hopes, would run away into the night.

Pharez complained, "I can't walk or drag you if you insist on holding my leg."

"Pick me up and carry me. I know that you can't leave me if you are holding me."

He pushed Pharez past his limitation of temper.

"All right, I will carry you, but you have to let go of my leg."

Pharez bent over so that he could get his arms under the man's withering body. As he did, the beggar repositioned his death-like grip from Pharez's leg to his arm. Being accustomed to hard work made it easy for Pharez to lift his unwanted patient off the ground, but the partially paralyzed parasite would have preferred the ground if he knew what was in his Pharez's mind.

"He wants water; water he will get."

As they neared the pool, the grateful beggar loosened his hold on Pharez's arm, expecting to sit by the edge so he could hold on to the side with his iron-like arms and dangle his useless legs in the water. But instead, with one mighty thrust, Pharez tossed the man into the water without giving thought to how deep the water was or how the helpless cripple would get out. He quickly turned to leave before some other stranger could lay hold of him. He nearly reached the gate before hearing the first frantic cry for help; unmistakably, from the one who spoke his name and sought his help just moments ago.

"Helllllpppp." Then silence. Again, "Helllllpppp."

"What in G-d's name?" Pharez grumbled aloud. "Am I cursed to spend the entire night here?"

He looked over to see the gate's guard staring at him.

"Good, a way out of this mess," he thought. Then, without rank or authority, he ordered, "Guard, go help him. It is your duty."

"Go help who, go help where? If I answered every call for help that came from the worthless vermin that laze around that pool, this gate would go unattended. I have more important things to see to," the gatekeeper argued.

Their argument was interrupted by a gurgling, "Helllll," that had no finish.

Pharez remembered the words, "You are known here for your kindness," and that is all it took to put him in full stride back to the pool. Without time to disrobe, he dove into the darkness of the deep water and began groping around, hoping to feel a strong hand grab hold of him. He came up for a breath, and he saw the man thrashing the water with both arms and both legs. No, he was not swimming; he did not know how, but he managed to keep his mouth and nose out of the water just enough to avoid drowning. Nearing exhaustion, he would soon go under for the last time, unless someone helped. Pharez's body surged with fear-induced strength. He swam close enough to grab hold of one of the man's previously paralyzed legs, now kicking away at the water. Pharez feared the beggar would drown them both before he got them to the safety of the steps of the pool. Once Pharez had a breath to spare, he used it to reprimand the swindler.

"You deceived me. You are not cripple as you said. We both could have drowned. How many years have you been out here stealing while you could have been working like most of us?"

Pharez's report came as a revelation to the beggar. He had been so busy kicking that he had not noticed that his death struggle brought life to his paralysis. Then, a rush of pain shot down his legs as the few piteous muscles he had began to cramp up. They hurt so bad that he had to laugh at the pleasure of feeling anything in his legs, even if it was pain. The legend of the angels in the water was sure to grow in the days to come when the people that knew the cripple would see him walking, but G-d did not need to perform another miracle to be G-d. He had a different purpose in mind, a lesson every bit as great as seeing the lame leap for joy.

Pharez shivered as he walked past the apathetic guard and out of the sheep gate into the cool of the early night. He hurried to be with the shepherds, who by now would have a fire built to warm themselves as they prepared their evening meal. He was too tired to be hungry, but would welcome some dry clothes and more so, a chance to put today behind him with some restful sleep. Two more small hills stood between him and the shepherd's camp, when the shrill bleating of a lamb caught his attention. Though Pharez wore costly clothing indicative of his social standing, they covered the heart of a shepherd. He listened closely so that he could fetch the little wanderer who strayed from its family and cried for its mother to find it. Hearing it appeal again, he headed off to bring it in. The next cry told him the lamb was close by, but the fearsome snarl of a desert wolf closing in to kill the helpless lamb dispelled hopes of an easy rescue.

Nature prepared its own for this kind of fight. The wolf winded Pharez and with its eyes made to see in the dark of night, it had no problem locating its enemy. Using its sense of smell, the wily predator cunningly circled around back of his stalker. Without concern for his safety, Pharez pulled his knife from its sheath and crept toward where he believed the wolf to be. Pharez was not as well adapted as the wolf, but many nights out in the fields sharpened his senses. He felt the presence of the wolf as it leapt for the back of his neck. Instinctively, he spun around with the blade of his knife extended in front of his face. The knife found its mark as skillfully as it would have if its bearer had seen the target. It pierced the beast's heart and with little more than a whimper, it lay dead at his feet. The only harm done was his blood-covered garment. The lamb let out another lamentful cry, and Pharez ran to gather it in his blood-covered arms. Pharez said to the lamb, "Bloody but safe, covered in crimson but safe we are."

He was too tired to tell the story to the inquisitive shepherds. Without warming himself or asking for dry clothing, he grabbed some covering and disappeared into the flickering shadows created by the campfire as it slowly died down.

Exhaustion did a quick work on Pharez, and he went to the place where men let down their guard and leave preconceived notions behind as they enter the world of dreams. It is a spiritual place where G-d, angels, and spirits visit, causing hardened men to cry, brave men to tremble, and the stubborn to become willing. Pharez's soul left the pastureland on the north side of Jerusalem and traveled to Kidron. His dream placed him sitting on a large boulder alongside his brother. He recognized the place as his mother's burial tomb.

Zerah was oblivious to Pharez being present. Pharez assumed that he could get Zerah's attention and spoke to him asking, "What are you doing here?"

No answer.

"Zerah, don't you see or hear me?"

No reply.

It was then that Pharez realized he was there as a witness and nothing else.

Zerah spoke up, "My mother, I am here for the last time. I told you this once before, but somehow I made it back. Now that I am back, I wish I never made it home. I know father's servants resent me—I represent more work for them—and father's friends came to the celebration for the food and the wine. I heard them talking behind his back and they think he is crazy for caring for me. He and Egla are the only two people who ever loved me, and I let her go to her death without defending her. She was everything to me; you would be if you were alive. I may have caused your death just as I participated in hers. Most of all, I fear that my return may hurt father even more than my leaving did. I also feel for Pharez. I do not blame him for hating me. I envied him so much that I taunted him, teased him, and would have killed him given the chance. He had what I wanted, the birthright, a relationship with father, everything. I came here to be done with all of this. Please give me the courage to do what I must. When they find me here, they can quietly bury me with you, and tell everyone that I left again, avoiding any further embarrassment." Zerah reached down by his side, picked up some crimson-colored rope, and tossed one end over a stout limb that hung like a canopy over the cave.

Pharez heaved in sorrow, having heard a side of his brother's life that he never knew existed. He perceived Zerah as carefree, devoid of devotion, and incapable of sincere thoughts. He waved his arms furiously, but Zerah chose not see him. He screamed, "No, no, no, don't do this. Please Zerah, do you hear me? Don't do this."

He watched in horror as Zerah made a loop, pulled the rope up tight to the limb, and continued making a noose out of the remaining end, placing it around his neck. Pharez was helpless. He looked close at Zerah's expressionless face. It was frightening to see the emptiness, especially his eyes. There were not any tears, not even a hint of fear, just a far-off blank stare.

His last words pierced Pharez like a warrior's spear, "I love you, Ammah. I love you, Abiel. I love you, Pharez."

Pharez jumped in front of him and said, "I love," but he did not get to finish before his brother's body passed through him, and he turned to see it swinging from the rope. Evidently, the fall broke his neck because Zerah's hands were free, but he never reached for the rope to stop choking. There was no sound except the eerie creaking of the rope rubbing against the limb. When the body stopped swinging, Pharez finished what he had began to say, "...you too, Zerah."

Pharez wiped his teary eyes to make sure he really saw a "Shining Being" cut the rope and take Zerah into his arms. The Being turned to face Pharez, addressing him by name, saying, "Pharez, you are a good man who found favor with G-d because of your obedience to your father on earth and your Father in heaven. No man is blameless and you must put away fighting with your brother. The things that happened to you last night were G-d's way of speaking to you. If a man crippled from his birth can walk again because someone will go through the deep waters of trouble with him, likewise your brother is not hopeless as you have supposed, but he will drown in the depths of his despair unless you are willing to save him. You fought a wolf for a defenseless lamb. Will you fight to save your own flesh and blood? Is your brother's life of lesser value than that of a lamb? The beggar and the wolf were two witnesses from G-d. I am the third, establishing that this is his will and his word. Go now before it is too late."

Pharez awoke with the words of his unfinished sentence, "You too, Zerah" ringing in his ears. I have to go and find him. He must hear me say, "I love you, too Zerah, before it's too late."

He made haste to let the shepherds know that he was taking one of the donkeys and he would be back later on. He rode as fast as one could on a beast of burden, headed toward Kidron even though the last he heard, Zerah was at home.

On the other side of town under Abiel and Pharez's roof, a somewhat similar scene played out. Abiel and Zerah's prayers relieved Zerah's anxiety just enough for him to drift off to sleep. His dream took him on a walk through Toph, where he followed at a distance behind Pharez. Pharez raised his voice in anger, cursed at G-d, and said terrible things against Abiel. "There must be something to the worship of Baal. I should renounce the G-d of my fathers. How have they rewarded me? I serve my father night and day, all of my life, and make sacrifices to G-d sparing nothing. What did it get me to give the first fruits of my labor? I have not had any fun or adventure that my brother has had, and he is a servant of Baal."

Zerah tried to speak up, "Pharez, listen to me," but it was to no avail. Pharez did not hear him.

Pharez continued, "Zerah gets his inheritance, leaves home, spends everything, and now he is back for the rest of what belongs to me. It seems that Baal will see to it that he gets it. I am a servant of the highest G-d, but my brother who serves other gods wears my robe, has father's ring, drinks my wedding wine, and feasts on my calf. I have never been with a woman. I devoted myself to my father and our business, never even taking time to love a woman."

Zerah knew the danger in this kind of talk. He pled, "Pharez, please hear me. It is not the way you think."

He peered through the smoke of Tophet to see Qadashu in all of her purple finery, her golden jewelry making its familiar seductive sound as she walked toward Pharez. He looked back at Pharez who was obviously captivated by her beauty as he opened his arms to embrace her.

"Don't, I beg you, don't go with her. She is the mother of all temptation and if you defile yourself with her, you will be open to every evil thing," he reasoned, but to no avail.

Just before Pharez disappeared into the smoke with Qadashu, he turned around staring straight at Zerah and said, "She is exactly what I want. I want to open up to everything, all the things that I deprived myself of for nothing."

As he spoke these words, the smoke cleared long enough for Zerah to see an image of Baal. As he watched, the idol's belly opened and swine came running out. Zerah recognized the swine as the ones that the spirits possessed back on the banks of the Jordan River. Pharez grabbed one of them to sacrifice to Baal. When he cut its throat, the spirits that Zerah was free from entered his brother's body. Zerah grimaced in pain, fully understanding the lies and promises of promiscuous life. He had lived what Pharez was in for. Another pig came out of Baal's belly and ran to Pharez's feet. It regurgitated the scarlet cord that Zerah threw over the fence as he said goodbye to Canaan. Pharez picked it up and tied it around his neck. Zerah screamed at Pharez, "Do not put it on. For G-d's sake, for your sake, do not put on the cord of rebellion." Pharez, Qadashu, the swine, and the evil spirits disappeared into the belly of Baal.

Just as his brother did, Zerah awakened with a sense of urgency to go to Tophet, Hinnom, and on to Kidron.

"If Pharez decides that my life has been better than his and he chooses to follow in my footsteps, I must go and stop him. He has to know that the road I chose was not a path to freedom but a pit of torment into which I fell. I will stop him at all costs."

Zerah was up and out of the door of the house first, but Abiel was not far behind him. Disturbing dreams rousted Pharez and Zerah up early, but Abiel, ever full of faith, awoke refreshed, in anticipation of answer to his request of last evening. He tapped lightly on Zerah's door and upon receiving no response, he eased the door open, to find the room empty. He made his way to the kitchen where he inquired if anyone knew of Zerah's whereabouts.

"Master, I saw him leave awhile ago. I knew that you would probably want him followed. I'm afraid that he headed straight for the Dung Gate, and you know what that means."

Abiel would have none of it. "Don't speak foolishly. You have no idea what is happening. Quickly, have someone saddle my ass. I must be about my Father's business."

The servant muddled under his breath, "What business does the old man Hiphil have this early in the morning?"

The servant misunderstood the Father of which Abiel spoke!

Meanwhile, Pharez being the first of his family to rise, and riding instead of walking, had already made his way through the Dung Gate, not realizing that Zerah and Abiel were not far behind him. He was glad to be riding. It got him in and out of Toph quickly. The hair stood up on the donkey's back as well as the back of Pharez's neck as he kicked hard at the donkey's flanks to make it move faster through this forsaken place.

Zerah walked as fast as possible. His heart sank as he questioned the guard at the Dung Gate as to whether or not his brother Pharez had passed this way recently.

"Yes, as a matter of fact he did come through here awhile ago. He seemed to be in a big hurry," the guard reported.

The sentinel's words caused Zerah to relive the terror of his night vision and the reminder put him in a panicked hurry.

Pharez arrived at his mother's tomb relieved at not seeing his brother's body swinging from the huge tree that shaded the family sepulcher. His vision was so vivid that he wouldn't be satisfied that no suicide had happened here without securing a second witness. He walked away to look for the gardener. Surely, he would know if any such thing happened.

Zerah reached the bottom of the hill, searching for his brother amidst the smoke and stench of the place that sent him into a downward spiral straight to hell. He frantically called out his brother's name.

"Pharez…Pharez…Are you here? It is your brother Zerah. Pharez…Please answer me. Pharez." A soldier misunderstood him and answered back. Zerah no longer feared arrest of anything but his heart. His apprehension was almost unbearable. Looking around here made him aghast that he ever found anything to like, much less worship in a place like this. Now was not the time for reflection on the past. Pharez was gone and he had to make haste to catch up to his brother. He determined to follow Pharez, even if it meant going back to Canaan. As he hurried through Hinnom toward Kidron, his bigger concern became what to do if Pharez was possessed of demons when he found him. It occurred to him that he should have brought some water. His experience of deliverance took place in the water and that certainly was the first place that the pigs headed to purge theirselves of the demons. Nevertheless, water or no water, he was not going to back down from anything or anyone. He was the one who opened the gate of rebellion to this family, and he was willing to die closing it. With his mind racing as fast as his feet, he came up on the place that always brought him peace. If he had to choose a place to die, this would be it. He had been to his mother's tomb many times; enough to know that by climbing on top of the craggy rock that sealed the opening to the cave, he could see much of the valley. It was a logical spot to save a lot of time searching for Pharez. He scurried to atop the tomb to see if he could tell the direction that Pharez traveled.

Pharez located the skittish caretaker, addressing him as he approached, "Sir, please do not be afraid. I intend you no harm. Just a question."

He grumbled, "What is happening out here? One day a pauper, the next day a prince, asking questions."

"Yes, yes. What is it that you ask?"

"It is about my brother. I fear that he came here to kill himself, and I know that you see everything that happens here. Have you seen a young man out here by himself today?"

"Master, it is not yet the third hour of the day. No one but you has been here. Certainly no one trying to die."

"Thank you, kind sir. I must be in time."

Pharez turned to go back to Ammah's tomb where he would wait.

The gardener stopped him saying, "There was a young man here yesterday. He, like you, asked about death. He wanted to know if any of the house of Abiel and Ammah had died. But, he could not be the one of whom you speak. He was nearly naked and half crazed. You look like a man of wealth. This man was a vagabond. Never could he be a brother of yours."

Pharez did not know what to make of what he heard. "Yesterday?"

"Absolutely, it was yesterday," the caretaker asserted.

Pharez knew that he had to get to Ammah's grave and quick. His dream was real. Zerah's sole reason for coming home was to kill himself and be buried with his family. He ran furiously, all the while convincing himself that if any of his dream was real, then all of it was, and he would get a chance to save his brother.

The gardener scratched his head and wondered, "He said he was in time. In time for what?" Out of curiosity, he slowly made his way behind Pharez.

Pharez passed a small stand of olive trees that blocked his view of the family's sepulcher, only to see the scene that he dreaded was more than just a dream. Zerah was standing atop Ammah's tomb close to the limb from which Pharez saw him hang himself. He was not near enough to see if he had a rope or not. He tied to run closer, but it felt like his feet were in deep mud. All he could do is scream, "No, no, no don't do it. I am here for you. I love you. I love you, Zerah. Please, I love you my brother."

Zerah was so startled by Pharez's screams that he stumbled and slid off the side of the big rock and out of Pharez's view. He heard his brother scream, "Nooooooo, please G-d, no." Zerah feared that Pharez was screaming at his demons.

Pharez reached for his knife, it still caked with the blood of the wolf, and finally got his feet moving. "If I can get to him, I will cut him down before he dies."

Zerah stood up, dusted himself a bit, and prepared for the worst. Someone out there acted possessed and he suspected it was Pharez. Pharez ran around the side of his mother's tomb, shocked to see his brother alive and standing without a rope around his neck. Zerah stared back at Pharez's neck and was just as shocked not seeing a scarlet rope around his neck, but then his eyes went to the bloody knife.

Zerah's voice shook with emotion, "It is true. The dream is true. You did offer a pig to Baal."

Pharez's face knotted with confusion as he was on the verge of stuttering for the first time in years. "Whaat? What are youu talking about? The dream is no...no...not true. I will not let you kill yourself."

"Kill myself! What do you mean? I have no reason to kill myself. You seem ready to do that for me, but I don't care. I would rather be dead than know that you are with Qadashu."

"Qadas-who? I have no idea what you are saying."

"But your bloody knife. I saw you sacrifice the pig to Baal."

"Zerah, I have never sacrificed anything to Baal, nor will I ever. When did you see me sacrifice a pig?"

"In my dream. You were upset because father killed the calf and welcomed me home. You thought my life was better than yours was, and you decided to do what I did. You offered sacrifice to Baal, and the spirits that possessed me went into you. That is how I know you can kill me. There were days when I wanted you dead."

Zerah never took his eyes off the knife. Pharez calmed down enough to notice.

"I would never kill you. The blood on my knife came from a wolf I killed last night. A wolf came to kill one of my lambs and I protected it with my knife. Then I dreamed that you were like a lamb in danger and I did nothing to defend you. I felt guilty that a lamb meant more to me than my own brother."

Pharez looked up from his knife to his brother's face. Zerah stood there rubbing his neck. Zerah did not have to say one word. His scar did all the talking! Pharez thought back to the day when the red rope around his brother's neck infuriated him so, that he almost killed Zerah. Pharez felt the knife slip from his hand. "Brother, I lied to you. I could have killed you; I wanted to. I wanted you dead, too. I never ran away as you did, but I am every bit as guilty of destroying our family. You took your inheritance years before it was rightfully yours. From the time we were children, I took father's love and treated it as if belonged to me only. What I did was worse. Will you forgive me?"

Those four words broke the curse of the crimson cord forever.

Zerah's answer came quickly as he, the second born made the first move, but not to fight or kill anyone like the last time that they were together. Abiel rode over a small rise just in time to see his sons awkwardly leap at each other. If this would have happened before last night, Abiel would have been frightened. While providence visited his son's dreams, angels whispered the end of the story to Abiel; or was it the beginning? The saga came full circle. The struggle that started in Ammah's womb reenacted itself. They rolled against the stone that sealed their mother's body in death and embraced one another at their mother's feet. This time, they were not struggling for supremacy. They held each other tight to sweat out all of the strife that had separated them. Abiel wept as he watched. It reminded him of the story of the patriarch Ya`aqob wrestling with an angel. He heard Pharez say, "I said will you forgive me?"

Zerah replied, "You must forgive me first."

Pharez countered, "I will not let you go until you forgive me."

Abiel stayed out of it. He knew at last that they were learning what it meant to be brothers—together in their differences, together in their likeness. Om and Ot. Shalemu and Shaharu. Dawn and dusk. Pharez and Zerah. Finally, they wrestled to the conclusion that the only way to end this was to say it together; two voices in unison, "I forgive you my brother!"

Abiel could not resist. He ran and fell upon the both of his sons, not to protect them from harm, but to cover them in love.

The scene thoroughly confounded Kidron's caretaker who peered from behind an olive tree at the sight of grown men rolling on the hallowed grounds of their family burial site. He was convinced they were crazy. Walking away he recounted, "Two of them came to me asking about death and burial. They meet up and begin fighting each other as the older man watches. Then he jumps on them and they all laugh. Do they not know there is to be no joy in this place until Messiah comes here to raise up his dead ones?"

The gardener, like so many before and after him, misunderstood. The Messiah comes and goes in his own way, in his own time, and we miss the resurrection.

Changed men got up off the ground, resurrected from their living tombs that proved darker, colder, and crueler than death itself.

The sun was straight up and down as the three of them walked out of Kidron together. No dawn, no dusk, no morning, no night, no shadows: everything equal and new. The long, trying, arduous journey came down to a short walk home. As they left the valley, the gardener overheard Pharez say, "Bloody but safe," Zerah continue, "stained in crimson," and Abiel finish, "but safe we are." The legacy of the love of these three men continues until this very day.

0-595-33372-9